The Trumpets of Jericho:

A Romantic Novel About Bands and Musicians in the American Civil War

By

Victor H. Thompson

authorHOUSE™

1663 LIBERTY DRIVE, SUITE 200
BLOOMINGTON, INDIANA 47403
(800) 839-8640
WWW.AUTHORHOUSE.COM

This book is a work of fiction. Places, events, and situations in this story are purely fictional and any resemblance to actual persons, living or dead, is coincidental.

© 2004 Victor H. Thompson.
All Rights Reserved.

No part of this book may be reproduced, stored in a retrieval system, or transmitted by any means without the written permission of the author.

First published by AuthorHouse 12/11/04

ISBN: 1-4184-9113-6 (e)
ISBN: 1-4184-9112-8 (sc)
ISBN: 1-4184-9111-X (dj)

Library of Congress Control Number: 2004096064

Printed in the United States of America
Bloomington, Indiana

This book is printed on acid-free paper.

For my wife Sharon, who patiently led me through all the battlefields of the Civil War in her native Tennessee.

PREFACE

"And the seven priests shall bear before the ark seven trumpets of ram's horns:
and the seventh day ye shall compass the city seven times,
and the priests shall blow with the trumpets.
And it shall come to pass,
that when they make a long blast with the ram's horn,
and when ye hear the sound of the trumpet,
all the people will shout with a great shout;
and the wall of the city shall fall down flat,
and the people shall ascend up every man straight before him."
Joshua 6: 4-5.

In describing novels, literary historians tend to make rather arbitrary distinctions between realism and romance. Cooper wrote romantic novels; Hemingway wrote realistic ones, and never the twain would meet. In realistic novels, bad things happen to good people because that is the way the world really is. At the end of Hemingway's A Farewell to Arms, the hero's essential goodness does not entitle him to a happy ending: he loses the girl and all sense of future happiness. In the romantic novels of James Fenimore Cooper, on the other hand, life is better than reality; virtue is always rewarded, and bad things never happen to the irrepressibly good Deerslayer. In The Trumpets of Jericho, I abandon these distinctions between realism and romance to develop an unlikely genre, the realistic romance. It seems to me that pure romance and pure realism can often miss one of the most astounding truths of human existence: sometimes the most amazing and improbable events are also true. The improbable is also the heart of comedy, a temporary triumph over life, and in this sense <u>The Trumpets of Jericho</u> is a comic novel much closer to the absurdities of Cooper than to the tragedies of Hemingway.

In writing <u>The Trumpets of Jericho</u>, I attempted to anchor the most incredible events to the bedrock of facts. The Union assault on Missionary Ridge, for example, never should have happened in the world of realism. How could an army--without orders and without a battle plan--ascend a two-hundred-foot cliff and defeat an enemy shooting at them from the top? Virtually every attempt of a Civil War Army to take a position from an entrenched enemy failed. The accuracy and killing power of the mid-nineteenth century weapons simply over matched the 18th century frontal assaults by massed infantry. The Union Army had attempted a well-organized attack against entrenched Confederates at Fredericksburg and had suffered a disastrous defeat. The Confederates did the same thing at Gettysburg with the same results. And even before Cold Harbor, Grant was beginning to suspect that hurling masses of infantry against these modern weapons was suicide, and when Sherman moved South against Atlanta, he generally flanked Confederate defenses rather than attempting to go through them. The situation at Missionary Ridge looked so similar to the disasters before it, that Confederate troops taunted the Union troops below with the words, "Remember Fredericksburg." What made Missionary Ridge different? Military historians can no doubt find military reasons for what happened. The guns at the top of the ridge were over shooting their targets below; the defenses had been weakened by troops pulled from the ridge defenses to fight Sherman who was coming up from Tunnel Hill. But mere science can not fully explain what happened on that November day in Chattanooga, Tennessee. In defiance of Grant's orders, a Union Army went up a nearly vertical 200-foot cliff and defeated the Confederate defenders. The victory was so unlikely, that Shakespeare might have said, "If this were played upon a stage, I would condemn it as an improbable fiction." However, that is exactly what happened, and the whole event has been amply recorded by eyewitnesses and historians.

The events of The Trumpets of Jericho are all based on events and places described by eyewitnesses and historians, but as Samuel Clemens observed in Huckleberry Finn: "He told the truth mainly. There was things which he stretched, but mainly he told the truth." I have taken the facts and stretched them into a work of the imagination, but the essential truth remains. At the battle of Hoover's Gap, a Union soldier was mortally wounded, but before he died he was determined to destroy his Spencer Rifle to keep it out of the hands of the Confederates. Unlike the single-shot, muzzle-loading Enfields used by most infantry, the Spencer was a clip-fed seven-shot repeater, and this soldier, with his dying breath, wanted to keep the enemy from using it against Union troops. This whole incident has an aura of unreality about it. Why would a dying man be more concerned with keeping his gun out of the hands of the enemy than with his own death? But an eyewitness, Major James A. Connolly of the 123rd Illinois Mounted Infantry, describes this event in his journal, <u>Three Years in the Army of the Cumberland</u>. In <u>The Trumpets of Jericho,</u> I transform this incident to fit the purposes of my novel. One of my main characters discovers the dying soldier, and the soldier tells him to destroy it. My romantic hero can't help thinking of the dying Arthur casting away Excalibur, and for a few moments considers keeping this wonderful rifle. With such a rifle, he could protect himself and the woman he is with from the real dangers of war privateers. But tormented by the pleas of the dying soldier, he smashes the gun against a rock and breaks the stock from the barrel.

Several other incidents of my novel are adaptations of events related by Connolly, including the story of a young southern girl who reluctantly gives her favorite horse to a Yankee. I am also indebted to Connolly for my understanding of weather and road conditions in the summer of 1863. It was a particularly rainy summer, and the dirt roads were essentially troughs of thick mud. When my heroine makes her way through the mud on the Nashville Pike, she is historically accurate. She, however, is a personage of my own imagination. She is a montage of all the strong, intelligent, and capable women that I have known in my own time, but I have put her into a distant past. I would like to have given her some advantages of modern clothing such as blue jeans, sweat shirts, and running shoes but had to make her true to her time. According to Juanita Leisch in her book, <u>Who Wore What? Women's Wear 1861-1865,</u> women wore those long bulky dresses for all occasions, even in the fields. The only exceptions were women who disguised themselves as men to serve in the army, but my heroine is every inch a woman and has nothing to hide.

My understanding of the military strategy, the battles, and the men, comes mainly from <u>Echoes of Battle: The Struggle for Chattanooga</u> by Richard A. Baumgartner and Larry M. Strayer, <u>The Shipwreck of Their Hopes</u> by Peter Cozzens, and <u>The Civil War Day by Day</u> by E. B. Long with Barbara Long. For the specific engagements and movements of the Seventh Pennsylvania Cavalry--the unit of my hero--I have referred to the regimental history, <u>The Saber Regiment</u> by William B. Sipes. My great-grandfather fought with the 7th Pennsylvania Cavalry, and I have given him a place in the novel under his own name, Corporal Morgan Davis, and related some family anecdotes about his war service. All the military engagements covered in the novel are accurate in detail, but I have added the imaginative perspective of my fictitious hero. The 7th Pennsylvania did hold Reed's Bridge against the Confederates in the Battle of Chickamauga. In fact a monument still stands there to commemorate their heroic stand, but my hero's actions in the battle are imaginary.

My hero is also a musician, and to make the actions of musicians in the Civil War historically accurate, I have referred to <u>Music and Musket: Bands and Bandsmen of the American Civil War</u> by Kenneth E. Olson, and <u>A Pictorial History of Civil War Era Musical Instruments and Military Bands</u> by Robert Garofalo and Mark Elrod. Here again facts often defy realistic expectations. The modern military band plays for ceremonial occasions and for troops not in combat. Thus the modern reader might be surprised to find a band in the thick of a battle, but the Union General Sheridan often sent the band into military engagements. At the Battle of Chancellorsville, the Union lost the fight, but a total rout was prevented by the timely arrival of the regimental band which brought music instead of guns. I assume the enemy fled, not because the music was so bad, but because the band rallied the Union Troops. In addition to maintaining accuracy of the bands in combat, I have used the actual instrumentation and music. When I have the Union Band on one side of the river having a joint concert with the Confederate Band on the other side, I may seem to be giving in to the excesses of romanticism, but such concerts actually took place. Music did seem to be a unifying element for the two sides and was a constant reminder that, culturally, North and South had much more in common than they had differences. For the purposes of my novel, however, I needed to move the concert from the Rappahannock River to the Tennessee River. My female cornetist may seem to be an historical anachronism, because in the 19th century the cornet was considered an instrument for males only. I presume that the sheer bravado of playing a cornet was considered a male thing to do, and playing loud and high was, perhaps, associated with the mating calls of large animals. Females were supposed to play the violin. But the International Trumpet Guild published an article about a celebrated female cornetist named Anna Berger who was internationally known shortly after the Civil War. People told her that women should play the violin. My heroine is loosely based on the real-life Anna Berger.

I specify cornet rather than trumpet, because the cornet was the preferred brass instrument until well into the 20th century. The great 20th century cornetist, Herbert L. Clark, could not even imagine trying to play solos on a trumpet. A trumpet has a shriller more piercing sound than a cornet, and for over a hundred years people preferred the smoother, more mellow sounds of the cornet. The modern trumpet player can never play too loud or too high, and so he or she generally prefers the trumpet. For my title, <u>The Trumpets of Jericho</u>, I used trumpets rather than cornets to keep in the spirit of the biblical allusion. The vibrations of trumpets would be more likely to bring down a city wall than the more mellow cornets.

My discussions of practice sessions and the details of learning an instrument are based on my personal experiences as a trumpet player. I do make one disclaimer here. The young woman who teaches my hero to play is not based in any way on my own excellent instructor and mentor, Dr. William Bartolotta of Old Dominion University.

My understanding of the daily lives of soldiers in the Civil War comes from several sources, but the most important was a pair of books, <u>The Life of Johnny Reb: The Common Soldier of the Confederacy,</u> and <u>The Life of Billy Yank: The Common Soldier of the Union</u>, both by Bell Irwin Wiley. These books told in detail what the soldiers ate, what they wore, what they did for fun. A little known classic, <u>The Story the Soldiers Wouldn't Tell: Sex in the Civil War</u> by Thomas P. Lowery was also useful as were <u>Civil War Medicine</u> by C. Keith Wilber, and <u>Arms and Equipment of the Civil War</u> by Jack Coggins. The baseball scene in a Confederate prison was inspired by an article in <u>The Civil War Times.</u>

Finally, the geographical details of my novel are accurate. All the action takes place in the Western theatre of the war from Nashville, Tennessee to Macon, Georgia, and most of that from Murfreesboro to Chattanooga. I base my movements of characters and troops on a Civil War Military Map "Showing the Theatre of Operations in the Tullahoma, Chickamauga, and Chattanooga Campaigns." All distances and places are accurate for 1863. I have also traveled the modern routes and seen the actual places and regretted that everything has been changed by time and progress. The dirt road to Hoover's Gap that my hero and heroine traversed in a heavy rain is now an interstate. Even the sense of a gap through a mountain has been destroyed by the leveling force of dynamite. I have visited the battlefields and stood on Orchard Knob where Grant watched his troops disobey his orders and storm Missionary Ridge. Where he saw open fields, I saw houses. I even climbed up and down the side of Missionary Ridge to see what the troops of both sides had literally been up against. The Nashville & Chattanooga railroad that plays a part in my novel appears on the military map.

In a world of interstate highways, I tried to imagine what it would have been like traveling on foot or horseback along muddy dirt roads and did my best to estimate travel times. Basing my estimates on Civil War journals, I concluded that twenty miles a day on foot would have been possible but somewhat remarkable. Since my heroine is a remarkable girl, I let her travel twenty miles a day.

In this world of Civil War fact, I allow some very romantic things to happen. As in a Cooper novel, the right people often run into each other at the right times. Sometimes in our lives most of us have had such improbable meetings. In a college classroom, I found myself sitting next to a lost cousin from Denmark. We didn't even know of each other's existences but soon found that we had the same Danish uncle. In most romances the hero arrives at just the right moments to rescue the hapless heroine. In <u>The Trumpets of Jericho,</u> the roles are reversed: the heroine always arrives just in time. This may be perceived by some as a feminist revision of Civil War history, but then as now, there were many courageous women like Clara Barton who--wearing long dresses-- walked out onto battlefields to rescue men. The book, <u>Women in the Civil War</u> by Frank Moore examines the lives of forty women who risked their lives for their country and for the love of their men.

<u>The Trumpets of Jericho</u> is a love story set in the most deadly war of American history, but it is also about the power of music. The hero--a mediocre cornet player--is committed to a single idea: music is a peace maker. If people would sit down and play music together, or even listen to music together, they would find no need for war. They would recognize that the language of music transcends all languages and find in music a profound sense of shared humanity. In music, they would hear the voice of God and with it find the power for world peace. This seems like an improbable dream, but in the mind of my hero, anything is possible.

Victor H. Thompson
Hampton, Virginia

CHAPTER ONE
To Murfreesboro and Beyond

"Sigh no more, ladies, sigh no more
Men were deceivers ever;
One foot in sea, and one on shore;
To one thing constant never."

Shakespeare, <u>Much Ado About Nothing</u>

On the afternoon of June 20th, 1863, a heavy rain fell on Murfreesboro, Tennessee, and gusty winds stirred the leaves on limbs that had been shattered by the leaden hail of the Battle of Stones River. As if driven by the wind, a petite young woman with flaming red hair and deep blue eyes made her way briskly along the Manchester-Nashville Pike. She was Rita Goldstein of Cairo, Illinois, and she was about to descend like a wolf on the long-folded Union Army that lay stretched out unsuspectingly on the long-quiet battlefield. She was "a woman scorned," and as the poet said, "there could be no greater fury on earth." Her slender shoulders were draped with a black wool cloak, and with each step she swung a large lace reticule like a pendulum. And with each step she knew that she was moving closer to that lying Yankee who had left her standing alone with the Justice of the Peace. He could hide in the ranks of the Union Army, but by God she would find him if she had to search every army camp on the North American Continent. And she knew she was not the only woman who had been seduced and abandoned by a nefarious son of man. Adam had probably done the same thing to Eve, and she felt she was doing this for all women. She, Rita Goldstein, would bring Man before that great bar of justice from which there is no escape.

The muddy road was deeply scarred by the footprints of 80,000 soldiers, but Rita Goldstein made her inexorable way through the crevices and holes without wavering, without changing direction, and without even looking at the ground. She seemed to be driven by a demon force as she plunged towards the unsuspecting town of Murfreesboro, Tennessee.

Rita had started walking from Cairo, Illinois on June 9th, and eleven days later her long slender legs were still carrying her small body ever further into the dark heart of the South. The places she had passed and the dim recollections of filthy inns and muddy roads in Benton, Cadiz, and Clarksville, were of little consequence to her. What did they matter? She only knew that Private 1st Class Butch Lassiter was more than two hundred miles away and that she needed to walk more than twenty miles a day to catch him before he could run and hide. Only Nashville and Murfreesboro mattered. In Nashville she was in striking distance of the Union Army, and now she was near her target in Murfreesboro.

As Rita plunged along the muddy turnpike into the outskirts of Murfreesboro, Tennessee, the Army of the Cumberland was beginning to stir from its winter lethargy like a giant grizzly stretching its huge paws to the sun. Lincoln had unleashed this great beast of over 60,000 men to destroy the Confederate monster,

Treason, but after a bloody and inconclusive battle at Stones River in the cold final days of 1862, the Federals hibernated in Murfreesboro, and the Confederates dragged themselves across the Duck River in Tullahoma and hid themselves in the earth. But as the days marched on into summer, General Rosecrans, the master of the Federal beast, a man named affectionately by his troops, "Old Rosie," stepped from his tent and sniffed the sweet fresh wind that blew gently across the rolling hills of the Cumberland plain. Even in the steady drizzle, there was a faint fragrance of honey suckle blended with the rank smell of damp, newly plowed earth, and the old general almost forgot the death and destruction of six months ago. In fact, he had already transformed the near disaster of December into a kind of summer victory, and as his orderly handed him his morning coffee, he longed to complete his destruction of the Confederacy.

Before him lay the Cumberland Mountains, and he knew that the only roads to Tullahoma were through Hoover's Gap and Liberty Gap, both heavily defended by his ever-watchful and cautious enemy General Bragg. Old Rosie spoke in the general directions of the mountains and to no one in particular and almost affectionately, "Bragg, we're coming for you now, and this time you won't get away." Rosecrans knew that if he could take the gaps, he could flank Bragg at Tullahoma and move into Chattanooga. From Chattanooga, he could launch the forces that would destroy Atlanta, Savannah, and ultimately the South.

As she approached the vast Army of the Cumberland, Rita Goldstein knew nothing of these great prospects, nor would she have been particularly interested in them. But, like Rosecrans, she was ready to do battle, not with Bragg and not necessarily for the Union cause but with the man who had left her to join the Union Army. With each step, she felt a peculiar surge of anger tempered by something like love, and even she wasn't sure what she felt. "Butch must have had his reasons," she said in one moment, but in the next she said, "I swear I'll shoot that man." The only thing she knew for certain was that she wanted to meet Butch Lassiter face to face and ask him why he had left her with the Justice of the Peace and no bridegroom. In her mind's eye she saw Butch running up to her and hugging her and explaining that he had been kidnapped and forced into the army and wasn't able to see her, but she also saw the crestfallen face of a man caught in a lie. "I just want him to tell me to my face," she said to herself as she climbed over a fallen tree. The same scene played itself before her again as it had a thousand times before. She had waited all night by the old oak and had seen the damp darkness give way to a sickly yellow sky before she resigned herself to the fact that he wasn't coming. She was about to make her way home when she heard a mocking voice.

"Butch said to tell you that he won't be coming tonight or any other night. He's 'listed. Become a soldier boy to fight them Rebs." The speaker was one of the boys who had never let her forget that she was Jewish and that Cairo was a Christian town.

"That's a damned lie," Rita screamed. "Butch would never do anything like that without telling me."

"Suit yourself," the voice squeaked. "If you don't believe me, ask his Pa."

Butch's Pa didn't care a thing for Rita, and she knew he just might spit in her face, but still she ran to the log house on the edge of town and pounded on the door.

Pop Lassiter was already drunk as he opened the door and gazed into the face of his son's pretty girl friend. Rita could smell the whiskey as soon as the door opened and almost wished she hadn't come.

"Well ain't you a pretty sight! Butch ain't here, but you and me sure could have a little fun. Come on in."

"Where is Butch?" she had demanded.

Pa Lassiter laughed and said, "I reckon as far away from his Jewish princess as he could get. He joined the 123rd Illinois mounted infantry just so he wouldn't be tempted no more by some Jesus-killing bitch. It's really a matter of religious scruples if you get my drift. Ain't nothing wrong with a romp in the hay but to marry a Jew. Why he's got his soul to worry about."

As Rita turned to walk away, she heard the door slam shut, but she could feel his eyes from the window undressing her. "I'll find that man if it's the last thing I do," she resolved. "Exactly what I'll do when I find him, I'm not sure."

And so this petite young woman with flaming red hair and deep blue eyes was about to throw herself between the powers that would eventually destroy over 450,000 lives. By June 20th, 1862, Americans had been killing each other for about two years, but the job was only half done. The earth would circle the sun two more times before the last victim would fall. It was late in the afternoon when she approached the huge Federal camp at Murfreesboro. It had been raining the entire eleven days she had been on the road, but she was a philosophical young woman whose father had taught her that all things were for the good.

If this is "The best of all possible worlds," Rita muttered to herself, "why is Tennessee so wet and miserable?" As she felt her shoes suck at the thick mud, she remembered listening to her father reading <u>Candide</u> and laughed. There she was by the big iron stove in Cairo, and her father--with his deep warm humorous voice -- was reading her the words of that delightful hypocrite, Pangloss. In the book, ten thousand men died in battle to make a point, and now here she was walking across a bloody battlefield of the Civil War, and just what was the point?

"The point is to find Butch," she exclaimed to the trees. "I'll find him and bring him back dead or alive." Suddenly the road began to descend into what had once been a lovely forest but was now a hideous wasteland. Huge pines lay on their sides with grotesque gashes that revealed the white flesh under the bark. Bent trees stood with limbs shot away, and wide tears in the forest revealed a bleak montage of scrub timber and standing water. Even the face of the earth had been gouged into irregular furrows by some terrible invisible hand. "So this is the Inferno," she muttered to herself. "And so where is Virgil to help me?" She tried to make light of her situation but felt herself being swallowed by the dark vastness of an old battle field. *What am I doing here? Am I really going to find Butch here alive, and what if I do find him? Do I say Butch I love you, or Butch you son of a bitch. I hate you for running away from me without so much as a word. How could you have done this to me Butch?*

In her day dreams, she was with Butch in the old barn on that clear, cool October night, and as he clutched her to his breast, he was saying over and over again, "I love you, I love you." *He was so gentle and kind and the other boys in Cairo had seemed so rough and cruel. He stood up for me. He said he would marry me.*

One voice within her head said, "He is so good and so loving, that he must have his reasons." But the other voice said, "If he has another woman, I'll tear his heart out." She couldn't decide which voice to believe, and for the hundredth time she said to herself, "I will meet him in Murfreesboro and make him explain himself to me face to face."

As she was changing her mind about Butch for the thousandth time, she became aware of someone looking at her. Then she saw a tall young man leaning against a boulder on the side of the road staring intently at her. She remembered all those rude young men from Cairo who had leered at her and made obscene remarks and gestures, and so she brushed back her damp red hair with her hand and stood up straight and strong. As she drew near him she said, "What's the matter, haven't you ever seen a girl before?"

"I'm sorry Mam. I didn't mean any harm. It's just that the world around here is so blamed ugly, and you are so pretty, that I couldn't help myself." Although he was over six feet tall, Rita thought at first that he was rather short, because he was all hunched over when he stood. When she drew closer, he stood straighter but with his eyes looking at the ground. He almost whispered, "I'm sorry that I made you uncomfortable. I wouldn't have hurt you for the world."

To Rita his voice was surprisingly sweet and gentle, masculine but boy-like and innocent. She was about to move past him with a mocking, "I forgive you," but he seemed so vulnerable and sweet, that she stopped next to him. He was not wearing a military uniform, just some home-spun wool pants and a dirty cotton shirt. His light blond hair was pasted to his forehead and neck by the rain, and he looked like he had just come in from the fields.

"So what are you doing here?" Rita asked gently. "Do you want to be a soldier?"

The young man laughed. "No Mam, I'm really not much into killing folks. I'd much rather make peace. As the good book says, '"Blessed is the Peacemaker.'"

"So are you some kind of preacher then?"

The young man laughed again and then spoke very seriously. "I'm a cornet player."

"A cornet player? And so how do you expect to be a peacemaker with a cornet? Where I come from, cornet players disturb the peace."

The young man suddenly developed a pained expression on his face and said, "Where I come from it's the same way. You'd think that on a farm there'd be plenty of place to practice, but every time I start to blow, they start to mock me." The young man spoke in a rural accent.

"'Hey Joe, the cow sounds mighty sick, don't you think?' Or, 'I don't know what's got into that old mule.' Even my dog howls when I start to play. Hey Bugle?"

As he said this, a little red and white hound came out of the trees and sat at his feet. "Mam, this is Bugle, and my name is Sam Fletcher. I'm here to try out for the brigade band. Tryouts are today in that clearing just past the tents."

Rita had been so obsessed with finding Butch, that every second of delay was painful for her, but in this young man, Sam Fletcher, she had found a surprising source of joy that for a moment pushed back her anxiety and pain. She too loved music and could not just walk away. "You may find this hard to believe," she said excitedly, "but I am also a cornet player. My father sold band instruments and gave lessons in Brooklyn, New York, and when I was five, he started me on the cornet. It was about the only instrument small enough for me to hold. What kind of horn are you hiding behind your back?"

Sam stood up straight and spoke rapidly with the excitement of a child, "It's a B-flat cornet. Just wish I could play the thing." He handed it to Rita who cradled it like a baby before she worked the rotary valves with her fingers and studied the inscription on the bell. "It's a really nice instrument. Made of German silver by Isaac Fiske of Worcester, Mass. Four side action string rotary valves." As she held the instrument, she was so still and quiet, that she seemed to be somewhere else, and Sam finally said, "Mam, are you all right?"

"I'm sorry. I was just thinking of something that happened a long time ago. It's really not very interesting."

"Mam, if it has anything to do with cornets I'd sure like to hear about it."

Rita laughed and said, "I've never met anyone in my life who is so crazy about cornets, but then I'm a little crazy myself. I had a horn just like this, and I was in the parlor of our house in Brooklyn. My mother was accompanying me on her piano, and Dad was smiling ear to ear. The relatives couldn't believe that I could really play, but when that huge sound came from such a little person, they became believers at once. I've loved the cornet ever since, but those days are over. Here's your horn. Play it well."

As Sam took back his cornet, Rita looked away and started down the road to Murfreesboro. He shouted after her, "I've enjoyed talking with you, Mam," but she just raised her hand in a farewell. He watched as she slipped in the mud but didn't go down. With a twist of her shoulders, she regained her balance without losing a step, and then with her head held high, she disappeared in the abyss of the forest. Sam didn't want her to go, but he didn't know how to keep her either, and so he started to run after her. In his desperation, he slipped, but he didn't want to let go of the cornet, and he didn't want it to hit the ground, and so with the cornet held above his head, he fell in the muddy road and plowed a broad furrow with his face. After he struggled to his feet, he started running again and finally came behind Rita just as she was coming into another bombed-out area of the forest. He shouted after her, "Mam, could I ask you a big favor?"

When Rita turned and saw this creature of mud slugging along behind her, she burst out laughing.

"What's so funny?" panted Sam as he licked the mud from his lips and tried to spit it out as gracefully as he could.

"Sam, you are quite a sight. What time is this audition?"

"Oh, my God, it's about now. I was supposed to see Schmertz right after lunch, and I lost track of the time."

"Sam, you're a mess. You start talking to a strange woman, and then you forget about the most important thing in your life, the tryouts? You need someone to look after you."

Before Sam could say another word, Rita had pulled out a handkerchief from her bag and was wiping the mud from his face. "You know Sam, half of being a successful performer is image, and what an image you have! Now what were you going to ask me?"

"Mam, could I talk you into hearing me tryout? I'm pretty bad, but maybe even if I don't make the band you could give me some pointers."

Rita laughed and said, "Look, I'm trying to find someone important. I don't have time to listen. Now good-by and good luck." When she saw the sadness creep over Sam's face she said, "I'm sure you'll do fine." Then she said, "all right, I'll go but only if you stop calling me Mam. My name is Rita."

And so she and Sam started down the muddy road side by side The road turned into a little clearing in a pine forest, and at first she thought she was in hell. The clearing was apparently man-made, a casualty of the war with tall trees lying on their sides torn by cannon balls into rubble. A tall, white-bearded Satan wearing a huge white shako with a tall blue plume was standing in the middle of the clearing shouting for Sam to hurry up because he didn't have all day. He motioned for Sam to sit down and "play der damn horn." Sam put the cornet to his lips and a trembling blast of a sound ripped through the forest like a cannon ball, and at almost the same time, the frantic braying of mules came in a counterpoint from all directions. Sam paused briefly, as if to allow the choir an opportunity to make its entrance and then began a plaintive rendition of "Aura Lea."

As the wavering notes floated through the trees, the mules mimicked them, and the white-bearded man waved his wand. At the same moment, the little red hound threw back his head and bayed the mournful song of hounds, a song that made Rita think of millions of frantic rabbits one step ahead of millions of baying hounds in millions of ancient forests somewhere in the beginning of time. "And in Cairo, Illinois, when you are Jewish," she thought, "the hounds are men."

At this sublime moment, the white-bearded man, threw his wand into the ground and began to scream hysterically, "Nein, Nein, Nein! Take that cornet and throw it in the river. You will never play in my band!"

Sam sat for a moment dazed as if he had been hit by something, and then he rose slowly to his feet.

"But why sir? Give me a chance. I'll practice hard. You won't be sorry."

The director took off his tall-plumed shako hat, threw it on the ground and began to curse in German. After he had calmed down, he screamed,

"You have no musicality, no intonation, no rhythm, only noise. Now get out the hell out of here before I get really angry."

Just as Sam was about to retreat, Rita stepped forward. She was short, barely five feet tall, and slender, barely 100 pounds, but even in her lady-like bell-shaped dress that barely cleared the ground, and her dainty parasol, she was fierce.

"Not so fast General," she said to the director. "I think you're being a little hasty."

"And who the hell are you?"

"It doesn't matter who I am; you're being a little hasty. This young man has potential. Don't destroy his hopes."

"What the hell do you know about cornet playing?"

"She turned to Sam and said, "Let me borrow your cornet."

Sam smiled at his champion and handed her his most prized possession. She looked at it intently as if waiting for it to speak and worked the valves. Then she put the mouthpiece to her lips, and out came a clear strong rendition of the D Major scale. When she was finished playing, the young man reached for his horn, but she said, "One more thing." Then she stood still for a moment staring at the instrument and listening for something in her head. Then she put the cornet to her lips again, and the beautiful first movement of Haydn's trumpet Concerto pushed back the heavy June air. Even the mules and the hound listened in silence. When she had finished the third movement, the old bandmaster had tears in his eyes.

"So beautiful," he said; "it reminds me of my youth in Germany. It's too bad women cannot play in the band. You should play the violin. Now go home. I need to audition some more cornet players."

"I studied with the great Laura Berger, and everyone told her the same thing. Play the violin. Cornets are for men. But the point is, I don't want to play in your band. I just want you to give him a chance."

She pointed towards Sam and then turned back to the director. "You don't just kill people's dreams like that. You've got to give them hope. People need to dream, and after all, anything is possible." As she said this, she imagined herself in Butch's arms standing on the porch of their beautiful Nebraska farm looking over endless fields of corn.

The director was about to argue with her, but when he looked into her deep blue eyes, he was powerless. He remembered his girl back in Germany, his little Hilda, and he whispered, "And so what do you expect me to do, give him lessons?"

"No. Just give him something to practice, and let him try again."

"When he can play the Haydn Trumpet Concerto like you, then we talk again." He jammed the shako on his broad white head and walked rapidly towards the woods.

Rita put her arm around Sam's back and said, "Cheer up. There's always hope. Don't throw your cornet in the river." She paused for a second as she looked into the young man's sad blue eyes. Then she brushed her hair back with her hand and said,

"If you'll help me find my fiancé, I'll teach you how to play the cornet."

"Fiancé? You have a fiancé?" Sam had difficulty suppressing his disappointment, and the proposal struck him somehow as against his own best interests, but how could he not help this young woman who had already given him so much hope? He smiled and said, "Rita I reckon I'd get the better of that bargain. There are probably 70,000 men who would love to help such a pretty lady as you, but only a real angel, maybe Gabriel himself, could teach me how to play. I have worked on this thing for months, for hours a day, and even the cows can't stand me any more. My family has about disowned me. They say, 'You certainly are loud,' and then they laugh as if I'm the greatest darned fool in the world, and then they tell each other, 'Sam can certainly play loud,' and then everybody laughs again. I guess it was crazy of me to think that I could ever play in an army band. I'm really a hopeless case as a cornet player, but I'll help you find your boyfriend. What's his name?"

Rita was astonished that Sam had taken her absurd proposal seriously and was about to say, "I was just kidding," when she found herself saying instead, "Butch Lassiter. He's with the 123rd Illinois."

"I'll find him for you," Sam replied in a loud confident voice that belied his shyness. "Meet me at the band tent in two hours, and I'll give you a full report."

Rita was about to say, "Don't go. I was just kidding," but something about Sam's determined stride across the mud made her hopeful instead. She watched as Sam disappeared into the trees and saw his huge footprints filling with water. "Anything is possible," she whispered, in 'this best of possible worlds.'"

Sam emerged into a huge clearing where he saw thousands of white canvas tents. Most of the tents had small fires burning before them, and the men seemed to be cooking supper. Sam could smell the bacon and the hot corn bread as he approached six men sitting on the ground eating from tin plates.

"Howdy men, I see you're eating, and so I won't take up much of your time, but do you know a fella named Butch Lassiter? He's with the 123rd Illinois."

A long-legged soldier spat into the fire and replied, "Suppose we does? What's it to you?"

"Well his fiancée is lookin' fer him, and I reckoned you might be willing to help out Cupid a little." A fat soldier laughed and said, "I don't know nothin' about this here Cupid feller, but if the gal's purty, send her over; maybe we could help her out. I got plenty of room in my tent and ain't had a gal there in a coon's age."

"Why you pig-assed bucket of lard," the long-legged soldier replied. "What kind of gal do you think would sleep with you?"

"Only if he paid her a thousand dollar," chimed in a red-faced soldier, and the rest of them laughed.

"And so how much does this gal charge?" asked the long-legged soldier? "I just may be Butch Lassiter myself."

"No you ain't," the fat soldier said, "I'm Butch Lassiter."

"No, I'm Butch Lassiter," the red-faced soldier said.

A gray-bearded soldier finally stood up and said, "Let's not give this feller such a hard time."

"Son," he said to Sam, "give me five bucks, and I'll tell you where the real Butch Lassiter is."

The other men made hissing sounds, but Sam pulled five silver dollars out of his pocket and handed them to the gray beard.

The gray-bearded soldier started pushing the money back to Sam, but when Sam smiled happily, gray beard stuffed the money in his pocket and said, "This gal must be pretty special to son you if you gives five bucks to help her out." Sam blushed and said, "She's kind of a sister to me, and we both play the cornet."

As Sam emerged from the trees, Rita's heart began to race, and she felt sick to her stomach. It seemed to take forever before he crossed the meadow once again and stood by her side.

"I have good news," he said happily. "The 123rd Illinois has gone on a foraging expedition near Tullahoma, and Butch is with them. If we start walking tomorrow morning, we can be there in about two days. Let's start packing."

Rita threw her arms around him, kissed him on the cheek and said sweetly, "We musicians--we stick up for each other. We are brothers and sisters of the Great Order of the Cornet." Since all either of them had was a knapsack with a little food and a change of clothes, packing was simple, and by dawn they were on their way but not before Sam had his first real cornet lesson in the rain under the shelter of an old pine tree.

Rita tried to sound serious when she said, "Let me hear you play the C major scale," but Sam was so intense, like an evangelist in search of sinners, that she could not suppress a smile when he took a huge breath and splattered a low C against the sky.

"Take it easy," she said. "You're not trying to kill anyone. There's no need to knock down the walls of the city." But when she saw the hurt look on his face, she said gently, "It's really a pretty sound, but if you don't blow so hard, it will be even prettier. Watch what I do." She took the cornet in her hands and took a deep full breath that lifted her breasts to the starchy limits of her tight bodice; then as she slowly exhaled through her pursed lips, Sam watched her breasts sink slowly back into place. "Fill your lungs and hold the air as if you are going to blow out a candle, then tighten your stomach muscles like a bellows and force a steady flow of air through your lips. Don't squeeze your lips too tightly together, and don't push too hard against the mouthpiece; let the air do its work."

Rita took another deep breath, and Sam watched again as her bosom rose within her dress, and when she put the cornet to her lips and played a clear, lovely middle C, Sam thought it was the prettiest note he had ever heard. And when she said, "Put your hands on my stomach and feel how I control the air flow," Sam's whole body trembled, but he put his hands around her little waist and felt the muscles tightening under his touch.

"Now you try it," she said, "And let me feel your stomach." Sam tried to think of Molly, the girl he left behind in Des Moines," but when Rita placed her hands on his stomach, he felt the electricity of her touch. And when she said, "Take a deep breath; hold it; now let it go slowly," he thought only of the lovely woman by his side. When at last he played the C Major scale, he knew he was playing it for her alone, and wished that he could make it sound beautiful.

Back in camp the word spread quickly that some gal was lookin' for Butch Lassiter. When word finally reached Butch, the story was much improved. A young lieutenant in the 123rd said, "This gal was so pregnant, that she waddled like an old sow, and her Pa was with her with a shot gun." Butch went to the commanding officer at once and asked to be assigned to another foraging detail, in Georgia if possible.

CHAPTER TWO
"Tenting on the Old Campground"

"The soft sweet moss shall be thy bed
With crawling woodbine over-spread
By which the silver-shedding streams
Shall gently melt thee into dreams."

Robert Herrick, "To Phillis, to Love and Live With Him"

The sun was hidden behind heavy rain clouds as Sam, Rita, and Bugle started wending their way along the Manchester Pike towards the rain-drenched Cumberland Mountains. Sam and Rita walked side by side, but Bugle ran in ever widening circles in front of them and behind them. They didn't know that the whole Army of the Cumberland was about to move in the same direction. The next day at dawn, Wilder's brigade was poised to make a lightening strike against the Confederate defenders in Hoover's Gap, but as Rita and Sam walked side by side, as alone as Adam and Eve in the garden, they had their private struggles. For Sam, each step was Herculean. Instead of simply lifting his feet, he was swinging great balls of Tennessee red clay that clung like droppings from the Augean stables. Moreover, his clothes were so wet, that he seemed to be carrying the world upon his back. But when he looked at Rita, she was almost dancing. In reality, her feet also sank into the mud above her ankles, and she too was soaked to her beautiful skin, but love and hope seemed to make her lighter than earth.

"How come you're so happy?" Sam blurted out in exasperation.

"Oh Sam, have you never been in love? When you are in love, even the rain and the mud are beautiful. I know that each step takes me that much closer to Butch. Someday, I hope that you too will find someone to love you, and then you will understand."

"If this Butch is so special, how come you're the one trying to find him? If I were Butch, I certainly would never have left you. Why I'd be the one climbing the mountains and swimming the rivers."

"Sam, you are so sweet. I certainly wish Butch thought the way you do, but Butch has a wandering spirit. I was never really enough for him. He always wanted to be on the move seeing new things, meeting other people." Rita stopped, threw back her head and sang, "Men were deceivers ever, with one foot on land and one on shore, to one thing constant never." I guess Shakespeare said it best. He always does. But I really do love Butch and will be so happy when I see him again. I know we will settle down. He promised that we would buy some land and have a farm in Nebraska. Then we are going to have six children, three boys and three girls. When we're settled, I want you to come and visit us. We're going to have cows and horses. In Brooklyn I didn't have cows and horses. Bring your cornet. By then you will be rich and famous, and everyone will want to hear you."

"This is really none of my business, Rita, but who are you trying to convince? Where I come from a man who leaves his woman is a disgrace. There's nothin' else to it."

"All right, I was lying. You probably will not be a great cornet player. I've heard some good ones, and you aren't even close."

"How about if I really try?"

"If you really try. But this is ridiculous. What are we talking about? You think Butch and I will never get together again don't you?"

"Anything is possible. Sometimes the most incredible things happen. Someday I may play a cornet solo for Mr. Lincoln."

Rita stopped walking and turned towards Sam. "You know we are both dreamers aren't we?"

Sam smiled, put his hand on her shoulder and said, "And so what wrong with that? Most people don't dream enough. They spend the best years of their lives seeing nothing but the rear end of the mule pulling their plow. Isn't it pretty to imagine something better? If this Butch is your dream, I'll find him if I have to climb every mountain in Tennessee."

"And I'll teach you to make that cornet sound pretty if it's the last thing I do."

It was about noon when they came upon a white frame house a couple hundred yards off the pike. Sam thought of that hard tack and water that they had packed for lunch and suddenly had a better idea. "Let's visit those folks and see if we can buy a little milk and fresh bread. Maybe we could even come out of the rain to eat it."

"I'm not sure," said Rita. "They're probably rebels and would have no use for a couple of Yanks."

"Come on Rita. We may be from the north, and we both do talk kind of funny, but we ain't exactly in the army, and wouldn't it be nice to have some fresh food and to be dry for a few minutes?"

"Well I suppose we do need to eat, and being dry would be nice."

And so they made their way up a little winding road lined with flowering cherry tress and found themselves face to face with a very pretty lady of about sixteen. She was standing on the porch looking out over a beautiful flower garden next to her white frame house. Everything about the house and girl was neat and beautiful, a picture of the old South before the war. Rita imagined herself living in such a place with Butch.

Sam spoke to the girl. "Miss, do you suppose you could help out a couple of soaked hungry travelers?"

The girl came to the porch rail and said, "Well, you poor things. Come in out of the rain before you catch your death of cold." Then she yelled into the house, "Maw we have a couple of visitors. Tell Sally to put out a couple more plates."

A gray-haired lady stepped to the door and said softly, "Yes do come in. Welcome to the Hoover House. I am Mrs. Hoover, and my husband, John Hoover will be joining us shortly. I do declare this is certainly Yankee weather we're having here. Come on in." Then she ushered Rita and Sam into a large dining room dominated by a long, highly polished, mahogany table. Two young men and three young ladies, all in their twenties, and an old man with a grizzled gray beard and no teeth were already seated at the table. As Rita and Sam entered, everyone at the table stood up, bowed, said "Welcome," and sat down. A Negro servant with a lace cap stood in a corner holding a pitcher of something. At the center of the table was a bright silver candelabrum with six tall whale oil candles that radiated brilliantly across shining silver serving dishes piled high with greens, and meat, and potatoes.

The young girl said, "Let me take your coats, and then sit down." Right after they were seated, a large gray-haired man walked into the room and took his place at the head of the table. He nodded at the guests and said, "Welcome strangers. May the peace of the Lord be with us all." Then he bowed his head and said the blessing. "Oh Lord thank you for all this food which you have so bountifully given us to nourish our bodies and help us to use it and all our many blessings in thy service." He paused uncertainly and then continued, "Please forgive the Yankees for what they are doing and please protect us from their diabolic fury. Amen." His wife, who sat at the other end of the table said, "Sally, make sure that our guests have plenty to drink." The maid glided soundlessly to Sam and Rita and filled their glasses with cold tea.

John Hoover began to fill his plate and passed the silver dishes around the table. When everyone had something, and after his wife had had the first bite, he began to eat, and Sam and Rita began to eat. Sam had just savored that first taste of corn bread dripping with butter when he heard the distant splashing of horses' hooves in the thick mud. John Hoover apparently heard the sound too, because he stood up suddenly and said, "Excuse me a moment folks, I'll be right back." He opened the door and stepped out on the porch. In a few seconds, the sounds of many horses and the voices of many men were suddenly audible to everyone in the dining room. And then a loud northern voice shouted, "Pops we've come to help ourselves to your horses. It's for a good cause though, to save the union."

John Hoover spoke loudly and distinctly. "I have no horses. A bunch of thieving Yankees took them all last week. Now if you'll kindly excuse me, I'd like to finish my dinner."

The loud northern voice said, "Ah dinner. My boys and I could use a little sustenance. Ain't that right boys?" and a cheer went up. Then the front door flew open and about twenty blue-clad Union soldiers led by a young Captain crowded into the dining room. One of the young men at the table stood up and pointed a pistol at the Yankee Captain, but before he could shoot, a voice from the rear said, "Better put that gun away or everybody in the room is dead." The young man dropped the gun and sat down.

The Captain spoke again, "We'll let you finish up your dinner while we scout around the barn for horses. Swanson, take your squad outside and start looking." A tall, slender Nordic-looking fellow saluted and said, "Follow me boys," and, all but five of the troopers filed out the door. From the window Sam could see them fanning across the farmyard in the rain. The Captain said almost kindly, "I could sure use some of that milk and cornbread." Mrs. Hoover nodded to Sally, and Sally fixed a plate and brought it to the Captain. The Captain sat down next to Rita and while munching on his corn bread said almost apologetically, "I don't really mean you folks any harm. I just need some horses so we can end this bloody war. If you hard-headed Southerners would just listen to reason and obey the laws of this country, we will all be better off."

By now the Captain was the only one sitting at the table. Everyone else was standing and moving as far away as possible, and no one said a word.

Suddenly a bay mare moved across the window being led by one of the blue coats, and the youngest Hoover daughter, Meg, screamed, "Oh no. Please don't let your men take my horse. I raised her from a colt, and she's the only horse I have." She was crying now, and the Hoover men looked on helplessly. Suddenly a sharp voice from Brooklyn split the silence.

"Captain, don't you think you're being too harsh? After all, she is a kind young lady and never did you any harm."

The Captain looked at Rita and laughed. "Don't tell be that we've got Rebs all the way from Brooklyn, New York. Well listen my dear compatriot; we need horses. Soon we're going to take this great state of Tennessee and put it back in the Union, and we're going to need good horses to do it. I too hate to make a girl cry, but this is war."

Rita stood next to the Captain and said, "Well at least you can let the girl decide who will own her horse."

The Captain took a swallow of milk and said, "Well my sweet belle of Brooklyn, it shall be done." The Captain turned to the young Hoover girl and said, "Look over my men and pick the one you want to have your horse."

Meg was about to argue, but Rita looked at her and said, "With these people, it's best to give them what they want. Sam, take Meg outside to meet the soldiers."

Sam was happy to be able to actually do something, and he walked with Meg slowly out to the front porch. "Well Meg," Sam said softly, "which of these fine gentlemen is most worthy of your horse?"

Meg scanned the row of blue-coated troopers and finally said, "I like the shy young man with no beard" and pointed to a young Yankee of about seventeen. The young man looked at the ground and then shyly into the young girl's eyes. Finally he spoke, "Miss, I am honored to have your horse. I promise I will take care of her." Meg put the reins into his hands and hugged her mare around the neck for the last time. Then she clasped the young trooper's hand and squeezed it gently. As the troopers finally started down the cherry blossom road leading every horse from the farm, about ten animals in all, the young blue coat turned in his saddle and waved to Meg, and Meg waved back. Sam noticed that the maid Sally was riding with them and next to her on a sorrel horse was a big, muscular black man. Mr. Hoover was now standing next to Sam muttering, "It wasn't enough they took my horses, but they had to take my two best niggers as well."

Sam intended to be sympathetic to the man who had been so kind to him, but he wanted to clap his hands and scream for joy when he realized that two slaves were now free to have lives of their own. He turned to Mr. Hoover and said, "God bless Mr. Lincoln. I think I finally understand this war."

John Hoover looked like Sam had just hit him in the stomach, and when he had regained his breath said with great dignity, "I would be most obliged if you damned Yankees would vacate my premises immediately. You were hungry, and we fed you, and what thanks do we get? According to the Bible, you could have been angels, but you turned out to be devils instead. Now both of you get out of here."

Rita appeared at the door with Sam's coat and pack, and as they started down the aisle of cherry blossoms, Sam shouted, "Thank you for your hospitality. Just be grateful they didn't steal your silver, and violate your women, and burn your house." All the men suddenly appeared on the porch with rifles, and Rita said to Sam, "Just shut up and keep walking as fast as you can."

When they reached the Pike, Sam shouted, "Free the Slaves, free the slaves," and he could hear bullets buzzing by his head like a swarm of bees. Rita said, "Shut up you fool," but Sam just shouted louder, "God bless Abraham Lincoln. You know Rita, being shot at with real bullets for a good cause is rather exciting after all."

Rita said, "Being alive is exciting. And I've not sure that being dead is exciting at all. The next time you want to give your life to free the slaves, leave me out." She walked quickly ahead of Sam in silence.

Sam said, "What did I do wrong?"

Rita stopped walking and looked into Sam's gentle blue eyes. "Sam," she said. "You almost ended both of our dreams." You want to be a great cornet player, and I want to be a happily married farmer's wife with a lot of children. If we're dead, none of that can happen. Now don't be an idiot. Be a live coward but not a dead idiot."

"So that's your dream is it? It's not just Butch; it's being a farmer's wife. I don't know why anyone who can play the cornet the way you do would ever want to be a farmer's wife. I grew up on a farm, and I can tell you there is nothing there but hard exhausting work that never ends. Every morning you get up at dawn to feed the livestock and milk the cows. There is no break here, no day off. Then depending on the season, you plow or plant or hoe or weed until it's too dark to see, and after eating dinner, you fall asleep and start all over the next day."

Rita said, "On my farm it's going to be different. Butch and I will love every minute of our work. As we plow and sow together on God's good green earth, our children will labor with us and our lives will be lives of the seasons, and we will think no evil. It will be just the way it is in <u>Candide</u>: We will 'cultivate our own garden.'

"I can tell you from experience that playing a cornet is not all that great. No matter how much you practice or how well you play, there will be other musicians trying to bring you down a few notches. Every error you make will be magnified, and the better you play the more the others will hate you."

Sam laughed and said, "You have it all wrong. In my dream, music will bring world peace. When God created this world, I think he created it with music. Out of a chaos of sound, God made melodies and harmonies, and these became the world. The problem is, mankind doesn't always listen. In fact, people are generally the most quarrelsome creatures on this earth. Even my own family fights over things of no consequence. One Sunday an army band came to town and played on the town green. I had never heard a band play before, and so the music they made seemed to come from another world. As I listened closely, I realized what they were doing was something my family had never done; they were working together in the most wonderful way. The cornets came in for their licks, and they all stayed together, and no one tried to drown out anyone else. And then the cornets gave the clarinets their chance to speak, and like the cornets, the clarinets all played together. The drums kept everyone on the same beat, and even the big saxhorns didn't steal the show. From this mass of totally different instruments came these lovely sounds. And I thought to myself, life should be like that. In spite of our differences, we should all be working together to make beautiful music. I looked at the audience, and they were all at peace too. There was a happy smile on every face, and I knew right then that I wanted to be a part of a band and to make people peaceful and happy. And where could I do the most good? In a war of course. Where else was peace and harmony more needed? Maybe music could even end this awful war."

"Sam, you're crazy. The world can never be like that. People are mean and hateful, and they always will be."

"And I suppose this Butch of yours is an exception. How can a man like that be in anyone's dream? I haven't heard any good reason why he's worth all the trouble of tracking down and bringing back."

"Sam, that's really none of your business. You're almost as bad as my father. I love Butch because he stood by me when no one else would."

"What man wouldn't stand by you? You could have counted on me."

"Look, I was a Jewish girl from Brooklyn in a community of Baptists. Butch was the only one who even gave me the time of day. You weren't there. After my Mom died, we moved to Cairo, and Dad tried to set up his music business, but no one was interested. I was his only pupil, and he taught me everything he knew about the cornet, but I was non-paying. Consequently, he opened a general store instead and soon had a thriving business. Unfortunately, he was too good. He drove the other store out of business, and there was a lot of resentment. The other store had been cheating people for 20 years, but it was run by Presbyterians, and people thought that the expensive shoddy goods they bought were somehow predestined to show them the vanity of this life. Anyway, they put up with Dad for about eight years, and almost everyone owed him money because he was such an easy touch. Meanwhile I grew up and started teaching in the one-room school house. These were poor kids, and when Christmas came around, some of them didn't even have a Christmas tree. Heck, I was Jewish. Why should I care? But I did care. They were real suffering kids, and I thought that I could help. Dad and I cut some trees from the forest, gathered up some small gifts from the store and delivered them late at night on Christmas Eve. The kids were absolutely delighted, but their parents were not. Someone had seen us driving by in the night and word soon got out that "Santa Claus is Jewish." My father made a joke of it by saying, "But so was Jesus, and wasn't this his birthday?" But the locals were not in a joking mood. It was the first time anyone had called me a Kike and spat at me. And it was the first time I had seen someone paint a Star of David on an outhouse. The guys had never paid much attention to me before, but now they were just plain ugly. They called me Jewish bitch and Jewish whore. The only one who didn't was Butch. He came by the house late at night and told me he wasn't like the rest of them. In fact he loved me, and if I gave him a chance, I would see. He never took me anywhere by daylight, but one night we went into the barn and made love. Then he promised to marry me. He said he knew of some good farmland in Nebraska, and we would move there and start over. Then we made love, and I never saw him again."

"That son of a bitch," yelled Sam. "If I had him here, I'd tear him into little pieces."

"Sam, I think you're jealous. Why don't you make me jealous? Tell me about your girl friend. Now isn't this cornet business just a way to win some girl's heart?"

Sam chuckled and said, "To the contrary. The cornet just about busted up my relationship with Molly."

"Ah, so there is a love in your life. Now who is this Molly?"

"Molly is the girl I grew up with. She was from the next farm over, and we did just about everything together, barn dances, state fairs, hayrides, skating on the pond, bobbing for apples. Everybody just expected that we would get hitched some day. I even started saving some money for us and had put away about $50.

"Then one day this fellow came to our farm and asked if he could sleep in our barn. Pa told him he could sleep in the house if he wanted and to bring in his bags. Now one of the bags was kind of small, not much longer than an egg crate and a quarter as wide "What's in the bag?" Pa asked, and the fellow said, "Why it's a b-flat cornet." I could hardly believe my ears, and I asked, "Can I hear you play it?" and he just nodded.

Well as soon as the fellow came down for dinner, I asked him again, "Can I hear you play the cornet? And before I know it he had it out and was blowing out the sweetest sounds you ever heard. "Play Annie Laurie," I said, and he did. Then I asked him to play some more, and every song I asked for he played, and they were more than pretty. As he was putting the horn back in the case, I said, "I wish I had a horn like that," and he said, "How much you give me for it?" Before I could even think I said, "I'll give you $50, no more." Then he shook my hand and said, "Sold."

Now Molly was sitting there watching this, and she suddenly started to cry and left the room, but I was on my way up the stairs to get my money out of the mattress. After the man left, I begin to blow on the horn, but nothing came out. Molly, screamed at me, "You damned fool. That money would have bought me a nice engagement ring. Then I heard the door slam as she ran out of the house."

"And so what did you do to make poor Molly feel better?" Rita asked.

"I explained to her why playing the horn meant so much to me, but she just kept saying that if I had really loved her I wouldn't have bought it."

Rita asked, "Did you tell her how God created music to bring world peace?"

Sam laughed and said, "She started punching me with her little fists and walked out of the room. So much for a peacemaker. If beauty won't work, maybe just volume will. If the Jewish people could bring down Jericho with a thousand trumpets, a couple of hundred guys like me with cornets could bring down the whole Confederacy. I'm just loud enough and mean enough to do it."

"So what does Molly hope for?"

"She hopes that I will make the Army band, earn a lot of money, and then come home to get married."

"What do you think?"

"I think maybe Bugle is the only one of us with any sense."

"I don't know about the wisdom of dogs. In Brooklyn, the only dog I could have was stuffed."

"Well you've seen what old Bugle has been doing all day. When he puts his nose to the ground and picks up a scent, he is absolutely happy. He takes off into the woods singing and waving that white flag of a tail just above the top of the grass. He wants us humans to run with him and sing his happy song, but he doesn't seem to understand that we can't share his excitement. He smells things and hears things that we can't even imagine. It sort of the way we hear and love music that most people can't understand. Look at that smile on his face."

"Dogs can't smile. Their mouths are too droopy."

"They smile mostly with their eyes and tail, but believe me they smile."

"So why are dogs happier than we are?"

"That's easy. They are true to their natures. Old Bugle does all day what he was born to do: sniff the ground and hunt for rabbits. We humans, on the other hand, don't know what our nature is. If we play music, we come close to understanding our humanity, but we can't play music all the time. We worry about finding boy friends and girl friends. We worry about finding food, clothing and a place to stay. But old Bugle doesn't worry about any of that. In his own way, he knows that God will provide. When he barks, he is saying, "Take no thought for the morrow, for sufficient onto the day is the evil thereof."

"Are you saying that a dog is the greatest of philosophers?"

"I'm just saying that dogs are too smart to make war."

They had traveled about fifteen miles across the Cumberland plain and were now gradually climbing into the pass called Hoover's Gap. It was getting dark, and the little farm houses and Negro shacks that had been everywhere seemed to have disappeared. Now there were only the soft dark outlines of pines and the harsher jutting boulders. Sam looked off to the right side of the turnpike and noticed a small outcropping of rock that might give at least some shelter "The swallows have their nests, he thought, and the foxes their dens, but these children of Adam have no place to lay their weary heads."

"When I was coming from Cairo, I just put down a blanket in the leaves and fell asleep."

"Well this time, dear Rita, you're going first class."

Sam disappeared in the woods for a few minutes and returned with two sections of fence rail. He leaned them against the rock ledge about six feet apart and then took a sheet of oil cloth from his pack and suspended it over the two rails and the rock ledge. Finally he anchored the bottom and top corners with rocks. It was open at both ends but still kept off most of the rain. He made the sounds of a trumpet fanfare with his mouth and announced, "Your chamber, madam, has been prepared." When he looked at Rita, however, he noticed that she was shivering, and her teeth were chattering. Although it was a night in early summer, the steady rain had kept the temperature low in the mountains, and the night breeze against the wet clothes made Rita think of winter. In the vicinity of rebel troops in the gap, Sam didn't want to be conspicuous, but he knew they needed a fire.

After Rita entered the shelter, he broke off some dead lower branches from a nearby pine, tore them into little pieces and placed them in a small pile at the edge of the shelter. Then he broke off some larger branches and fashioned them into a small log cabin around the pile. Finally, he reached into an inner pocket, pulled out a miraculously dry Lucifer and started the fire. The twigs began to glow reluctantly at first, but they finally burst into a small yellow flame, and just when it looked as though the twigs were going to burn out, the larger pieces caught fire, and soon a small fire was reflecting its heat and light from the side of the rocks.

Rita was still shivering, and Sam knew that she would become ill if she didn't become warm and dry very soon. He pulled out the wool blanket that he had rolled up in the oil cloth and spread it out on the rubber ground cloth.

"I'm embarrassed to ask you this," Sam said gently, "but you need to get out of those wet clothes and cover yourself with the blanket. I'll go outside while you change."

When he came back in, he saw her wet clothes spread out on the rocks to dry and Rita shivering under the blankets. In a trembling voice, she said, "Lie down beside me to keep me warm."

"But what about Butch?"

"I'm not talking about making love, just keeping warm."

"I'm not sure that I could just lie down with you, but I'll sure try."

"Just think of Molly, and nothing will happen. Her spirit will protect you from an evil person like me."

"I'll find another fence rail and put it between us like a bundling board. Grandma said in the old days when it was too cold to rock on the porch, the young couples would get under the covers with a board between them. That way they could keep warm and virtuous at the same time."

"Forget the rail. Just get under the blanket with me."

Sam was still not certain what was right. His Dionysian body struggled against the starchy limits of his Presbyterian soul, and in "dubious battle," the outcome was not yet certain. He could spend the night in his wet clothes sitting by a dwindling fire, or he could take them off and crawl under the blanket with Rita. When Rita said once again, "I'm cold," Sam slipped out of his wet clothes, hung them on the rocks, and crawled under the blanket.

"I promise I won't do anything to you Rita," he said.

"I'm not worried," she said. "You are much too good."

Sam turned his back to her, but she wrapped herself around him shivering. As he felt the heavy softness of her breasts against his back, he didn't dare to move. He didn't even dare to turn around and face her. "She belongs to someone else," he said to himself, "and that wouldn't be right. The Lord would punish us both." Sam lay awake for a long time and soon felt Rita's body relaxing into a deep slumber. He was about to drift off himself when he smelled the heavy musky odor of wet dog and said, "Bugle, you rascal. You always know how to find the best places." Bugle licked Sam's face, and after turning in tight circles, in the manner of dogs, he settled down at Sam's feet and fell asleep. Sam whispered, "Rita, I told you this dog is no fool," but she only answered with a gentle snore.

Sam lay awake for what seemed like hours worrying about life in general but particularly about the lovely woman at his side. He loved her for the way she played the cornet, but was that all? What right did he have to love her at all? As he worried, he watched Bugle running in his sleep doing beagle work even in his dreams. Hours later, Sam at last fell asleep.

He dreamed that he was playing a cornet solo for Mr. Lincoln, but before he could play a note, he heard the unmistakable sounds of musket fire. He peered through the gap between the rock and the oil cloth and saw Wilder's cavalry riding by at full gallop. "Rita," he whispered. "I think we are in the middle of a battle. Stay here while I see what's happening." Sam struggled into his wet underwear and ran out into the open plain.

Even though she was cold and naked, Rita suddenly thought that Sam needed her. "Wait and I'll go with you," she muttered, but Sam was already gone. Rita pulled on her wet clothes, picked up the cornet, and ran after him.

CHAPTER THREE
The Battle for Hoover's Gap

"Farewell My Child, farewell my wife,
The bugle sound I hear;
It calls me to the bloody strife,
It calls the volunteer."

Song, "The Dying Volunteer" by G. Gumpert

Dressed in only his underwear, Sam rushed out on to the windy plains of Hoover's Gap to share the fate of two army's intent upon destroying each other. Without the slightest idea of what he hoped to accomplish, and swept up in the mindless excitement of men rushing to battle, he found himself running as fast as he could in the direction of the Union cavalry. His legs felt strong as he leaped over fallen trees and boulders, and he rejoiced in the power of his lungs and beating heart. So this was war at last. In his exuberance, he almost ran right into the back of a tall dismounted union cavalryman. The man turned suddenly pointing his rifle in Sam's face.

"Well I'll be damned," he muttered. "I heard them Rebs was short of clothes, but this here's the first I ever seen almost as he come from his mother's womb, so to speak. What yaw have to say for yerself, Johnnie?"

Sam was so astonished, that he just stared for a second and finally blurted out, "Don't shoot me. I'm a Yank. Well at least I'm trying to be a Yank if you'll let me."

"So if you ain't a Yank yet, what are you now?"

A group of troopers now surrounded Sam as he tried to explain that he was actually an Idaho farm boy who was trying to join the 7th Pennsylvania Cavalry.

"So they don't wear no clothes in Idaho, do they?" asked a sneering old man with white whiskers. Sam could hear laughter from the crowd. "I understand they've got pigs in Idaho too. Maybe you're just an Idaho pig. Let's see you root around in this Tennessee mud. Go on, get down there. Sam felt the rifle barrel pressed against his back, but before he could move, he heard a shout from down the long blue line. "Here they come, boys. Hold your fire until you hear the bugle. Jake, stand here and blow that thing when I tell you to."

From out of a curtain of rain and mist a huge wave of men in butternut moved up into the gap. As they got closer, the mountain echoed with a fierce yell, and Sam heard in that cry a time of darkness before men had words to push back their fears, and with the yell came the shrill cry of the bugle followed by the crackle of musket fire and then the whistle of Minie balls. It all seemed like musical theatre, even as a tall soldier threw up his hands and then settled slowly to the ground, as if to take a nap. As the masses of butternuts seemed on the verge of rushing over the men in blue, the bugle suddenly blasted the order to fire, and sheets of flame illuminated the blue line and sent the butternuts staggering. Hoping to take the battery before the men in blue could reload, the butternuts yelled and charged once again, but the men in blue kept firing. Sam then realized that the Union had Spencer repeaters, and the outgunned Confederates retreated rapidly down the mountainside with Wilder's dismounted cavalry right behind them.

However, the tall napping cavalryman did not join them. In the silence of a mountain pass, Sam heard the man groaning and rushed to his side. Sam could see the huge red stain on the man's blue coat, and he kneeled down to help. He unbuttoned the heavy wool coat and tried to stop the bubbling spring of blood which now completely soaked the white shirt. "Don't worry old fellow. Everything's going to be all right." Sam had seen the deaths of many farm animals as the blood gushed from their innocent throats, but this was the first man. As he watched the blood flow, he thought of the little lamb that his father had killed for an Easter dinner. "The lamb don't hurt," his father tried to reassure him. But the shocked look of terror in the lamb's eyes haunted him all his life. The lamb seemed to be saying, "I was your friend. I loved you. How could you do this to me?" He couldn't save the lamb, but maybe this time things would be different.

The napping soldier whispered to him, "Look son, I know I'm a dead man. When one of them minies gets you in the chest, they ain't nobody can put you together again. But I want you to do something for me. Take that there Spencer and bust it up good. I don't want any Rebs using it against old Abe Lincoln."

Sam picked up the rifle, and it felt good in his hands. He had fired many musket balls at squirrels and rabbits on the farm, but this was the first breech-loading repeater he had ever seen. He liked the feel of the wood and the balance. This was a gun that could make you feel safe.

"Bust the thing against a rock. Don't want no Rebs..." He gasped, and Sam thought that he was gone, but then the whispered words returned, "Don't want no damn Rebs. Son I want you to have this coat. No sense in you running around in your underwear. Take my coat."

"No sir. You need it more than I do."

"Don't be a jackass. Take the coat."

With a great gasp the man rose to a sitting position and peeled off his coat. "Now put this on and bust the gun."

Sam put on the coat and felt the cold blood oozing against the top of his underwear. As he moved towards a huge boulder with the gun, he thought of the dying Arthur and Excalibur from the McGuffy's readers. If I don't destroy it, he will know. And so with great reluctance, Sam swung the beautiful gun against the boulder, and the stock and barrel broke in two. Then he beat the barrel against the rock again and again, but the gun was too well made, and chips of stone began flying in Sam's face. He dropped the barrel and returned to tell the dying soldier what he had done, but when he got there, the soldier was dead. He touched the face, and it was already cold. Then he placed his hand on the bloody chest and felt for the silent heart. For a moment he was the last man on earth, and before him all was but desolation and death. But suddenly he hard Rita's clear soprano voice calling for him, and there was life again.

She emerged from behind some boulders and rushed into Sam's arms. "Sam, I've been so worried about you. Thank God you're safe."

"Rita, for God's sake, I told you to stay hidden."

"Sam, you should know by now that I'm not the kind of girl who hides from anything. As Shakespeare once said under other more pleasing circumstances, 'I may be little, but I'm fierce.'"

She looked at the body of the fallen Yankee and said, "We need to start walking to Tullahoma, but we can't just leave him here there. We need to get the spade from the shelter and dig him a grave."

Dragging the barrel of the ruined Spencer and wearing the dead man's coat, Sam looked for the boulder that marked the entrance to their lean-to shelter, and just as he was about to tell Rita that he had found it, men in butternut stepped out of a stand of pine trees with their rifles pointing at him.

A Reb with corporal's bars on a dirty brown jacket spoke first. "Drop your gun and put your hands up. I guess you'll be working for Jeff Davis from now on."

"Just a minute, Reb," Sam replied. "I'm a civilian. You've no right to…"

"Sure you're a civilian, and Abe Lincoln can fly. If you're a civilian what are you doing with that Yankee coat and part of a Spencer? You're one of them bastards who gunned down sixteen of Hardee's boys in the gap. I oughta blow your damned head off, but that would be too kind. I reckon I'll take you to Tullahoma instead. Now get on this horse before I shoot."

Sam was climbing aboard a small sorrel mare when Rita came out from behind the boulder and yelled, "Let him go. He's no soldier. He's a cornet player."

The Rebs were astonished at the sudden appearance of a pretty young woman but unmoved. "He's going with us Mam," the Corporal shouted, and then he yanked on the lead rope hooked to the mare, and the six men disappeared into the forest. Rita ran after them shouting, "He's no soldier. Let him be." But she was soon standing alone in the drizzling rain, and her words died in the muffled heavy air.

Sam tried to remember details of his journey so that he could find his way back to Rita, but the road was a devious one. Since the Yanks occupied the Manchester Pike beyond the gap, the Confederates made a long westerly loop through the forest, and the loblollies all looked too similar to be remembered. Towards dusk, the horses crossed a river and finally came into an open countryside. In the gloomy distance, Sam saw the outlines of massive earthworks, and within a few minutes he was inside one of the most ominous looking fortifications he had ever seen. "My God, he thought. The Yanks will be slaughtered if they try to take this place. Fredericksburg will seem like a minor skirmish in comparison."

A sentry blocked their way into the earthworks, but when the corporal saluted, the sentry stepped aside and motioned for the horsemen to pass. Sam tried to memorize every detail, so that he could plan his escape. Every pile of dirt every wooden paling, even the river itself were gigantic barriers between him and Rita. Once inside, the horsemen rode up to an old warehouse and stopped.

"Well Yank, this will be your home for a long time. If you cooperate and tell us what Old Rosie is up to, your stay here could be quite enjoyable. If not, well we don't even want to think about that does we boys?" The corporal chuckled and a spat stream of tobacco juice towards the warehouse door.

"Zeke, take him inside and show him his accommodations." A large barrel of a man slid off his horse and told Sam to do likewise. Then pushing Sam from behind, he lurched towards the heavy wooden door. Sam could feel the rope cutting into his wrists, and he worried that somehow his cornet-playing fingers would be made useless. When the door creaked open, Sam could see the forms of many men in various positions of repose. When his eyes became accustomed to the light, he recognized the blue coats of the Union Army. He heard the massive oak door snap shut behind him and suddenly he was surrounded by men in blue.

A hoarse voice broke from the shadows: "The Johnnies claim they whipped us out in the Gap and that Old Rosie is headed back to Washington. What do you have to say to that?"

Sam paused for a second to savor his position as truth-bringer before he answered. "Pack of lies. Wilder's brigade drove the Rebs through the Gap this morning. Rosie and the whole damned Army of the Cumberland will be here before you know it."

Then a chorus of cheers filled the old warehouse, and for the first time in his life Sam felt like kind of a hero.

An old whiskered fellow slid by his side, and asked, "Ya got any grub on ye? They ain't fed us in two days, and we's getting kind of hungry and thirsty."

Before he could answer, the door to the warehouse creaked open, and two Confederate soldiers with Enfield muskets stood in the opening. One of them them hollered, "We come for Sam Fletcher. The Colonel wants to see him."

Sam stepped towards the door and said, "Well here I am. I'm not going anywhere." The soldiers led him across the muddy parade ground of the fortification and into a small room built into the side of the wall. Here a fat-faced soldier with a red beard and moustache was sitting behind a rude oak table. "Sit down, Yank," he said in a most civilized southern voice. "We thought that you might be of some service to the cause of states rights."

Sam felt his whole body go tense, and then he blurted out, "States Rights, hell. You're all a bunch of damned traitors. I'd rather help hang old Jeff Davis from a sour apple tree."

The red-bearded Colonel looked Sam right in the eye and said, "Perhaps you don't fully appreciate your situation here. You are my guest. Now kindly tell me what you know of Rosecrans' intentions."

"Look colonel. I'm only a cornet player. I know nothing of what Old Rosie has in mind."

The colonel tapped a pencil on his desk like a drum stick and then said with a rasp in his voice, "So a cornet player you are. Let's hear a few tunes."

"I can't. I left my cornet in Hoover's Gap. If you traitors hadn't unlawfully dragged me away from it, I could play you a Yankee song or two, but I can't do anything now."

The Trumpets of Jericho:

The Colonel grinned and said, "That's all right boy. I'm sure we can find you a cornet around here someplace. Hey Joe. Go ask Bill Forrest to bring me his cornet. I'm sure he's not using it now." A young soldier saluted and went out the door.

Sam stood in silence, and the Colonel smiled and said, "That's a pretty good story about the cornet, but I won't believe it until I hear you can play " Dixie.'"

Sam said, "I don't play Rebel songs."

The Colonel's face turned red; then he said rather harshly, "Stop calling us rebels. We're not Rebels. We are an oppressed people fighting for our natural rights. Didn't the Declaration of Independence guarantee that all people have the natural right to change governments when the existing government wasn't doing its job of protecting 'life liberty and the pursuit of happiness?'" Without waiting for an answer, he shouted, "Well that government in Washington with that baboon Lincoln in charge ain't protecting the 'life, liberty, and happiness'" of southern people. I, for one, ain't happy at all. Slaves are our property, and the Feds are going to take them away from us. Do you call that protecting our property?"

The colonel's rant ended suddenly as the door swung open, and a short, heavy Confederate bandsman walked into the room cradling a cornet in his left hand. He was about to salute, but the Colonel said, "No need to stand on ceremony here. We are about to have a cornet solo."

The Confederate bandsman, Bill Forrest, blushed and asked, "What would you like me to play sir?"

"Not you, Forrest, him." The Colonel jabbed his thumb towards Sam and said, "Give your cornet to him. I want to hear him play 'Dixie'" The bandsman, paused for a few seconds, and then asked softly, "Am I being replaced, sir? I have always worked hard and tried to do my best."

The colonel laughed and said, "Of course we're not going to replace you. We just want to see if this lying Yankee can play the cornet. Give it to him Forrest. You'll get it back. I promise. You hang on to that thing as if it's the Holy Grail or something. It's just a piece of metal."

Forrest hugged the cornet to his chest as if it had been his sweetheart, and he was about to be separated for a long time, and then he handed it to Sam. With a pained expression on his face Sam grasped the instrument in his left hand and worked the valves rapidly with his right. "Don't like the movements on these valves," he muttered. "Too slow." Then he put the mouthpiece to his lips and blatted out a C major scale.

The Colonel went to the door and said, "Hey boys, come on in. We're going to have ourselves a little concert."

The two guards with muskets and three men with officer's bars walked into the room, and the Colonel said to Sam, "Play 'Dixie.' It's our favorite."

Sam blew some air through the horn and tried to imagine the tune for "Dixie" in his head. Then he filled his lungs, gripped the instrument as if he were about to strangle it, and let the air loose into the mouthpiece. All at once the room was filled with the echoes of vibrating brass but no identifiable tune. Sam tried to start it on an F, but when he reached for the next note, the correct interval was not there, so he stopped and started again with a G, but that didn't lead anywhere either, and so he started again with an A. In the distance a hound began to howl.

"Stop," the Colonel screamed. We will not let you make a mockery of our song. You have insulted us, but I understand. You can probably do a great job with that cursed abolitionist tune 'Battle Hymn.' Play it."

Sam tried to imagine the "Battle Hymn" and trusted his fingers to push the right valves, but like his attempt at "Dixie," this one ended in complete failure. The Colonel roared, "Cornet player, my foot. This man doesn't know the first thing about the cornet. Put him with the rest of those damned Yankees in the stockade."

As the guards dragged Sam back to the warehouse, the Colonel muttered, "Yankee son of a bitch. I'll teach him to mock us."

CHAPTER FOUR
Lost Dog

"She was the most faithful dog I have ever known"
Konrad Lorenz, <u>Man Meets Dog</u>

Bugle had watched his master disappear into the woods with strange men on horses, but he never heard the words, "Come Bugle," and so he stayed near the camp until he picked up the scent of a rabbit and followed it, sniffing excitedly and yelping all at the same time. He thought the rabbit would appear at any moment, and there would be the big boom from Sam, and the two of them would share the hot-blooded meat. But the scent suddenly disappeared in the smell of horses hooves. Bugle sniffed briefly at the smell of horses but turned again to find that elusive rabbit. The world was becoming dark when Bugle's nose was overcome by man smell, a smell so strong, that he could not even distinguish a single man. It was time to settle down with Sam for the night and curl up by Sam's feet, but there was no Sam smell.

Bugle vaguely approached the man smell still looking for Sam but suddenly heard a strange man voice.

The voice was soft, and a hand touched his head and rubbed his ears. Then there was a cap full of water, and Bugle lapped it until it was gone and then drank another. Then the hand reached behind him and produced something small. It smelled like food, something Sam had given him when there was nothing else. Bugle crushed it in his teeth and looked gratefully into the face of the kind man who had given it to him. From then on he followed the young man and went wherever the 2nd Tennessee volunteers went. Bugle felt a sense of uneasiness and sniffed every man who came near hoping to smell Sam, but with each day, the memory of Sam became less intense, and Bugle slept at the feet of the young man with food and water.

Life was tough with the 2nd Tennessee, and food was scarce, but these men in gray treated him right. One day Bugle even went into the woods and helped track down some rabbits. The men in gray killed them and shared some of the meat. It was almost like old times, but something was missing.

One day the men packed everything away including those oily-smelling things they slept under, and they rode off on horses. Some of them walked, including the man who gave the food and water. And so Bugle walked with the men in gray and slept with the man who fed him; by and by everyone was running, and he was running with them.

In a couple of days the men and horses were moving again, and this time they set their sleeping places on the top of a tall hill. From the tent of his new master, he could look out over a large clear grassy area below. Life stayed like this through many darknesses, and life seemed good for Bugle, but he still yearned to find the man smell that had been with him from the earliest days he could remember.

CHAPTER FIVE
Saved by A Cornet

"Blown harshly, keeps the trump its golden cry?"
Robert Browning, "Pictor Ignotus"

Rita felt as if her lungs would burst, but still she kept flying over rocks and fallen branches. "Let him go," she screamed into the afternoon shadows, "let him go." But as if a magician had waved his wand, Sam and the Confederates had already disappeared behind a curtain of white pines. The show was over, but Rita kept running, running until her foot caught a root, and she fell on her face in the mud. She felt the cold sticky mud across her mouth and face and turned on her side. She lay still for what seemed like hours and then crawled slowly to her feet and sat on a rock.

"It's all my fault," she mumbled to herself. "If I had done this alone, there would have been no problem. Once you let other people in your life, you only create problems."

She walked slowly back to the little camp and began piling her things in the rubber ground cloth. There was a box of hardtack, a little dried fruit, a small bag of cornmeal, wet clothes, and the sheet of oil cloth. She rolled the ground cloth into a sausage-shaped bundle, tied it together with a rope and slung it over her shoulders. Then she saw Sam's cornet lying in the mud, and resolved at once to leave it where it was. "I've got to think of saving myself now," she muttered. "What could be more useless than a cornet?" But even as she made her resolution and walked the first hundred yards towards Tullahoma, she was thinking of how much that cornet had meant to Sam. "I never knew a man who loved a cornet that much," she said. "He can't play it, but the mere hope that he will learn some day gives him a reason for existing that I can almost understand. But I can't carry the damned thing. It's all I can do to save myself. Besides, I'll probably never see him again. Like everything gentle and good, he will be swallowed up by this terrible war, and God knows I don't need a cornet."

With tears in her eyes, Rita walked the hundred yards back to the shelter and picked up the cornet. She rubbed it against her dress to take off the mud, put the mouthpiece to her lips and started to play the haunting first notes of "Aura Lea."

"This is absolutely crazy," she said, as she tied the cornet to her pack and slung it once again over her shoulders. As she walked into the dusk, the cornet banged against her back with every step.

After she had walked for about two miles, she suddenly came upon a riderless cavalry horse with US branded on his right haunch. The horse was drinking from a narrow stream and had his saddle still cinched to his back. "At least he's a Union horse," Rita thought happily and shouted, "Any Federal troops around here? Hello! I'm a friend. Born and raised a Yankee." But there was only the soft sound of the rushing stream for an answer.

"I suppose I could borrow this horse from Abe Lincoln," she said aloud, "if I promise to take care of it and bring it back." It was a big black horse with a white blaze on his forehead, and as Rita touched him, he pressed his muzzle against her face. "Good boy," she whispered gently and patted him on the muzzle.

She slung her pack over the horse's back and tied it to the saddle. Then she put her foot in the stirrup and pulled herself up onto the horse. With this great horse beneath her, she felt strong and hopeful again and started riding into a stand of pines.

She followed a narrow, well-beaten path for about an hour and was now about to climb a small incline when she saw a large shadow fall across her trail. As she came closer, she noticed that the shadow was a large man on a mule. He had pulled across the path and was holding a rifle in his hand. Rita was about to turn her horse around and gallop in the opposite direction, but a loud hoarse voice froze her where she was.

"I wouldn't try that if I was you. Old Betsy here can drop a coon at 500 yards, and a damned Yankee at a thousand. Come a little closer, so that I can get a good look at you."

Rita rode slowly towards the voice and noticed that the man wore no uniform. He had on brown homespun trousers and a blue wool shirt. A brown slouch hat covered a shaggy head of black hair that reached below his shoulders and seemed to frame a heavy black beard.

"Well, I be swan," he said softly. "So them Yanks is putting the gals in the cav'ry now. I know's they's a bunch of yellow-livered cowards, but if this don't beat all. Come here sweetheart. Let me get a look at them breasts."

He kicked his mule and rode closer to her and said, "My ain't they big ons. I'd sure like to get my hands on those."

Rita could smell the alcohol in the air and shuddered as he slid off his mule like a snake and grabbed the reins of her horse. She kicked her heels into the flanks of her mount, but the man held tightly to the reins, and the horse did not move. Then she clutched her only weapon, the cornet, and swung it at his head, but he ducked and dragged her from the horse. She could feel the immense strength in his big hairy hands and was completely overpowered. But she hit him in the nose with the cornet, and he screamed and let go. "Why you little bitch, you've broken my nose." As he grabbed for his nose, Rita started to run, but she found herself boxed into a little canyon of rocks. As the man lumbered toward her, she put the cornet to her lips and played the bugle call "The Run." The urgent sounds of the call were loud and clear and echoed among the boulders. But before she could play it again, he was on her. He snatched the cornet from her hand and hurled it to the ground. Then grasping both of her hands in one of his, he began to tear at her dress. She suddenly felt the cool air against her bare breasts and then his hand was between her legs, and she was flat on the ground. She couldn't breathe with this mountain of foul-smelling flesh crushing out her life, and as he fumbled for the soft hollow of her chamber of Venus, she was aware of a mosquito landing on her face and absurdly wondering how she could swat it. Then she could feel his coarse hand fumbling between her legs like a hairy spider, and she screamed a most blood-curdling yell.

At just that moment, the man mountain suddenly fell away from her, and she found herself staring at the blue pants of a Yankee cavalryman. She sat up and saw her attacker clutching his head which was now a mass of blood and a tall Yankee holding a Spencer by the barrel.

"Are you all right Mam?" the Yankee asked in a deep gentle voice.

Rita pulled her torn dress over her breasts and said, "Thanks to you. Another minute, and I could have been, worse than dead."

"I was going to put a bullet in him a while back but was afraid that I might hit you. I'm sorry that I couldn't have helped you sooner."

As he spoke, the Yankee took some rope and tied the hands of the dazed attacker. Then he hurled the man across the mule and tied him on like a huge sack of flour. "When I heard that bugle, I came as fast as I could."

"Saved by a cornet," Rita said. "There seems to be a message here somewhere, but I'm not sure what it is."

"I've got an extra jacket here. Why don't you put it on? I know a lady in Manchester who will be able to put you up for the night, and tomorrow you can tell me what I can do to help. By the way, my name's Morgan Davis, Seventh Pennsylvania Cavalry. We're camped just outside Manchester."

And so Morgan Davis and Rita, leading the mule with the fallen attacker, made their way slowly towards Manchester.

Rita knew that she should have been grateful to the man who had saved her honor, but she was beginning to resent Morgan's patronizing attitude towards her.

"Morgan," she said more sharply than she intended. "I'm a grown up woman, and I don't need some soldier to tell me what to do. What makes you think you're so damned smart?"

Morgan leaned over and grabbed the reins of Rita's horse and brought the two horses to a standstill. "Young lady, if I were your father, I'd take you across my knee and..."

"But you're not my father. Look, you saved me from that monster back there, and I am grateful to you. But I'm going to do what I need to do, and no one can stop me, not even you."

Morgan said nothing but led Rita's horse and rode his own into a little clearing next to a brook. "This place will suit us fine." Then he climbed down and motioned for Rita to do the same. She was about to protest, but Morgan's confident manner mesmerized her, and so she complied.

They sat next to each other on a fallen oak, and Morgan began to talk.

"I don't mean to sound like a know-it-all, but I've been in this war for about three years now, and I know what can happen. I've seen lots of folks killed for reasons that I hardly understand. I was in the big battle at Stones River and captured twice, but each time I managed to escape."

"Well you must certainly be some kind of hero," Rita jeered.

"No, not a hero exactly. I was just trying to save my life. I've heard about guys that get sent to Rebel prison. Their lives aren't fit for much. They treat hogs better."

"So do you enjoy killing rebels?" Rita asked sarcastically. "What's been your favorite part of the war so far?"

Morgan looked at the ground and said softly, "I'd appreciate it you would stop making fun of me. I don't enjoy the killing at all. When I enlisted in Harrisburg at the beginning of the war, I thought all southerners looked and acted kind of like Satan himself. Any people who would keep slaves and treat them worst than livestock surely had to be devils, and killing them didn't seem like a very hard thing to do. About a year ago the Seventh Pennsylvania galloped into Huntsville, Alabama intent upon killing a few Rebs, but when we reached the center of town, there were no men there. It was so quiet that we could hear the hum of insects and a few birds chirping in the bushes. At first I thought we had rushed into an ambush, but by and by an old woman in a shawl poked her head out a window and said, 'Put away them guns and swords. Ain't a man within twenty miles of this place, except maybe a few old sick ones.'

"I expected to hear gun shots, but nothing happened, and finally a few women came out of their houses and looked at us. A little red-haired girl came up to me and said, 'You're one of them damned Yankees who killed my Papa.' Then she began to punch at my leg, but she could barely reach my shoe. I felt her little fists thumping against my horse and reached down and touched her head. She was sobbing so hard the words hardly came out, but she did manage to bite my hand pretty hard. It still hurts a little.

"In any event we soon realized that all the men had run out of town for various reasons and left the women folk to fend for themselves. We also realized that most of them didn't have any heat in their houses or any flour to cook.

"Well my real job back in Pennsylvania is digging coal, and I'd much rather do that than kill people anyway. So I got a bunch of the boys together, and we opened up an old coal mine and started to dig. It felt good to have a shovel in my hand instead of a saber, and it felt even better to bring some warmth into those cold houses. In a couple of weeks we turned up enough coal to last them the winter.

"While we were digging coal, a few of the boys noticed that the town had a mill, but it wasn't working, and so they took a detail and fixed it. Now there was flour to be cooked. When we left a few weeks later, the little red-haired girl came up and gave me a big hug. To me that's been the best part of the war so far. The killing part makes no sense. God wanted us all to get along gave us all plenty of everything. There's no sense in fighting."

CHAPTER SIX
Ira Goldstein Finds a Band

"We are coming father Abraham,
Three hundred thousand more,
From Mississippi's winding stream
and from New England's shore."

Song, "We Are Coming Father Abraham,"
L.O. Emerson

Ira Goldstein had left Cairo, Illinois at three in the morning, and as his canvas-covered buckboard bumped along the dirt road towards Murfreesboro, the sun was beginning to rise above the broad cornfields in front of him. "God be praised," Goldstein said to the sun. "I am still headed East, and soon I will see my baby girl." Ira gave his mule a gentle tap of the whip and began to hum the "Brandenburg Concertos." "Yes, Old Sally," he said gently to his mule. "This is indeed the best of all possible worlds. The goyim burn down my store and seduce my daughter, but still God has a purpose for everything. I am alive and can still make music. Who knows what wonders God has in store for me? My people were slaves for a thousand years, but God led them through the Red Sea and to the Promised Land. Blessed be the name of the lord.

"I should be bitter, but I still got my musical instruments and ten barrels of apples. God does provide." Goldstein turned and looked back into his wagon where he saw crates of cornets and saxhorns of every kind. As if speaking to a customer he said, "We got them all made in Ohio. Soprano over-the shoulder, tenor and base pointing straight up, valved cornets, keyed bugles. You name it, I got it. My prices are good too. I sell for 5% over wholesale." He pulled a fiddle from under his seat and began to play the opening bars of Mendelssohn's violin concerto.

He had barely started the second movement when he saw a file of men walking up the road towards him. As they came closer, he could see that they were wearing Union Army uniforms but carried no weapons. They were singing that maudlin old war song, "Tenting tonight on the Old Campground," but they weren't weeping as the words would suggest. They were laughing and smiling. But as they approached Ira's wagon, a short, skinny man with a black spade of a beard sprinted ahead of the others, and as he came closer Ira saw that he had a pistol in his hand. He pointed it at Ira's head and said, "Whatever ya got in that wagon belongs to me."

Ira heard the metallic click as the hammer went back and threw his hands over his head. "Great Jehovah, am I to become another Job? Naked I came from my mother's womb...."

"Just shut up and get off the wagon."

Ira felt his knees shaking and a tightness in his throat as he began to climb down the side, but before his foot hit the ground, a booming voice shattered the silence.

"Jack, you old idiot, put the damned gun down and let the poor fellow alone." Ira turned around and saw a giant of a man standing next to him. He was broad-shouldered and blond and for an instance seemed to be an angel of the Lord.

"Praise the God of Israel," Ira chanted. "When I need help he sends me an angel."

The blond soldier laughed, and snickers of laughter broke out among the twelve men who now surrounded the wagon.

"He ain't exactly an angel," came a voice from the other side of the wagon, "but he's a damned good man. Hates the Rebs and loves Uncle Abe." A gray bearded fellow of about fifty stepped up to Ira and extended his hand. "Name's Myers, Fred Myers. This here feller who saved your life is Bill Hancock, a Harvard man. Thinks the niggers should be set free but otherwise he's a pretty smart man."

Ira shook hands with the man named Myers, nodded at Hancock and profusely thanked them both. In the mean time the little skinny man had moved off in the distance about fifty feet from the other men. Hancock pointed his thumb in his direction and said, "The rascal who tried to rob you is Jack Wilde. As a human being he's absolutely worthless, but he can play piccolo with the best of them. That's why we don't just shoot him."

Myers spoke suddenly, "Hey Pops. You got any food in that wagon? I'll pay you good Federal dollars for anything fit to eat."

Ira smiled and said, "I've got ten barrels of apples and nothing else. But apples will keep you alive. They fed Adam and Eve in Paradise. I'll let you have them three for a nickel. They're usually a nickel apiece but for you boys in blue, I have a special deal."

"Ya, some special deal, I bet," said someone with a heavy Swedish accent. "Soak the veterans. Make them pay through the nose. I know how you people operate. Besides look what happened to Adam and Eve after they ate the apple? Without the apple we not have this lousy war."

"Swede, don't you never stop complaining? Was you born with no Mama to love you?" A big Man with an Irish accent had stepped in front of Swede and said, "Sure we'll take some apples and here's the first nickel."

Soon all twelve men had paid their nickels and were sitting on the ground in a circle nibbling on their apples.

"These apples is sort of like manna in the desert," said a gruff voice in the circle.

"Ya," said Swede, "but the Lord don't charge no nickel."

Ira felt like the host at a banquet as he looked over his circle of guests. "So where are you boys headed?' he asked pleasantly.

Hancock spoke for the group. "We're heading home to Des Moines. Had enough of this terrible war."

"So you fellows have mustered out, have you?" asked Ira.

"Actually we was kind of fired," said the squeaky voice of Wilde. "Gov'ment said no more money for regimental bands. We stayed around for awhile and helped with the wounded but got tired of working for grub. Them soldier bastards was making $13 a month but we musicians, nothing."

"So you're musicians," Ira said excitedly. "I'm a musician myself. Taught music in New York City for 30 years. Ran a music store and played in three bands. Those were the days. Nothing but music day and night." Ira closed his eyes and looked into the window of his memories.

"So why did you quit?" asked a young man with an ostrich plume in a broad-brimmed Black Watch hat. Weren't ya good enough?"

Ira looked at the ground, and when he spoke the words were barely audible. "Wife died. Poor Estelle. She was in such pain at the end, cancer, but still she said, 'Ira don't worry about me. Think of your music. Think of our daughter Rita. Promise me that you will take good care of Rita. Teach her music.' And then she was gone. One minute I got a wife who is the reason for everything I do, and then like some magician snapped his fingers, she is gone. Like a dream. She looks like she is still there with me in the room asleep, but I know she's gone. God rest her soul. Then I don't see no reason to stay in New York. The music don't mean nothing without Estelle. I did everything for her, and now the whole city of New York is not big enough to hide me. I go to the Park and think of concerts there. Everywhere I see places we been together. I feel like I can't breathe any more. And so my baby Rita and I went West. Horace Greely said, 'Go West,' so we done it. But things didn't work out. The West is a tough place for Jews. I had a grocery store, but they burned it down. But still we got music, right boys? And I got a whole wagon full of instruments. They burned down my store, but the instruments was safe in my shed. See the Lord does provide, and this is the best of all possible worlds, am I right boys?"

Ira waited for a reply but heard only the sound of twelve people munching apples. Finally, Hancock spoke. "I'm really sorry about your wife's death; and I am really trying to feel how sad the loss of loved one can be, but after Stones River I can't really feel that much any more. It's as if something in me has died. I've seen so much death, that death doesn't seem to really matter anymore. When my grandma died, I thought that death was something profoundly individual, profoundly sublime, a "transition from this world to the next" as the preacher said. But now there is something absurd about the whole thing." Hancock paused and took a swig of water from his canteen and continued.

"My best friend from Des Moines and I enlisted together, and we went with the 123rd to Stones River. We're standing there eating breakfast together when suddenly his head disappears, taken off by a cannon ball from nowhere. In a sense it was absurd like when we play peek-a-boo with children. The face disappears behind the napkin and then suddenly reappears, and the child laughs at the incongruity of the whole thing. The face is gone and then, like magic, it is there again. So a part of me is thinking, Bill put your head back on. Stop fooling around, but the headless body lies bleeding on the ground, and there is nothing in my experience to make sense of things. I don't even have time to grieve the loss of my life-time companion because soon Rebs are everywhere. Bullets are whizzing by my head like bees. In fact they almost seem harmless as bees until I see people around me fall in pools of blood, and then I realize that I've got to run. I can't stay to help my companions. I've got to run to save myself. How strange, I think. Back in Des Moines people would be everywhere helping the injured, but here….How strange. The human race survived for millions of years by helping each other, and here we are running, running….I'm really sorry Ira."

"So who burned down your store?" Ira thought that a girl had spoken and looked towards a slender soldier sitting cross-legged at the opposite end of the circle.

"I don't really want to talk about it, because I ain't a complainer. 'The Lord God giveth, and the Lord God taketh,' and the goyin of Cairo were just helping the Lord. They took what they wanted and burned the rest, but the Lord spared my instruments. Speaking of instruments, you boys have any music? I lost all mine in the fire."

A deep voice with a heavy German accent said, "Ve all gotts music. The gov'ment takes back der instruments, but we all gotts der pouches of music. Ve gotts enough to play fer three hour."

"So you got the music, and I got the instruments. How interesting," exclaimed Ira. Then he looked at the circle of musicians and asked, "How long since you last played?"

"Three months, maybe more."

"Sure miss it."

There was a long silence, then Ira spoke. "This sounds a little crazy, but would you boys like to play a few tunes before you head back to Des Moines? For old times sake?"

"Hell, no! I want to get back to my wife. I suspect that she's been fooling around with old Jake Horner, and I aim to find out what the hell's goin' on." As he said these words, a large man with no hat and shaggy shoulder length hair stood up and headed towards the road.

"You damned fool, Jeff Little. Nobody in his right mind would have any doings with that woman of yours. She's as hard-headed as a mule and twice as ugly." Fred Myers had stood up and was addressing the group.

The man called Jeff Little ran towards Myers with his fists clenched and was about to throw a punch when Hancock stepped between the two men. He said, "Little, there is no need for more fighting. God knows we've seen enough of that. Besides, Fred didn't mean any harm. He was just trying to reassure you that your wife has certainly been true to you. Now sit down and relax." A faint ripple of laughter went around the circle.

Little scowled at the circle of laughing men and then sat down on the ground near the road. Hancock continued. "We've been on the road for a long time without music. What do you say we play a few tunes? Everybody pull out "The Battle Cry of Freedom," and Ira, pass out some of those instruments. The men will tell you who gets what."

The men were used to doing what Hancock said, and they opened their leather pouches and pulled out the music. Then they lined up at the wagon to get their instruments. As he passed out his precious cargo of saxhorns, drums, cymbals, and one piccolo for the would-be robber, Wilde, Ira whistled "The Battle Cry of Freedom." "I'll probably never see that piccolo again, he thought, but I never did care much for the sound of peanut whistles. God save my saxhorns."

After each man had an instrument, Ira was pleased to see that he had players on just about all parts. He even had a snare drummer, a boy of about twelve years old and an American Indian on bass drum. Hancock had an e-flat cornet, "the instrument of the brightest and most talented" thought Ira. The men formed two rows with the e-flat and b-flat cornets in front and the bass and baritone saxhorns in the rear, and already the sounds of a band warming up broke the silence of the summer morning. The cacophonous blasts of the bass saxhorns cut across the mellow runs of the cornets, and Ira felt a lump in his throat as he stepped up in front of the group with a stick for a baton. He held the stick high, and the group fell suddenly silent. Then Ira turned to the empty road and announced,

"Ladies and gentlemen, welcome to this first ever concert by the Ira Goldstein Concert Band. Our first number is a piece that you will all recognize. It rallied our boys at Charlottesville, and Antietam, and it will rally them until every rebel has laid down his guns. It is the wonderful "Battle Cry of Freedom."

Then he faced the band, raised his stick, and when he brought it down, the cornets burst into the melody, and the deep saxhorns played a kind of counterpoint. The boy on the snares and the Indian on the bass drum matched Ira's beat perfectly. However, the cornets soon rose to such a volume, that nothing else could be heard, and Jacques Flambeau, the flamboyant Frenchmen with the ostrich plume hat could be heard above everyone else. His face had turned red as he blasted louder and higher than anyone else. Ira motioned with his hand to play more softly, but Flambeau and the cornets played even louder. Finally Ira brought down the baton and said, "Stop. The cornets are making me deaf. Now I know how those damned trumpets could bring down the walls of Jericho. You men need to play softer. Give me a pretty tone, not a blast of thunder."

Flambeau said, "I don't need to take this. No one tells me how to play the cornet." Then he started to walk away, but Hancock called, "Do you always have to be such a Jackass Flambeau? We're here to have fun. Now get back here and play right." Everyone made Jackass sounds as Flambeau slinked back to his place.

Then Ira said, "Now we try it again, softer for cornets, louder for everyone else."

This time the beautiful harmonies of the "Battle Hymn" drifted across the still Illinois cornfields, and everyone knew it was good.

When the piece ended, some of the players started to head towards the wagon with their instruments, but someone said, "Let's do 'Aura Lea,'" and after they played all the verses of "Aura Lea," they dug into their pouches for more: "All Quiet Along the Potomac Tonight," "Yankee Doodle," "Just Before the Battle Mother," "We Are Coming Father Abraham." They played for over another hour, and no one complained. Everyone wanted the music to go on and on. As long as the music played, life was good, and the war and all its horrors seemed far away.

Hancock thought, "Only here does life make sense. Stones River was unreal. This was real. This was the way life should be."

But lips get tired, particularly lips that haven't played in three months, and soon not much was coming out of the horns. Hancock finally said, "Let's return Ira's instruments and get on our way."

The men slowly filed up to the wagon and gave Ira the instruments, but more than one player continued to work the valves and to look fondly at the instrument like a mother holding a child. A few blew a tunes from memory while waiting in line. When the instruments were back in their crates, the men lined up and started to file up the road.

Ira waved, and they all waved back, and Ira had what he knew was an utterly insane and improbable idea. It was so improbable, that it might actually work. He ran up the road and breathlessly caught Hancock's arm. "What do you say we play a concert in Shelbyville? It's a union town, and the 4th of July is coming up. We could probably make a few bucks, and I'm sure your boys could use some cash."

Hancock laughed, and said "That's the craziest thing I ever heard. Shelbyville is three days traveling in the opposite direction. And we've already been there. Nobody would be crazy enough to do that. Would you boys?" But even as he spoke, Hancock was hoping that maybe someone would contradict him. He thought of the music, and he thought of returning to his law office in Des Moines, and the law office seemed dead by comparison. There he would sit looking at endless deeds and wills and spend days trying to settle the petty disputes of people obsessed with who owns what cow or horse while his mind would be drifting back ceaselessly to that field in Tennessee where he saw that nothing was really important. Nothing, he suddenly thought, except maybe music.

The procession had stopped, and the men had gathered around Ira and Hancock to see what was going on, and when Hancock asked them again if they wanted to play in Shelbyville, everyone began to laugh.

"What kind of lard-headed idea is that?" asked Jeff Little. "Here we are three days from home, and this fool thinks I'm going to play in a concert in Shelbyville? I'll be damned first."

"I'm certainly not going," said Fred Myers. "Hell would have to freeze over first."

Soon everyone in the band had agreed that going to Shelbyville was about the stupidest thing that anyone had ever thought of, and they began laughing in Ira's face.

Ira had turned and was walking towards his wagon when he heard Hancock start to speak.

"You fellows are certainly right. Going to Shelbyville to play a 4th of July concert is, as this world goes, totally foolish. You would have a hard time explaining to anyone why you did it. But how many of you love to play music?"

A couple of hands went up, and then soon twelve hands were waving in the air. "And how many of you have instruments at home and a chance to play when you get there?" Not a single hand went up, and a kind of gloomy silence enshrouded the group. "So you're all going back to boring jobs in Des Moines and may never play again. Is that right?"

Suddenly Fred Myers spoke up. "Damn you Hancock, you're a lawyer through and through. What's with all those leading questions? If we say yes, we're agreeing that doing the sensible thing is stupid. But you've got me so confused now, that I don't know which way I'm going. If we go to Shelbyville, what then?"

Hancock looked at the ground for a minute and then said to Ira, "What then?"

Ira smiled and said, "How should I know? The Lord will provide. Ain't you guys Christian? Don't you have no faith?"

Hancock looked at the musicians and said, "The Bible says, 'Take no thought for the morrow, for the morrow shall take care of itself. Sufficient o to the day is the evil thereof.' Don't you men have any faith? What is this Jew going to think if you Christians don't believe that the Lord will provide? I say, on to Shelbyville!" As the late afternoon shadows fell on the vast cornfields of Illinois, a small caravan made its way down the dusty road towards Shelbyville. Ira and his mule-drawn wagon led the way followed by twelve musicians carrying an assortment of cornets, saxhorns and percussion. At the very end of the line, a small man played cheerful airs on a piccolo.

CHAPTER SEVEN
Sam Experiences Some Unwanted Southern Hospitality

"In the prison cell I sit,
Thinking Mother Dear of You
And our bright and happy home so far away,
And the tears they fill my eyes
Spite of all that I can do,
Tho' I try to cheer my comrades and be gay."

Song, "Tramp! Tramp! Tramp!" George F. Root

"Stone walls do not a prison make,
Nor Iron Bars a Cage."

Richard Lovelace, "To Althea: From Prison"

As his backside hit the cold stone floor of the warehouse prison, Sam screamed. "Damned Jeff Davis. I hope he rots in hell." And suddenly there were cheers from the darkness.

"That a way, Yank. That'll fix these Reb bastards. Send Jeff Davis to hell."

Sam was not used to the power of command, but as he sensed a crowd of Federal prisoners gathering around him, he felt suddenly invincible and began to sing as loudly as he could, "John Brown's Body." As his clear tenor voice echoed through the rafters, two other voices joined his, and soon dozens of voices from out of the darkness swelled to a mighty crescendo of joyous rebellion. The prisoners sang all the verses twice, and when they came to "Hang Jeff Davis from and old sour apple tree" for the third time, Confederate guards tried to shout them down, but the prisoners, led by Sam's mighty tenor, drowned them in an ocean of sound.

Even with the singing, life in the Confederate prison was at best tedious and at worst dangerous. The food was so poor and so scarce, that fellow Yanks sometimes fought among themselves for wormy hardtack and muddy water. Then there was the sickness. Sam found a tiny Yank in a corner burning with fever and calling for his mother. When Sam looked closer, he found that the lad couldn't have been more than 14 years old. He was lying on the cold stones with only an old fatigue coat for a cover. When Sam looked into the boy's eyes and felt the burning forehead, he saw the image of death. He took off his own coat--the bloodied coat of the dead union rifleman--and covered the boy with it. Then he went to the heavy oak door and called for help.

"What the hell do you want?" a voice yelled back from the other side.

Sam found a crack in the wooden door and said softly, "We've got a boy here who is really sick and needs help."

"This is a prison, not a damned hospital. What do you expect me to do, send a nurse?"

Sam said, "Yes send a nurse. Send us Clara Barton if you can find her."

"Look Yank, we never told him to leave his Mama and fight us God-fearing Confederates. It ain't our fault that he's fixin' to die."

"Look Johnnie, maybe someday you'll be the one needing help, and I'll be on the outside. This boy's an American just like you and me. He's also a fellow human being. Open the damned door and have a look at him."

Sam heard the loud jangling of heavy keys, and soon the thick oak door groaned open revealing three Confederate guards with Enfields. One was holding a flickering whale oil lamp, and behind him the greater lamp of a full yellow moon seemed to be mocking him.

One of the Confederates, a tall heavy fellow with a thick dark beard, set his rifle on the ground and looked at the sick Yankee on the ground. "Zeke," he said, "Run get me a bucket of water from the river. This boy's pretty bad."

One of the guards set down his gun and disappeared into the darkness. When he returned a few minutes later, the tall heavy Confederate began to mop the Yank's brow with a damp compress. "Got to get the fever down." Then the one who brought the water made a straw pallet in a corner and gently laid the young Union soldier on it.

"Poor feller," one of them said. "Ain't much we can do for him. I reckon typhoid's goin' to take him away before morning. Lookee here at these red spots all over his stomach. I seen old Jim Walker like this, and he was dead within twenty-four hours." The other

Reb, the one called Zeke, held his lantern near the youth and looked intensely at the hot, splotched face.

"Hell," he said, "the damned doctor killed old Jim. Bled him to death. I tell you what. I got me a tonic brewed from willow bark, dogwood, and poplar dissolved in whiskey. Let me give the kid a swig of that and rub a little turpentine on his chest. Can't hurt, can it? I hate to see the kid die and me do nothin' about it. Hell, I got me a brother about the same age Sure would want the Yanks to do the same for him."

Zeke got up and disappeared in the darkness, and Sam heard the heavy door slam shut. In a few minutes Zeke was back He was whistling a cheerful but slightly flat rendition of "Amazing Grace" as he plopped himself down next to the boy.

He propped up the boy's head on his lap and said, "Drink some of this son, and you'll feel as good as new." The boy was too weak to protest, and so Zeke poured some of his concoction into the boy's slightly parted lips All a once the boy shot up into a sitting position gasping and coughing, and Zeke said, "Praise the Lord. The medicine is working." Then he said, "Lie down. I'm going to spread some turpentine on your chest." When the first light of morning broke through the gray rain clouds, Zeke was still sitting next to the sleeping boy. Zeke said softly, "His fever is broke. He goin' to make it."

Sam said, "You know for Rebs, you're pretty nice guys. This kid could escape and come back to shoot you."

Zeke stood up, and in the gray morning light, Sam was surprised to see that he was a very tall muscular man. In the dark, the soft voice had made him seem small, but this giant of the morning put his hand on Sam's shoulder and said, "Let's not talk of killing. Don't you think we have had enough killing for one war?" Then he was gone.

The boy, Tom Williams, grew stronger every day, and every day, Zeke came to see him. One day Zeke made an interesting proposal to Sam. "Some of the boys is fixing to play a little baseball, but we're a little short-handed, and I know for a fact that you Yanks are crazy about this game. I was in Texas once and saw some of your boys playing a game between the lines. We shot and captured your center fielder, but you didn't quit until we captured the only ball in Texas. Anyway, we're gona play on the parade ground this Saturday, and I'd like you to organize some of these Yanks into a team. We'll have the North versus the South, and fight it out on the baseball field. What do you say?"

"So if we win is the war over?" asked Sam, "and is slavery dead?"

Zeke put his hand on Sam's shoulder and said softly, "I wish it were that easy. You know before this awful war started, they were fixin' to have a professional baseball team in Richmond, Virginia, and I was goin' to play on it. We could have played the Brooklyn Atlantics instead of shooting at those fellers in South Carolina. If we had, a lot of good people would still be alive today."

"So if we win, what happens?" asked Sam.

"If you win, we'll let you play us again every Saturday."

"Not much of a prize. How about if you give us some decent chow and let us out occasionally?"

"I can't promise you much. We ain't got much grub of our own, but I'll see what I can do."

After Zeke left, Sam shouted into the shadows of the warehouse, "All you guys who can play ball come out of the woodwork now." In a few minutes, about fifteen prisoners made their way to Sam. They were a motley bunch, half-starved and ragged, but they wanted to play ball.

On the morning of July 3rd, 1963, the sun emerged from behind the clouds that had hidden it for the past ten days, and two ball teams converged on the muddy parade ground. As North and South prepared for battle with bat and ball, Meade was winning at Gettysburg, and Grant was winning in Vicksburg. In the larger picture, things did not look good for the South. But this day, on a muddy parade ground in Tullahoma, Tennessee, prospects were much better.

The nine men of the southern team approached the parade ground in long-sleeved white wool shirts and gray uniform pants. The nine men of the north came in rags with no shoes. Moreover, they were a half-starved sickly-looking crew. There seemed but little chance of a Union victory here. Someone had placed a round tin plate for home and measured off forty-five feet for the pitcher. Pieces of board marked off the three bases in an approximate diamond shape. Along the sidelines and even slightly behind the outfielders a crowd of about two hundred people had already gathered. Sam could see that most of them were Confederate officers and men, but along the first base line, about thirty fellow prisoners were gathered with about ten Rebels with Enfields right behind them. There were also a few civilians including about a dozen or so Southern belles dressed in their long hooped gowns and coal scoop bonnets. As the Rebs took the field, the crowd cheered wildly, and some of the women blew kisses to the ball players.

The Rebel pitcher was a tall skinny fellow who threw his warm-up pitches underhanded with a high backward kick of his right leg. The ball came in from forty-five feet like a blur, and Sam couldn't figure out how anyone could throw a ball that fast. Sam batted first and stepped to the plate carrying a long thin wooden bat and tapped it lightly on the plate. It felt good in his hands as he swung it lightly backwards and forwards. With such a bat, he felt he could knock the ball over the fielders' heads. He cocked it behind his shoulder, and the lanky pitcher fired the first pitch like a bullet. It was already in the catcher's hands when Sam swung at it. The same thing happened with pitches two and three, and Sam was out. As the next Yankee batter stepped up to the plate, he yelled at the pitcher, "You better not be breaking your wrist. It's illegal you know."

The pitcher yelled back, "I'll show you bastards about illegal." The first pitch caught the Yank in the ribs, and he doubled up in pain. Three pitches later he was out, and three pitches after that the side was retired.

Most of the Yanks were pretty riled up by now. The cadaverous-looking first baseman, screamed, "You damned bastards. Let's see how you like some fast pitching. Let 'em have it Sam." Sam knew that the function of the pitcher was to simply serve the ball to the batter, but apparently these southerners didn't want to play fair. Sam made believe that he was throwing rocks at rabbits as he mowed down the first three southern batters.

With such pitching the game remained scoreless through six innings. Sam managed to tap a roller to second in the third inning and beat the throw to first. He even managed to steal second base but was unable to score. Zeke, the center fielder from the South, managed to hit a high fly to center, but the Yank center fielder caught it. By now the crowd had thinned out considerably, and Sam noticed that there was no one in the outfield beyond his own center fielder. As big Zeke stepped to the plate, Sam had an idea.

Zeke waved the bat back and forth, and Sam looped a slow pitch right over the center of the plate. Zeke was so astonished, that he swung with all his might and missed. "Damn," said Sam to himself. "The world's first change up and he misses it." Before the next pitch he said, "Here it comes again Zeke. Let's see what you can do with it." This time Zeke timed his swing perfectly, and the ball took off like a bullet towards centerfield. The center fielder just watched it go over his head, but Sam started running after it as fast as he could. Zeke was rounding second as Sam caught up with the ball near the outer edge of the parade ground, and as Zeke was rounding third, Sam ran past the ball and continued into the woods just beyond. Everyone was so excited about Zeke's home run, that for a while they didn't notice that Sam had disappeared. Some were slapping Zeke on the back, and others were taunting the Yanks. The pitcher shouted at the small knot of Yankee prisoners, "I guess that will show you damned abolitionists what we Johnnie Rebs can do. Just tell Abe Lincoln that his boys lost." Then the Southern team cheered, and the people on the sidelines cheered. About ten minutes elapsed before Zeke finally said, "Say what ever happened to Sam?"

One of the ladies said, "Well I saw him heading towards the woods. I thought it was nature calling, if you know what I mean."

Zeke turned to a sergeant and said, "Take your squad and go after him." A few minutes later a small group of men with Enfields was moving on the double quick towards the woods.

By this time, Sam had reached the Duck River and had to either hide in the brush or swim for his life. As he heard the footsteps crashing through the woods behind him, he pulled off his shoes and jumped into the water. As the cool water of the Duck closed around his body, he kicked his feet and flailed his arms against this sea of troubles and soon heard the plopping sounds of bullets hitting the water around him. He took a deep breath of air and dived as deeply as he could and groped in the mud for the distant shore. The dim green world of the river seemed quiet and safe, and Sam wanted to stay there forever, but as the water became lighter, he knew that he was bobbing dangerously near the surface. He drove himself deeper with his arms and desperately grasped slimy bits of river grass. But as his lungs seemed ready to burst, he let himself be lifted towards the surface and bullets. When his face bobbed to the surface, he heard no bullets but felt the warm sun on his head and took a deep gulp of air before diving again. This time he swam along the bottom as far as he could go and surfaced again about 20 yards ahead, and still there were no bullets. Finally he realized he was standing in the mud and began to walk as quickly as he could up the other bank of the river. With each step, he expected to feel a bullet, but nothing happened. While looking back for Rebs, he ran into a tree and fell in the maze of tangled roots and moss. It was an old hollow oak tree, and Sam quickly crawled inside. It was damp and musty, and for Sam, it was like Mother Nature's womb.

Back in the Confederate camp at Tullahoma, a nervous General Bragg had called in all his troops and was making an important announcement.

"Boys," he said "we need to leave Tullahoma immediately and camp in Chattanooga tonight. If we don't, that old rascal Rosecrans will have us caught like rats in the bung hole of a barrel." Bragg had been ready with one of the strongest defensive positions of the war, and in his heart knew that Rosecrans would come crashing right into it just like Hooker had done at Fredericksburg. That was the way this war was supposed to go. Outnumbered Confederates would dig in and decimate the superior Union forces that tried to drive them away. But the Yankees seemed to be getting smarter. Now they just went around strong defensive positions. If Bragg didn't reach Chattanooga, his whole army would be flanked. And so as the sun was beginning to set, long lines of Confederate soldiers and long lines of supply wagons began the journey to the most critical point in the battle for the west, Chattanooga, the railroad hub of the deep South.

Sam listened all night for the approach of the enemy, and of course, nothing happened because the only troops in the area belonged to Mr. Lincoln. As Sam peered from his tree he saw columns of blue-clad cavalry thundering by, and he rushed out of the tree waving his cap.

A burly red-bearded trooper pulled his horse to a stop next to Sam, and shouted,

"Look what we have here boys. A Reb who done lost his army."

Sam spoke softly, "No I'm not a Reb. I'm a Yank. My uncle's in the Seventh Pennsylvania."

"And so what unit are you with?" the trooper snarled. With that Reb cap I suspect that you belong to Jeff Davis."

"No shouted Sam. I am a loyal American." The trooper, pointed his carbine in Sam's face, and shouted, "Come with me boy. You're now a prisoner of Uncle Sam." Before Sam knew what was happening, he was being led at gunpoint to a small clearing in a stand of pines. In the center of the clearing sat a circle of blue-coated officers poring over a map. A tall bearded man said, "Them sons-of-a bitches" slipped out on us and are probably half way to Chattanooga by now." As Sam and the red-bearded soldier approached, the tall officer, shouted, "What are you doing here? You're supposed to be chasing Bragg."

"I may have something better for you here. Bragg left this fellow behind to spy on us, but maybe we can turn the tables here." Red Beard pushed Sam into the circle of officers with the barrel of his carbine and said, "Tell these gentlemen what Bragg is up to." The officers all looked at Sam intently waiting for some kind of response, but Sam only said, "I have nothing to say."

"Why nothing will come of nothing," said a young clean-shaven officer. "You know the penalty for spying, death. Maybe if you help us out a little, we could go easy on you."

Sam just hung his head and said, "I have nothing to say. I was a prisoner at Tullahoma and escaped just when you happened to come by. I know nothing of Bragg or his movements."

"And just how did you come to escape?" asked the red-bearded cavalryman.

After Sam finished telling his story of the baseball game, the tall officer laughed and said, "If that's not the most dad-blamed fantastical lie I ever heard, I don't know what is. This man is just wasting our time. We'll shoot him in the morning. In the meantime, keep his hands tied, and don't take your eyes off him. He's dangerous, I can tell you."

At first Sam thought the men were kidding, but when the red-bearded soldier marched him at gunpoint to a field tent, he began to feel a weakness in his knees. "My God," Sam said to the trees. "This can't really be happening." Night came too soon, and in the dark Sam said to the young private guarding the tent, "This is America, the land of freedom and justice. Whatever happened to due process and a jury of your peers?" The guard shrugged his shoulders and said, "This is war. They ain't no time for a jury of pears. If I was to fall asleep guarding you, they'd shoot me too. No doubt about it. No mercy in war time, No mercy at all."

Sam pitied himself immensely in the early hours of the evening. "If I hadn't done the right thing and tried to help my country, this wouldn't have happened. I'd still be back there on the farm in Illinois, maybe even out smooching with Molly in the barn. But because I wanted to save my country, my country is about to put me to death. My God, my God. Does even God care about me now, or am I just like all those other nameless souls buried in thousands of unmarked graves? And why did they all die like slaughtered lambs at Fredericksburg, Shiloh, and Stones River? Why did God save some and condemn others? It was all just too much of a muddle, and soon Sam slipped into a deep slumber. He dreamed again of playing his cornet for Mr. Lincoln. People filled the street in front of the White House, and when Sam played "The Battle Hymn of the Republic" in clear bright notes that floated like silver in a sweet April breeze, he was looking at Mr. Lincoln. He watched as a slight smile crossed that sad, care-worn face, and he knew that he had found the power of music to change the world. Mr. Lincoln was reaching out to shake his hand, as the sound of a bugle shattering the darkness brought Sam back to a field near Tullahoma, Tennessee. Then a gruff voice said, "It's time for you to die."

Two lines of soldiers with muskets filed on either side of Sam, and a drummer led the way. To the dead thump of muffled drums, Sam walked slowly towards his place of execution. A pole had been erected, and when the soldiers arrived, Sam's hands were tied around it. In the early morning light, he could see the drowsy faces of Union soldiers who, like him, had just left the mysterious Land of Nod. The tall whiskered officer rode forward on a big bay mare and addressed the group. "Let this be a warning to all traitors to their country. Firing squad, take your places." Ten young soldiers stepped forward in a line and raised their muskets. "And so all the music is going to stop now," thought Sam. "At least for me it will. I just hope there is music on the other side."

CHAPTER EIGHT
The Strange Case of a Female Who Does Not Want to be Rescued by a Big, Strong Man

"I see a woman may be made a fool
If she had not a spirit to resist."

Shakespeare, <u>The Taming of the Shrew</u>

The rain was still falling as Morgan Davis and Rita left the grove of trees just outside of the little town of Beech Grove, Tennessee. Rita kept saying, "I'll be all right now. Just show me the way to Tullahoma," and Morgan Davis said even more insistently, "This is no place for an unescorted woman. I won't feel satisfied until I know you're safe in Shelbyville." It was getting dark in the mountains as Morgan headed steadfastly towards the union town of Shelbyville. Even though Tennessee had officially seceded from the union and was now part of the Confederacy, Eastern Tennessee had many Union strongholds, and Shelbyville was one of the best of them. In just a few days, this little Southern town would be doing something extremely rare in Dixie, celebrating the 4th of July.

Morgan asked Rita what a pretty young girl like her was doing out in the woods in the middle of a war, and she told him of her search for Butch Lassiter and her concern for the fate of the young cornetist. Morgan was unmoved by these yearnings of a young girl's heart. "All the same you need to be somewhere safe. If you were my sister, I'd send you home to Cairo."

"But I'm not your sister. In fact, I'm an only child. I'm used to doing what I want to do when I want to do it."

"Well I suppose you have a Papa who's spoiled you rotten, but I ain't your Papa either. I'm one of Lincoln's soldiers, and I'm supposed to protect widows, orphans, and silly young gals like you."

"Who told you were supposed to protect silly young girls like me?"

Morgan laughed and said, "Maybe God told me. I don't know. Aren't all red-blooded American men supposed to look out for the safety of pretty women?"

"Well that's the first I ever heard about that," said Rita irritably. "I don't really need anyone looking out for me."

"Tell that to our traveling companion back yonder," said Davis as he pointed his thumb in the direction of the mule carrying Rita's assailant.

"But I'll be careful," Rita pleaded, but Morgan Davis plunged inexorably towards Shelbyville.

As they reached the top of a slight rise in the trail, Morgan saw smoke from a campfire about five hundred yards ahead and pulled up his horse short. He whispered to Rita, "Walk the horses back into the dell and wait until I come back" Then he slipped into the cover of a stand of pine and was gone. Rita briefly considered leaving

Morgan and trying to find the way to Tullahoma. "He treats me as if I were a child," she said to the horse. "I'm a grown up woman, and nobody has the right to tell me what to do." In the dusk, with her attacker still tied to the mule, she resolved to wait for Morgan's return and then to tell him her decision to leave him.

After what seemed to be a very long time and after the silver of dusk had descended into the black of night, Morgan crept back to her side. "It's a good thing we stopped. We're riding into the midst of a Rebel platoon. Another few feet and we would have run right into a sentry. The way I figure it we need to take a little detour and go by way of Fairfield."

"Look, Morgan, I appreciate what you are trying to do for me, but I don't really want to go to Shelbyville anyway. Just tell me the road to Tullahoma, and I'll be on my way."

Before Morgan could answer, they heard the sounds of men crashing through the woods, and Morgan said, "Get on your horse and follow me closely." They left the mule with the prisoner tied to a tree, and Morgan began retreating along the path through the woods. They could hear voices now. "Get your horses boys. I think some of those damned Yankees may be paying us a little visit."

Morgan whispered, "Let your horse have his head and move as quickly as you can." The earth throbbed to the beat of many horses' hooves as Morgan and Rita glided through the loblollies. As they went up a little hill, Morgan looked back and could see movement in the trees a few hundred yards behind them. "Move faster Rita. Fly."

Rita always thought that she was fearless, but as she heard the Rebs coming closer and closer from out of the darkness, she wanted to be back in Brooklyn, New York in that warm little parlor with her cornet and her adoring relatives, but here she was in the deep dark woods of the Grimm brothers being pursued by a host of wicked witches, and her heart was beating like a windmill, and her only comfort was a tall Yankee on a big gray horse.

The horses were lurching down a narrow trail that ended in a little brook, and with each step, Rita felt as if she were going to fall over her horse's head, but when they reached the brook, she was still aboard, and in the moonlight she could see Morgan motioning to her to follow him. There was a steep wall of rock on one side and an enclosure made by huge boulders on the other. Inside they were just about invisible.

Morgan slipped off his horse and gestured for Rita to do likewise, and they crept into a crevice formed by an overhanging ledge of rock and waited. Rita could see a little brook just beyond her den of rocks, and in the stillness she could hear it rippling down the mountainside, and she suddenly realized how hot and thirsty she was. How lovely it would be to creep out to the edge and dip her face into that wonderful coolness. Much to her horror, the two horses had ambled to the edge of the stream and were drinking deeply. "Damn," Morgan muttered softly. "I should have tied them to a tree." But it was too late to do anything now. The ground was trembling with a cadence of its own, and the enemy would soon be near. "But what enemy," Rita mused? These men in gray seemed to have little to do with her life. She had no animosity towards them and supposed they had none for her either. Suppose I just walk out and say, "I'm not your enemy. I just want to go to Tullahoma to tend to my own business. What would they say?" She started to crawl out from her cover, but Morgan grabbed her arm. He whispered, "Don't count on no kindness from those boys. They'd figger that a northern gal down here was a hooker or a spy." Then a long line of Confederate cavalry emerged from the trees. They were riding slowly now and looking in all directions.

"They bound to be near here somewhere," a deep voice muttered. "No way they could have made it to the pike without one of the boys seein' them."

"They's always a way," said a high-pitched tenor. "I think they're in the next county by now. I say we go back to camp and get some shut eye. I tell you I'm just plain bushed."

A young officer with Lieutenant's bars rode up and said, "Let your horses have some water. Then we'll ride up the Shelbyville Road. The woman's probably that damned Yankee spy Pauline Cushman. Bring her in and Bragg will give us all a furlough."

Soon the narrow stream was lined with horses drinking, and what seemed to be a platoon of gray-coated cavalrymen talking softly to each other. Here and there Rita and Morgan could see the lights from cigars flashing like lightening bugs in the darkness, and a breeze brought them the acrid smell of burning tobacco.

"They're gonna see our horses," whispered Morgan. "We need to slip away before they do." In the moonlight the big bay horse and the sorrel mare looked huge, and the US brands on their haunches looked as clear as road signs, but somehow they were still invisible to the enemy. Morgan motioned for Rita to follow him, and they began to creep silently out of the overhang and behind some boulders. On the other side of the boulders, they saw a well-worn path that disappeared into a glade of pine trees, and they followed it as quickly and as quietly as they could. As they slipped into the pines, the ground was marshy, and Rita could feel muddy water oozing into her shoes. The strong smell of mud and rotting vegetation was somehow comforting to her, as if she had escaped into some corridor of time, a time long before this so-called War Between the States. She could no longer hear the voices as she and Morgan lay on their stomachs in a marshy hollow. She could hear Morgan breathing heavily and felt his strong arm over her shoulders.

CHAPTER NINE
The Pequod Meets *The Rachel* or Ira Goldstein Reveals the Real Purpose of His Journey

"Rachel weeping for her children refused to be comforted for her children, because they were not."

Jeremiah 31:15

The sun was just setting behind the rolling hills of Murfreesboro as what had once been the regimental band for the 123rd Illinois made its way slowly into the outskirts of town. Ira led the procession with his wagon, and the rest followed behind in little knots of twos and threes. The only exception was Hancock who now sat on the wagon next to Ira. Hancock asked Ira to give him the plan of action, but Ira remained wrapped silently in his own thoughts. At last Ira spoke.

"You got any children?"

"None that I know about," laughed Hancock, "but what the hell does that have to do with the plans?"

"Everything," replied Ira. "I've got this daughter, and they tell me she's in Murfreesboro. I gotta find her first. Then we talk about music. She plays the cornet beautifully, like an angel. We need her in this band."

Hancock looked off into the looming darkness and laughed. "So there's more to this business than the music, isn't there? You've brought back an entire regimental band to find your lost daughter. What idiots we are. So you've just been using us all along." Hancock was about to jump from the wagon when Ira grabbed his arm.

"Please don't say nothing to the boys. Let me explain." And so Ira told Hancock the sad story of his dead wife and of the sudden disappearance of his young daughter. Hancock listened in silence but the whole time was thinking that he should have gone on to Cairo. When he had finished his story, Ira said to Hancock, "I would sure appreciate any help you boys could give to me. If we all look around Murfreesboro, we can find her, and she sure could help this band."

Hancock was about to say something about the kind of women who follow soldiers, but when he looked into the sad, pleading eyes of Ira Goldstein, he changed his mind. The atrocities of war may have hardened his heart to the possibilities of human kindness, but when he looked at Ira Goldstein again, he changed his mind. "Sure we'll help. But what happens when we find her? Have you led us all this way to find your daughter, or are you really going to lead the band?"

"The band will play. I got nothing to go home to. What else is there but the band and music?"

Hancock replied, "You're right old man. What else is there but the band and music? It seems that half the people I knew died at

Stones River and thousands I didn't know went with them. And for what? After it was over we moved into Murfreesboro, and the Rebs went to Tullahoma, and the damned war still didn't end. It probably never will end. But in the midst of the battle, that mad carnival from hell, I could hear the rebel bands playing 'Lorena', and when they were finished, we let them have it with 'Aura Lea.' When we stopped playing, I could hear cheering from the rebel lines, and someone shouted, 'Play 'Dixie,' and we did. 'Dixie' really is one of our songs you know. It was written by a Yank but stolen by that rascal traitor, Jeff Davis. After 'Dixie,' they cheered again, and I was thinking, if Rebs and Yanks even love the same music, what the hell are they fighting about? I was feeling unaccountably happy with this thought until a bullet knocked my cornet right out of my hands. As my horn hit the ground, I thought that I had been mortally wounded. When I picked it up, I was actually crying and hugged it to my breast as if it had been a baby. It had a nick in the bell from a Minie ball, but I'm saying to myself, 'It's hurt but not dead. Praise the Lord, it's not dead.' Then I kissed it."

Ira laughed and said, "What kind of soldiers are you anyway? You go into battle with cornets instead of guns. What happens if somebody comes after you with a rifle?"

"We give 'em a blastisimo broadside with heavy brass, and they generally surrender," replied Hancock.

Ira scratched his head, and said, "You guys sure have guts. My people brought down a whole city with trumpets one time, but nobody was shooting at them. Those people in Jericho didn't have no Enfields and Minie balls."

The band was now entering the main street of Murfreesboro, and Hancock realized that a profound change had come over the place. The fields where soldiers had once cooked their meals and killed time, were now empty. Only here and there people wearing normal civilian clothes were quietly going about their business.

"Sure looks like the Army has left this place in peace," he muttered as he stepped down from the wagon.

"Say Sam, what's this daughter of yours look like anyway?"

Ira's old leathery face broke into a big grin, and he spoke rapturously. "She's an angel. Big blue eyes. Hair like a sunset. About five two and slender. When she smiles at you all your troubles go away."

"And what's her name?"

"Rita Goldstein. Jewish you know."

Hancock stepped down from the wagon and addressed his boys. "We're going to camp here tonight, but I want you all to help find Ira's daughter."

"Daughter? Ira's got a daughter? What the hell's she doin' around here?" said a voice in the darkness.

"What's she look like?" asked an old grizzled fellow.

"Like an angel" said Hancock with a smile

"You mean," said Jeff Little from the looming darkness, "she has breasts like ripe melons, lips like cherries, skin like alabaster, limbs of ivory, a voice like a silver stream, breath like roses, and when she walks, her feet don't touch the ground. Fish leap from rivers into her arms, little birds bring her fruit…"

"Something like that," replied Hancock.

"When we find her, I get to sleep with her first," chortled Flambeau.

"Shut up, ya old goat," shouted Little. "You wouldn't know what to do with her if you had her."

"I know a hell of a lot more about women than you do. Ya cain't even keep your wife from havin' a little fun on the side."

Little rushed towards Flambeau with his fist cocked, but Hancock intervened. "There will be no more fighting. God knows we've all seen enough fighting to last a lifetime."

Little backed away but said, "I'm not finished with you yet Flambeau."

Hancock stood on the wagon and shouted down to the band. "She's 23 years old, about five two, slender with flaming red hair and blue eyes. Gold to the man who finds her!" He waved a doubloon in the air, and as he nailed it to the side of the wagon, the men cheered. As the band members spread out their bed rolls on the ground, they talked of the Jewish princess, of their own uncertain future as bandsmen without an army, and of the gold doubloon. The next morning, the doubloon was gone. Hancock asked questions and certainly had his suspicions, but no one knew anything for certain. A week later, Flambeau appeared wearing a new wool jacket with gold braid and sipping from a bottle of French brandy.

The next morning, the twelve bandsmen and Ira scattered through the nearly empty streets of Murfreesboro in search of the lost daughter, their own Rachel. By noon everyone was back with different stories to tell.

"One thing's for certain," said Hancock, "the Army's gone to Tullahoma. Whether Rita is with them is a less certain matter."

Little said, "Hell, all the hookers in town have gone with the Army. She's probably in Tullahoma now snuggled up in the bed roll of some lucky Yank."

"That's the trouble with you Little," said Paddy O' Neil in a deep, rich, Irish brogue. "You think every woman is a tramp. Don't you have no romance in your heart?"

Before Little could answer, the deep bass voice of Olsen entered the conversation.

"I talk to old lady who say she saw girl just like Rita. She say the girl was with a young man walking down the street. They both have packs on their backs. Probably go away for a long time."

Ira began to dance in circles and shouted. "My baby girl is alive. Praise the God of Israel. He led my people out of Egypt, and now he has saved my Rita." Within an hour, the band was on its way to Tullahoma.

Dusk was settling over the low hills of Eastern Tennessee when Hancock announced that it was time to stop for the night. They had passed through Hoover's Gap and seen the fields strewn with bodies and were now about to enter the dark wood intersected by a narrow stream. Ira said, " This spot is as good as any on this good earth. The ground is flat, and we got water."

As the men were gathering wood for a fire, Ted Brown heard the distant yelping of hounds and suddenly nearby, the swish of underbrush and the crackling of twigs. "Bear!" he screamed and began to back away holding his ax above his head. A black head emerged from the underbrush, and before Ted could bring down his ax, a young black man fell at his feet. The young man's clothes were tattered and barely covered his gasping, heaving body.

"Please don't shoot me Massa. Please don't shoot. I won't run off no more."

"Hell. I ain't no Massa. I'm a Yank from Cairo, Illinois." The hounds were closer now, and Ted heard them breaking through the brush about 100 yards away.

Ted grasped the black man by the hand and pulled him to his feet. "I don't know what kind of trouble you're in, but I sure don't want to see you torn up by a bunch of Rebel hounds. Follow me."

The two young men ran back to the camp, and Ted shouted, "Look fellows. We done freed ourselves a slave"

"Holy Moses," said Ira. He looks like he's running away, and if I know anything about the South, Old Massa will be coming through these woods with guns and dogs. He ain't going to be a happy man."

Ira picked up the young black man in his arms and stumbled to the stream. Then he stepped in and walked through the water for about fifty feet and hid behind a huge boulder. Ira, the black man, and the block of granite became one in the growing darkness. Ira tried to control his panting breath, and when he did, he whispered to the young man in his arms, "Don't you worry. You may be in the Lions Den, but nobody's gonna hurt ya."

A moment later, four big tick hounds broke into the clearing with their noses to the ground. They circled and yelped excitedly, and in a few minutes three men with guns emerged from the brush. A tall, muscular man of about thirty-five with a slouch hat and a thick black beard almost to his waist spoke first.

"Got a run-away nigger come through here a minute ago. You fellers seen him?"

No one answered at first, but Hancock finally broke the silence. "We saw something come through the brush up yonder," and he pointed away from the camp to a small hill about a quarter of a mile away. "Some of the boys run after it, but when they seen it was a nigger, they figured he probably belonged to someone and was out on official business of some sort."

"Official business of some sort? What kind of blockheads are you anyways? That was our run-away nigger. If you see him again grab him. We'll make it worth your while. Let's go boys."

"Wait a minute," said an old grizzled fellow with bushy white eyebrows, and a snow white beard. If he went up that hill yonder, how come our dogs are sniffing around down here? I don't recollect old Blue here ever missing a track like that. I think these Yanks are sending us off on a wild goose chase. Bet that nigger's in this camp some'eres. Bob, check the wagon."

The third man was a kid of about eighteen. He poked his gun at Ira's wagon and walked slowly towards it. Then he said, "Nate, if you're in there you better come out now. We'll make it easy on you. Just cut off a foot so as you won't be in such a dad-blamed hurry to get away from them that owns you."

He poked the gun in the wagon and then looked in. "Nobody in here," he yelled, "just a bunch of shiny metal pipes and such truck."

The other two men went over and looked in, and the fellow with the black whiskers said,

"What is this junk? I never seed anything like it in my life."

Hancock replied, "Band instruments. You boys up for a little concert?"

"Hell no. I'd rather hear a wheel turning on a dry axle or cats in heat. We've got to find this nigger."

The hounds were circling around sniffing the ground and looking confused, and the black-bearded man kicked Old Blue in the side and yelled, "What the hell good are you anyway?" Blue yelped and slinked off with his tail between his legs.

"All right boys, let's head up the hill where these kind gentlemen said they seen old Nate. Much obliged Gents. If you catch him for us, there's fifty Confederate dollars for you."

"I'll give three blasts on my cornet if I see him," said Hancock cheerfully. Soon the men, with the dogs running in front went up the hill and disappeared in the darkness.

In a few minutes, Ira appeared from the woods carrying the young slave. "Hell, Ira. You can set him down now. He ain't your baby girl," said Flambeau.

"Don't want him leaving tracks and a scent," said Ira as he shoved Nate into the back of the wagon. Fred Myers watched these proceedings with some interest and finally blurted out, "For fifty bucks, I'll turn him in. Somebody give me a damned cornet."

The deep German voice of Axle Schmidt boomed from the darkness. "You touch that cornet, and I bash your head in with this stick." Axle came up to the wagon and faced Myers. "I come all the way from Germany to set the slaves free and find Yankees like this Myers trying to put the chains back on."

Myers spat a wad of tobacco at Axle's feet and said, "I'm sick of all you damned foreigners coming to my country and telling me how to live. You like the niggers, take 'em back to Germany with you."

"What's wrong with you Myers?" asked a high-pitched voice in the darkness. Don't you believe in the Bible? All men are brothers."

"Brothers, my foot. Listen I got this carpentry shop in Cairo, and business was pretty good. I do a few odd jobs and take afternoons off to do a little hunting and fishing. Then one day this nigger comes to town. Says he's been set free and shows everyone a piece of paper to prove it. Then he says he's a trained carpenter and wants some work.

"You wouldn't believe what happened next. All these women gathered around him crying and saying, 'Praise the Lord. In his mercy he has set free this black man and sent him to Cairo to do the Lord's work. He will be an example to others.' The next thing I know this nigger's building barns and fences and houses, and I'm just whistling 'Dixie.'

"I ask people, how can you hire this nigger instead of someone from your own race, and they say, 'He works harder than you, and when he's finished, the job's done right. How many years have I been asking you to fix that barn door, and you never done nothing about it.' Well that beat all. Hiring a nigger instead of a white man. That's how I got into this damned army in the first place. Nigger's got my job."

Suddenly out of nowhere the hounds appeared followed by the three men. The hounds circled the wagon and howled, and Old Blue put his front paws on the back wheel sniffing and barking excitedly.

"Dad blast it," the young man shouted. "He ain't in there." Then he kicked at the huge hound, but Blue ducked and dropped to the ground still staring intently at the wagon. "That damned dog ain't worth the food we're feeding him. Abner take him out and shoot him."

As Abner reached for Blue, a high-pitched voice broke against the gruff voices of the men. "Wait." Then Allen Richards, the tenor saxhorn player, stepped forward and touched Blue's head. Allen was actually Ellen, one of the many young women who disguised themselves as men to serve their country. Many of these young women died in battle, and only in death were their true sexualities ever known. However, there was little doubt about Ellen Richards. She tried heroically to flatten her breasts, but nature had been too prodigal with her gifts. Even with her soft brown hair cut short and covered with a military hat and even with her baggy Union coat and heavy wool trousers, she was every inch a woman. However, most members of the band kept her secret and never let on that they knew. She was like a sister to them, and no one doubted her good nature and kindness. Men would have died for her. "Please don't shoot the dog," she said softly and sweetly.

"Well I be swan," said the black-bearded man. "If you didn't have pants on, I'd swear you was a girl."

Allen blushed and said softly, "How much do you want for the dog?"

"Alive or dead," the young man asked?

"Alive, of course. Where I come from people don't shoot their dogs."

The young man stared intently at the musician and said gently, "You can have him for one U.S. dollar. None of that Jeff Davis trash."

Richards reached into her pocket and pulled out a battered silver dollar. "Here's your dollar, he said. The dog's mine now. Don't you dare shoot him."

The young man released his hold on Blue's neck, and Richards stroked Blue's head. "Old Blue, you're mine now," she whispered in the dog's large floppy ear. Blue watched as his former owners walked off into the night; then he licked Richards' face. "See," said Richards. "Dogs know who loves them. They are really very sensitive. They're better than most of the people I know." Blue leaped into the wagon and licked Nathan on the face.

At dawn, the band packed up and started down the road to Tullahoma, and as the sun finally broke through the heavy layer of clouds, Tullahoma stretched out before them bristling with the massive Confederate earthworks. The band went down the main street of town, but there was no Confederate army to challenge them. Hancock asked an old man sitting on a cracker barrel what happened to the army. The man spat a wad of tobacco at the ground and said indifferently, "I reckon they left."

"But where did they go?" persisted Hancock.

"They didn't tell me. Could be Shelbyville, could be Chattanooga, could be almost any damned place. I don't care. I'm just glad to see them go. Maybe we have some peace around here at last."

"I don't suppose you've seen a pretty red-haired gal around here have you?" asked Ira.

"Ain't no young gals around here any more. You might give Shelbyville a try. If this here gal is a Yankee, she's probably in Shelbyville. That's where all the local Yankees hang out these days."

And so the band started walking the road to Shelbyville. As the old man said, it was a Union town, and with the 4th of July coming up, they just might need a Union band to help them celebrate. Besides, Rita just might be there. As the band marched up the road, Old Blue ran ahead, and Nate stayed inside the wagon. In Shelbyville, even Nate might find a breath of freedom.

CHAPTER TEN
Rita Frees Herself from Her Big, Strong Man

"This is a way to kill a wife with Kindness."
Shakespeare, <u>The Taming of the Shrew</u>

As rosy-fingered Aurora crept slowly across the Eastern sky, Rita saw that the demon shapes of Confederate cavalry had departed, and in their place was a little grove of pine trees. From her hiding place she could see the stream where the horses had stood drinking and where the glow from many cigars had seemed like hell's fire. Birds were chirping in the trees now, and all was right with the world.

"Wake up Morgan," she said cheerfully. "This is the day the Lord hath made."

Morgan jumped up with his pistol in his hand, but when he realized where he was and whom he was with, he replied "Rejoice and be glad in it."

"Now which way is Tullahoma?" asked Rita. "Those big bad men are gone now, and I need to be on my way."

Morgan laughed and said, "Well you sure are one hard-headed girl. You're standing just outside of Fairfield, and Tullahoma is more than twenty miles from here. There's probably a Reb behind every tree, and every one of them is just itching to get his hands on a pretty Yankee gal like you. Just how do you propose to get to Tullahoma?

And if you do get there, just how are you going to sneak past the sentries?"

"Morgan, you keep talking about these Southerners as if they were the devil's children. I have no quarrel with them. I just want to find Butch."

"Young Lady, there is no middle ground. Either you're with us, or you're with them, and if you're with them how are you going to explain that to your Yankee fiancé? He's out there putting his life on the line every day being shot at by those damned rebels, sleeping in the mud, eating hardtack with worms, and you say you have no quarrel with them. Hell woman, if Butch's quarrel ain't your quarrel, I don't see much love there. Love is suffering together. Love is fighting together for what you believe in."

"But surely, Morgan, there must be some way for a sweet little gal from southern Brooklyn to get to Tullahoma." She said this with her best southern drawl and batted her eyes mockingly at Morgan.

"Hell woman, there is a way, and if anybody can make it, that somebody is you. It's a tough walk through the woods, but we're standing about five miles from the Nashville-Chattanooga Railroad. If the trains are still running, and if you don't mind traveling with a bunch of stinking Johnny Rebs, you could be in Tullahoma in the blink of an eye. I still don't know what you'll do when you get there, but I'll take you to the railroad."

Rita gave Morgan a big hug and said, "I knew you would help me. You're just a sucker for helpless women."

"Sucker am I? Well maybe I am. You sure are pretty."

There was a good road with no one on it, and in less than an hour the horses carried them to an opening in the trees. There, in the midmorning light, the thin line of rails that led to Nashville in the north or Chattanooga in the South glistened like a river in Paradise, but Rita just wanted Tullahoma.

They tied their horses to a little beech tree near the tracks, sat down on a boulder, and waited. Rita talked mostly about catching up with Butch and how surprised he would be to see her, but Morgan noticed how often she spoke of Sam Fletcher. "After I find Butch, the two of us will find Sam," she said so often that Morgan wondered at her disarming innocence. He wanted to tell her that her mission of love in the midst of thousands of men trying to destroy each other in the hatred of war was impossible and that she should go with him to Shelbyville where she could be safe and eventually return to her father. But she seemed so determined, that Morgan just sighed and resolved to help her. The sun was directly overhead when they heard a distant train whistle echoing mournfully through the pines. Soon they heard the panting roar and the clanking of metal on metal, and then there it was emerging from a grove of trees heading right towards them."You're lucky," Morgan grunted. "It's a Federal Train."

Morgan rushed out on the track, waved his arms, and the train began screeching to a stop. Rita thought that her black knight had at last arrived to carry her to her wayward prince, but from this shining armor came the most ungodly language.

"What the hell's going on here?" came an angry voice from the engine, and soon the cars were emptying themselves of men in blue cursing and jeering. Rita watched as Morgan gestured and talked and heard the engineer's words all too distinctly.

"You mean you stopped this damned train just so some wench could have a ride to Tullahoma? I got to get these boys to Chattanooga for the big fight that should end this war, and you want me to give your lady friend a ride. I ought to bust you right in the nose," and he might have done so if a young lieutenant hadn't suddenly appeared leading Rita by the arm.

He bowed mockingly to the engineer and said, "My noble Lord, I think we can make room for such a lovely lady. I found her under a tree looking for a succor, and she found us." The engineer was about to object, but he took one look at Rita and changed his mind. "All right. Put her on board and let's get moving. But I'm not responsible for her."

Morgan saw a little white hand waving to him from one of the cars, and he watched until the train disappeared into the mountains. Then he rode his horse across the tracks and headed towards Shelbyville.

CHAPTER ELEVEN
Rita Takes Chattanooga

"Tis not a year or two shows us a man.
They are all but stomachs and we all but food;
They eat us hungrily, and when they are full,
They belch us."

William Shakespeare, Othello

Rita could barely move as she stood crushed by the mass of blue-clad soldiers. With the lack of air and the stench of sweating, unwashed bodies, she could barely retain her balance, but as the train moved inexorably towards Tullahoma, she was almost singing. Soon her long journey would come to an end, and she would see her tormentor, her lover, face to face. But suddenly she heard the discordant screech of metal as the massive locomotive ground to a halt. Then she saw a tall lean cavalryman on a horse talking to a burly general by the side of the track. The general leaped back on the train, and she felt the hissing grinding beast of a locomotive lurching forward once again.

"What was that all about?" she asked a young soldier who was pressed against her side.

"Darned if I know Mam. The gin'ral must of got some news, but he ain't sharing it with the boys." But soon the car was ablaze with many-tongued rumor.

"Seems the Rebs have pulled up stakes and moved to Chattanooga. Ain't no point in going to Tullahoma now. We're movin' straight on to Chattanooga. Catch then Rebel rats before they can crawl back in their holes."

"So how can I get off this train at Tullahoma?" Rita shouted at the mass of blue clad bodies.

"What's your hurry sister?" came a voice from the writhing blue mass, and she felt hands groping her buttocks and breasts. She couldn't move but she screamed, "Get your hands off me you son of a bitch." Then she heard a deep voice mutter.

"What the hell's this? You got a brass wall around your middle?" Then she remembered Sam's cornet. It still hung on a cord around her waist and now thrust itself between her and her attacker.

"I sure do buster, and if you touch me one more time it will kill you."

Some of the men now realized what was going on, and laughed. "You watch yourself Zeke. Remember that whore in Nashville who darn near unmanned you?"

A high falsetto voice came out of the crowd, "You pay me white man or I'll make you sing soprano." A roar of laughter rolled through the car like a wave, and then the young lieutenant appeared from nowhere.

He was about 6 foot four, and his voice blasted like a bugle. "If anyone touches this young lady, I will shoot him." He brandished his pistol over his head and looked at the crowd, but the blue mass became suddenly silent. Then he made his way to Rita. He took her by the arm and said, "Come with me." He led her to a corner of the carriage and set himself like a Colossus in front of her. As the lieutenant took his position, the train was speeding past the deserted outer works of Tullahoma.

It was late afternoon when the locomotive screeched to a halt in Stevenson, Tennessee. In a gentle rain, the men disembarked and waited to board a train on the Nashville-Chattanooga Railroad. While they waited, the Lieutenant never let Rita out of his sight. He was 22-year old Lieutenant John Ashe from Erie, Pennsylvania and was with the 8th Pennsylvania volunteers. He had never seen a real Confederate but was eager to round up these devils and restore the union. Rita asked him about freeing the slaves, but he said that he didn't think it was right to steal another man's property. "But to break up the union! Why that was against God's plan."

Rita was going to argue with him, but when she thought of her precarious situation and of his simple good nature, she saw no reason to create ill will with the man who had protected her against the incivility of men. She stood with him in the rain waiting for a train to take her to Chattanooga.

About 8 p.m. of July 3rd, they saw the headlights of a locomotive dashing out of the darkness, and in a few minutes the huge black monster was wheezing and panting by their sides. "It almost looks alive," said Rita. "It's like one of those fierce dragons from the romances, but this one I suppose is friendly."

Lieutenant touched her arm lightly and said, "This dragon is on the side of God. This dragon will help us bring peace to our beloved country."

As Rita and the lieutenant climbed aboard a battered-looking railroad car, many a soldier looked on in envy. Here indeed was the most handsome young prince and his most beautiful princess bride. Even days traveling through the woods and sleeping on the ground could not dim the beauty of Rita's brilliant eyes or the grace of her movements.

About 9 p.m. the train stopped in the dusk at Wauhatchie. Out of the gloom of mist and fog rose the Cumberland Mountains, and cradled by the mountains was the Wauhatchie valley, Somewhere in the dark shadows of this long flat valley, the whole rebel army was waiting. As the troops emptied out of the cars, officers shouted orders and put the men in columns, and soon a giant blue snake was winding its ways through the trees in search of its deadly prey. Many of the Yanks had never seen those wicked butternut foes, and those who had, hadn't been this close in a long time. Not since the bloody massacres at Stones River six months before had the Army of the Cumberland come so close to such a host of Rebs. And Rita, that nice Jewish girl from Brooklyn New York, was in the midst of them. For days Rita had set her sights on Tullahoma, but now that Tullahoma was behind her she had no specific plans but only a vague sense of longing. Surely somewhere in this huge gathering of Yankees was the man she wanted to find. And so she too plunged into the darkness.

Young Lieutenant Ashe had some ambivalence about his beautiful charge. He didn't want to lose her but knew that she didn't belong with the army. And so they walked along side by side until someone on a horse rode by and shouted, "Damnation! What the hell is a woman doing? "Get her out of the way!"

Rita stepped back into the bushes at the side of the road as the army continued its advance towards somewhere. Lieutenant Ashe looked back and tried to catch her eye, but she was gone. After the army passed, Rita stood in the middle of the woods alone. A minute before she had been escorted by the most powerful army in the world, but now she was absolutely alone, and she felt suddenly very vulnerable. She had to go somewhere in a hurry but where? She started to run, and with each step, she felt the cornet beating against her back. "That damned cornet," she whispered and for the second time was about to hurl it away. But as she reached for the cornet, she felt her grip tighten on the valve casings. It was the grip her father had taught her in childhood, and as the fingers of her right hand began to compress the rotary valves, music filled her soul. Her eyes teared up as she put the horn to her lips and played the opening bars of the Haydn trumpet concerto. Then she sat down on a rock and played all three movements from her heart. The silver notes floated sweetly through the Wauhatchie valley bringing a sense of peace to the brooding darkness.

When she was finished playing, Rita remained seated on the rock, because for the first time in her life she didn't know what to do. But then she heard a crackling in the underbrush, and before she could be afraid, she found herself staring into the kind face of a slender old woman with snow white hair. "Land sakes child, what are you doing out here in the woods this time of night? Don't you know there's a war going on?"

Rita replied, "I wish I knew what I was doing out here."

"Well you sure can play that horn, but that don't really explain what you're doing here."

"So you heard the horn. I didn't know anyone was listening. I'm sorry if I disturbed you."

"Don't be sorry honey. I was feeling kind of sick at heart until I heard your music. Ya kinda picked me up if ya know what I mean. This war is making everybody sick at heart, and a little music sure helps keep up the spirits. I was chopping wood for the fire when I heard ya, and I come out to see if the angels had come down, and sure enough one of them had. By the way my name is Mrs. Gates, Mrs. Wilma Gates. My house is down yonder."

"Do ya need a place to stay the night? I'm kind of lonesome with all the men folk gone and could use some company."

In about a minute, Rita was entering the door of a log house on the side of a hill. There was a big fireplace at one end with several large logs burning down to coals.

"Let me warm you up a bowl of grits and some greens. It ain't much, but with the war going on food is a little scarce."

Rita had never tasted anything quite as good as that bowl of grits and the pile of greens. She hadn't eaten anything in about three days, and this simple fare tasted like food for the gods. After Rita finished eating her third bowl, the old woman said, "Now you need to rest."

Rita was sitting on a bed made of logs that jutted from the wall next to the fireplace and said, "Maybe I'll close my eyes for a minute or two before I continue on my way." She settled her head on a pillow of corn husks. When she opened her eyes again, the first rays of the sun were coming through the window, and she found herself covered by a light quilt of the log cabin design. Her grandmother had made one for her many years ago, but it had been lost somewhere between Brooklyn and Cairo.

Rita could hear the sounds of straw scraping against rocks, and when she looked out the window, she saw the old woman sweeping the front porch. The stone porch ran the length of the front of the house, and the roof was supported by four columns of stones cemented together in layers. About fifty yards from the front of the house Rita could see a dirt road, and in the distance beyond the road a mountain rose into a clear blue sky.

The old woman saw her looking out and came inside. "So how do you like my house? Isn't this the most beautiful place on God's green earth?"

Rita said, "Yes Mrs. Gates, it sure is lovely. I just wish I knew where I was."

"Child, you're on the side of Raccoon Mountain, and way off yonder are Abraham Lincoln's soldiers. A lot of the folks around her don't like those meddling Yanks, but I thank the Lord they are here. My grandpa fought in the Revolutionary War, and he hoped that one day this country of ours would be the biggest and strongest on earth. But now that rascal Jeff Davis wants to make us into two countries. Thank God for Abraham Lincoln. He'll make us one again. But let me fix you some breakfast."

Rita said that she had to go, but Mrs. Gates said there was no point in going unless she knew where she was going. When Rita finally explained her quest for the 123rd Illinois and Butch, Mrs.

Gates said, "I'll take you to the Yanks in a little bit, but first eat something."

Rita ate one bowl, but that was not enough to please Mrs. Gates. "I don't want you running off hungry. Sakes child, you're all skin and bones. You need to put some meat on those ribs. Can't have you coming down with consumption. There's a woman in the next valley didn't eat nothing, and she just passed away like a shadow."

After the third bowl of grits Rita, led by Mrs. Gates, crossed the dirt road and began the trip up the side of the next mountain. It was still early in the morning, and the dew was still on the grass as they approached a large encampment of Union Soldiers. As they came to the crest of the hill, Rita looked down the side of the mountain, and the valley looked like the night sky speckled with campfires like stars. They hadn't gone far when a sentry stepped in front of them and asked them to halt, but when he saw who was there he said, "Sorry Mrs. Gates. You just go on through."

They hadn't gone far before they heard the sound of muffled drums beating what seemed like a funeral march, and then they saw two short columns of blue coats with a man between them. The man's hands were tied behind his back, and the soldiers were dragging him forward. "What's that all about?" asked Rita.

"Just an execution. The young fellow in the middle must have fallen asleep at guard duty or forgot to salute a colonel. No telling what. It don't take too much to be executed in this war."

The execution detail was too far away to be seen clearly, but there was something about the intended victim that struck a shock of recognition in Rita. "I've got to get closer," said Rita.

"There ain't no use in you getting involved in something like this," said Mrs. Gates. "Executions ain't pretty. Besides they may wonder why you're so curious."

"Thanks for your advice, Mrs. Gates," Rita said, "but I think I know that man."

Rita started to run up the dirt road towards the execution party, and as she got closer, she was certain. The prisoner was Sam Fletcher. "Sam, she shouted. Sam!" She started to run again, but a big burly Yankee stepped in her path.

"Where ya going sweetheart?"

"I've got to stop this execution. There's no way that man is guilty of anything."

"Tell ya what. Let me see them breasts, and I just might help ya." He stepped forward and clawed at Rita's dress. Rita tried to punch him in the stomach, but he grabbed both her wrists in one huge muscular hand and pushed her to the ground. Rita tried to spring up, but he was upon her before she could get her breath. "Get off me," she screamed. "If Sam dies because of you, I'll tear your eyes out." Suddenly she slammed her knee into his groin, and while he doubled up in agony, Rita rolled away and started running up the road in the direction of the execution detail. They were out of sight now, and Rita could feel her heart beating like a funeral drum and her breath tearing at her lungs. Her side ached, and her body told her to stop, but she ran on and on over boulders, over fallen logs. Finally she came to a clearing, and there was Sam, tied to a tree and a rifle squad with their rifles pointed at her poor innocent Sam. A sergeant was about ready to yell the command, "Fire" when she burst into the clearing and screamed, "Stop! He is innocent." The sergeant was used to obeying orders, and so he changed the command to "rest arms." All the men seemed a little cowed by the sight of this beautiful woman who had commanded them to stop.

The Sergeant, a small skinny man, in a shiny new uniform finally regained his composure, and asked, "By whose authority do you ask us to stop?" Before Rita could answer, a loud female voice came out of the edge of the clearing.

"By my authority, you knuckle heads. Can't ya see you got the wrong man? What's the matter with ya anyway?" As Mrs. Gates stepped towards them, the soldiers took off their caps and looked at the ground. "Now untie the prisoner before I really get mad at ya."

The young sergeant went to the tree and cut the rope that held Sam's hands. When he was free, he rushed up to Rita and hugged her. "You saved my life. You really are an angel."

Mrs. Gates interrupted. "We're not out of the woods yet. We need to go back with these young men and do some explaining."

At first the captain was irate that his orders had not been followed, but when Sam's pretty advocate and the imposing Mrs. Gates made Sam's case, he changed his mind. "That's the trouble with this army," he grumbled. "You can't tell the civilians from the soldiers. You can't even tell the Rebs from the Yanks. But if these lovely ladies say you are a friend of the Union Army, I'm happy that my orders were disregarded. Now get out of here before I change my mind."

Led by Mrs. Gates, Sam and Rita crossed the mountain again and were soon sitting on Mrs. Gate's front porch watching the squirrels jumping from limb to limb on the great oak trees. "Just think," said Sam finally. "In another minute I would have been gone. These squirrels would still be dancing around the trees, but I wouldn't have been here to see them. It's really hard to imagine not being here."

Mrs. Gates said, "Well I guess I'll leave you two love birds alone for awhile. I know you have a lot to catch up on. There must be a million kisses you owe each other."

Rita laughed and said, "We're just friends. My fiancé is Butch Lassiter, and Sam here promised to help me find him. We give each other hugs but no kisses."

Mrs. Gates looked puzzled and then said, "So you're not the one? You certainly fooled me. I never saw a girl that concerned with saving just a friend." Then she fixed a bed for Sam upstairs. Rita remained in the bed by the fireplace, and for a time, Mrs. Gates had a family, a son and a daughter. Sam helped work the farm, and Rita helped with the household chores. Every evening Sam practiced his cornet, and Rita instructed him. After a couple of weeks, even Mrs. Gates admitted, "He ain't half bad now. Not good, I'm saying, but he don't frighten the life stock any more."

Every once in a while Sam said that he was going to see if the army needed a cornet player, but Mrs. Gates, said, "You ain't ready yet, but with a teacher like yours you will play a solo for Mr. Lincoln. Just listen to her and you will be all right."

Her other child, Rita, kept asking about Butch, and finally Mrs. Gates said that she would look for him herself. She left early one morning, and when she came back two days later, she said, "Sam I got a job for you."

Rita kept asking her, "Did you find Butch," but she just shook her head.

The next morning, Sam left for the main army camp in Wauhatchie.

CHAPTER TWELVE
The 4th of July in Dixie

"He has sounded forth the trumpet
That shall never call retreat;
He is sifting out the hearts of men
Before His judgment seat."

Song, "Battle Hymn of the Republic," Julia Ward Howe

It was mid afternoon on July 3rd when the Ira Goldstein Band approached the outskirts of Shelbyville, Tennessee. The fifteen miles through the mountains had been agonizing for them. The heat was unbearable, and nobody was in a joking mood when Ira called a halt and cheerfully said, "Ya know, it would be good if we marched into town playing. People would hear us and want to hire us for the 4th of July."

"You're full of crap Goldstein," said Flambeau. They ain't no way I'm marching and playing my way into this damned town. I should have gone home when I had a chance. Ain't that right boys?" But before anyone could answer, Hancock said,

"Ira makes a lot of sense to me. Do you fellers want to make some money or don't you? Why would folks pay you money to play if they they've never heard you? I tell you, you've got to give something to get something back. Old Ira knows what he's doing."

As Morgan Davis sipped his coffee in the Silver Dollar Café, he heard what seemed to be blasts of distant thunder, but as he stepped outside to cast a weather eye, the thunder turned into beating drums and the distant cry of cracked cornets. Down the main street of Shelbyville came the twelve members of the Ira Goldstein Band playing the stirring notes of "The Battle Hymn of the Republic." When the band reached the center of town, the music stopped, and Ira stepped on top of a horse mounting block and addressed the assembled crowd. "Ladies and Gentlemen, I am proud to present you with the world renowned Ira Goldstein Band."

"Can you boys play Dixie?" asked a rough voice in the back of the crowd, and people began jeering and hissing. "This here's a Union Town," someone shouted. "We got no need for such truck as Dixie."

"We ain't all Union here," came a harsh voice from the back of the crowd. About a dozen rough looking men walked forward with their fists clenched. Some had sticks brandished above their heads; others appeared to have pistols under their coats. Just when it looked like Yank and Reb were about to clash in the middle of the town, a tall man in a frock coat and stove pipe hat stepped between the two factions and shouted, "There's no call for any violence here today. We've got music not guns."

"He's right," said a deep voice from around the corner of a building and a man on a big bay horse rode into the middle of the street. "There will be no fighting here today. We've got enough fighting. Now we want music." The group of toughs fell back and melted into the crowd, and the man on the horse turned to Ira and asked, "You boys in town for long?"

Ira grinned and said, "As long as you people want some music."

"Good," said the man on the horse. "Tomorrow's the Fourth of July, and most of the folks in Shelbyville want to celebrate it. Our beloved state may have left the Union, but as far as we're concerned Shelbyville is still in the United States of America."

"Hooray," shouted hundreds of voices in the streets. "Hooray for the Union." Almost on cue Ira, yelled to the band, "Play the 'Battle Cry of Freedom,'" and soon the glorious sounds of the Union battle hymn flowed from the little brass band, and hundreds of voices in the street joined in singing the words,

"The Union forever, hurrah, boys, hurrah."

As the band walked towards Mrs. Willis' Rooming House, the man in the stove pipe hat followed them and began talking.

"I'm a preacher, and I know the people in this town. If we work together-- for Providence of course-- I think we could make a few bucks."

"What are you talking about?" asked Ira.

"You bring in the people with the music, and I keep them there with some inspired talking about the Lord's work. When we're finished, I pass the plate, and we divvy up the loot."

"You sure you're a preacher?" asked Ira. I don't know too much about Christians, but what about not laying up treasures on earth?"

"The Lord will provide for his shepherds," responded the man with the stovepipe hat. "That crowd could have killed me, but just like he did for Daniel in the Lions Den, the Lord spared me."

After the band checked in at Mrs. Willis place, Ira and the Reverend Belcher sat in the lobby and planned the program for July 4, 1863. Never had the promise of July 4th 1776 seemed more uncertain than now. From the Revolutionary War had come the foundations for a strong united democracy, but after Bull Run, Chancellorsville, and Fredericksburg, the Union seemed to be dissolving in a sea of blood. But as Ira flopped down on his corn husk mattress in the quiet of Mrs. Willis's boarding house, he said to himself, "Ya never know. Anything is possible. I may even find Rita tomorrow."

As the sun came up over the mountains and cast its rays on the little town of Shelbyville, Ira knew that it was going to be a hot sunny day. He threw off his blanket and stood by the window. "Praise the Lord," he said. "With God's help anything is possible."

The band began to assemble in Mrs. Willis' dining room, and when at last even Flambeau had been rousted out of his room, and his female guest of the evening had been dismissed to a chorus of boos, they all sat down to a real southern breakfast of grits and ham, eggs, corn bread and some chickery coffee. The sun was high on the mountains when the musicians arrived at the band shell in the center of town, and dozens of people were already sitting on the ground in quiet anticipation. Any kind of excitement was rare in a sleepy little rural town, north or south, and next to maybe having a circus, a real band was the best way to bring everyone together.

When the musicians had at last taken their places in the bandstand and warmed up with a cacophony of vibrating brass, and when Flambeau had played the tune-up note, and everyone was more or less in tune, hundreds of people encircled the bandstand in the reverent silence that occurs before a church service.

Ira nodded to the audience, turned to the band and said, "Pull out 'Lorena.' This crowd will love us." After "Lorena" had left everyone sobbing, an enthusiastic rendition of "We Are Coming Father Abraham" brought the crowd to its feet cheering. Then, as if he had ridden in on the wave of cheers, the Reverend Henry Belcher suddenly appeared on the bandstand. He held a big, black book over his head; then he lowered it and started to read in a deep voice that sounded like music. "The Lord has moved me to read from Joshua VI."

"So the people shouted when the priests blew the trumpets; and it came to pass, when the people heard the sound of the trumpet, and the people shouted with a great shout, that the wall fell down flat, so that the people went into the city, every man straight before him, and they took the city." When he was finished, he looked into the sky and paused as if awaiting a response. Then he lowered his eyes as if he had the answer and addressed the crowd that had already been softened by music.

"Now the people of Jericho were exceedingly wicked, and they did not walk in the ways of the Lord. My friends, they were filled with a false pride. They decked themselves out in all the finery of butterflies, but inside they were just grasshoppers hopping here and hopping there but never basking in the glory of God. But believe me God noticed them and sent the Israelites to warn them, but did they listen? No, they clung to their foolish pride. They thought they knew better than God and continued with their fornicating and stealing and murdering until God lost his patience. Now God is a patient God, but when he becomes angry, you all better watch out. Yes, my friends, the same God who sent grasshoppers to destroy the Egyptians and fire to destroy the Sodomites, sent trumpets to destroy the evil people of Jericho. Now you may think trumpets are innocent enough, just another kind of musical instrument you say, but there, my friends, you are wrong, dead wrong.

Trumpets can kill. There was a man back in my hometown in Bristol, Tennessee. In most ways he was a quiet sane fellow, but when it came to trumpets he was just crazy. Whenever a band came to town he went to hear the trumpets. He once said, "There ain't no harm in a trumpet anyway." He encouraged his boy to play the trumpet, and the boy brought home friends who also played the trumpet. And one Sunday afternoon, they played so loud, that the whole house fell down on 'em. Poor souls." Beicher paused and wiped his eyes with an enormous calico handkerchief and sobbed before he could continue. At this point, all the cornet players slipped out the back of the band shell and disappeared into the trees.

Now this same man had been talkin' about how Tennessee should secede from the Union and how them damn Yankees was a bunch of nigger lovers, and he was about ready to enlist in the Army of Tennessee when God struck him down, so to speak. Now the way I figure it, we've got ourselves a new city of Jericho right here in the

South. I'm not talkin' about Shelbyville. You are all God's people because you have stood up for God's U.S.A."

"Here, here," shouted someone in the crowd, and a thunderous applause ripped through the crowd like a giant wave. Belcher looked again towards the sky and waited for the applause to subside, and then he spoke so softly, that the crowd had to strain to hear him.

"The Jericho I'm talkin' about is the whole damned Confederate States of America. God is angry again my friends." Then his voice accelerated into a roar: "God created the United States of America, and I emphasize the word United." The crowd cheered so loudly, that the foundations of the town seemed to tremble, and when silence returned, Belcher looked them in their collective eyes and said, "When God created this country way back in 1776, he said through his servant Thomas Jefferson, that all men were equal, and he meant it. He didn't say that slaves were any less equal than anyone else." No one applauded, and there was kind of uneasiness in the crowd, and Belcher looked up to the sky again. "Of course the Lord don't necessarily mean that just because we're equal we've got to live together. I suspect that black folk would be happier living in their own country Africa. They'd be equal there."

"Amen shouted a voice in the crowd," and a thousand Amen's echoed through the trees.

"Now when God created this country," Belcher continued, "he wanted the United States to be his personal country just like the Israelites had been in the olden days. Just as God gave the Israelites their promised land, so did he give true blue Americans their promised land. Now the land he gave the Jews was a middlin' small bit of property, but with Americans he did much better. You see the Jews was always lettin' him down, going off and worshipping brass calves, lying, and cheating, and so God turned his sights to a bigger, better country. He gave his new chosen people a whole damned continent that stretched from coast to coast. Course the new chosen people had to chase out the savages that had been squatting there for about ten thousand years, but then God expected them to remain a United States. He didn't want a bunch of little foreign countries in this big land. He is God, after all, and God is big. God wanted a big country where he could stretch out and enjoy himself, not some dinky little foreign place.

"Which gets me to my point. God is really angry with these here Confederate States for messing around with his big country, and he is going to send those Confederate walls tumbling down." Belcher paused and pointed to a tall pine in the distance, and suddenly the blast of a comet filled the air. Then cornets sounded from all different directions at once, and blended into the "The Battle Hymn of the Republic." By the second verse the crowd was singing along, and the rest of the Ira Goldstein Band added the deeper sounds of the bass sax horns and the shrill sounds of the flutes and piccolos. And Belcher's voice carried over everything. "I hear Vicksburg falling; I hear Chattanooga falling; I hear Atlanta falling, and yes, I hear Richmond falling. Against the power of God's glory these Jerichos cannot stand. This is the Fourth of July my friends. On this day, God takes back his country. Alleluia."

The band played about ten more choruses of "The Battle Hymn of the Republic," and as they played, two men with baskets were moving through the crowd taking the collection. "For the Union," they shouted. No one questioned how their money was going to help the union. They just dug into their pockets and gave all that they had.

Belcher took the baskets from the young men, raised them to the sky and said, "Glory be to God. I've tried every scheme in the book, but there ain't nothing like trusting in Providence." He put one basket under each arm and had taken a few steps in the general direction of the woods when Flambeau suddenly appeared brandishing his cornet over his head like a sword. "Where ya goin' with all the loot?" he asked.

Belcher smiled and said sweetly, "Why to put it in a safe place in my room until we have a chance to divvy it up." The entire band now surrounded Belcher and soon escorted him back to the hotel lobby. There they sat down by a huge mahogany table where Ira dumped the baskets and counted out $112.16 Federal dollars, $52 Confederate dollars and a plug of Indian head tobacco. "Not bad for a morning's work," he muttered.

Belcher wanted to divide the cash, and so he pushed the Confederate dollars towards Ira and put 52 U.S. dollars by his place. "Now we take the rest, about sixty bucks, and cut it in half. I take thirty; you take thirty, and I throw in the 16 cents and the plug of tobacco."

"I don't know about those Confederate dollars," Ira said. "Where are we going to spend them when those walls come falling down? Now throw those 112 greenbacks back on the table, and we split them in half. You can keep the rebel trash. Show it to your grandchildren."

Belcher was about to protest, but when Flambeau raised his cornet, he said, "You win. You boys drive a hard bargain."

Ira stood up and stuffed the $56 in the pocket of his pants. He reached out his hand to Belcher and said, "Well Reverend, it's been a pleasure doing business with you. Perhaps we will meet again." Belcher smiled feebly and grasped the ends of Ira's fingers. "Yes, it's certainly been a pleasure."

"Now boys we head to Tullahoma where we will entertain thousands of people and make millions of dollars. But first we will buy some food. Follow me."

The band fell in step behind Ira as he led them to the general store just across the dusty street from the hotel. Ted Brown wanted some rock candy from the big barrel by the counter, and Axel Schmidt clamored for some sausage, but when the band started down the dusty road in the general direction of Tullahoma, Ira's wagon contained only two barrels of flour, a side of bacon, two bags of dried peas, and what was left of the apples. "We will follow this road until it's dark. Then we will camp."

In about two hours, they reached Mullins Mill, and Ole Olsen said, "Let's stop here. It looks like Sweden." But Ira didn't even slow down, and so the band continued to trudge after their next meal. Finally, Ira said, "We will stop here at Five Forks. Five is a lucky number. My Rita was born on May 5." He pulled the wagon off the road into a little clearing in a stand of loblollies, and the band followed him. "Get some wood for the fire," he said cheerfully and we will have bacon and biscuits. With twelve people scavenging for twigs and logs, and Hancock as the master fire builder, a fire soon pushed back the looming darkness.

Ellen Richards brought up a bucket of water from the Duck River and began fashioning biscuits. "A Little yeast would certainly help," she muttered to herself. "But these men know nothing of cooking."

The smell of bacon cooking on an open fire brought Hancock back to his childhood in a little woods near Cleveland, Ohio. He was with his father camped beside an enormous pine tree. He was just eight years old and a little cold and scared, but outside the tent, his father's shadow loomed large against the old tree, and he felt safe from all evil. His father had been dead now for ten or was it twelve years? He wished he could have one more conversation with him. He wished he could ask, "Dad, am I doing all right? Are you proud of me?" But there is no going back in this life.

After supper someone suggested that they take out their instruments and play a few tunes, and no one objected. They were exhausted, but their love of music drove back rivers of fatigue, and a few choruses of improvised melodies brought them all back to life. They had been playing for hours, but it just seemed like minutes, when they heard horses breaking through the underbrush and the loud shriek of a rebel yell. Hancock shouted, "Run into the woods and hide." Without comment, they all dropped their instruments by the camp fire and rushed into the underbrush. As the twigs beat against his eyes, and vines caught at his feet, Hancock could hear the other members of the band crashing through the brush all around him. And finally Ellen Richards dropped down almost on top of him. "What's happening?" she whispered? Hancock placed his hand gently over her mouth, and they lay together and waited.

In the light of the campfire, Hancock could see a larger group-- maybe thirty in all--of a very rough looking band of men. They were picking up instruments and examining them with some interest.

"Bunch of damned musicians," a rough voice shouted. "Don't see no infantry. Just a bunch of yellow-bellied musicians."

"Should we kill 'em?" asked a high pitched voice.

"Hell no. Ol' Bedford wouldn't even want us to waste the ammunition. Go ahead and gather up them instruments though. We may be able to get a few bucks for 'em over in Manchester." As the men gathered the instruments, they made musical sounds, and sang the words to "Lorena" in a mocking falsetto.

"So you bunch of yellow-bellied cowards won't even fight for your instruments will you? Well I hope you all sleep well and enjoy your stay in the great Confederate state of Tennessee." He pulled back on the reins, and his black horse reared up like an immense equestrian statue. In a few moments the men were gone, melted into the darkness as if they had never existed. But when the band members returned to the clearing, they found all the instruments gone. Even worse, the two barrels of flour and the two bags of peas had been scattered on the ground.

"They will pay for this," shouted Flambeau. "No one insults me like this. No one steals my cornet and gets away with it."

"Just shut up Flambeau," said Hancock.

"What are we going to do?" asked Ted Brown fighting back the tears.

Ira looked into the darkness and said, "We have no choice. We got to go to Manchester and get out instruments back."

CHAPTER THIRTEEN
A Mixed Blessing: Butch Lassiter Found

"Why don't you speak for yourself, John?"
Priscilla Mullins to John Alden

The cornet lessons had been going well, and Sam was particularly fond of his young instructor who seemed to have infinite patience and an inexhaustible optimism about his chances for success. The only impediment to his perfect bliss was the persistent shadow of Butch Lassiter. Whatever else his relationship with Rita was or could be, it was always tempered by Rita's unrelenting quest for her missing lover. Every morning, Rita walked down the path to the camp of the Union army, and every afternoon she returned in tears. Sam offered to look for her, but she just kissed him softly on the cheek and said that he was very sweet, but she had to find Butch herself. It broke Sam's heart to see her suffer, and so one day in mid-July he paid his own visit to the union camp in Wauhatchie.

The sun pounded on his head, and he felt a little dizzy as he approached the earthworks around the union camp. And when the sentry asked, "Who's there? Stand forth and unfold yourself," he was stunned and speechless. But at last he gave his name and the purpose of his mission. "I want to visit my Uncle Morgan Davis of the Seventh Pennsylvania Cavalry."

"So you're kin to Morgan are you? Go up yonder about a mile and a half, and you'll probably find him." The sentry pointed to a stand of pines in the distance, and Sam started walking. Soon, he saw his Uncle sitting in the shade and drinking a cup of coffee.

"Uncle Morgan, you've got to help me find somebody in the 123rd Illinois. It's very important."

Morgan looked at his young nephew quizzically and then said, "I bet you a Federal dollar, that you are looking for that rascal Butch Lassiter."

Sam was so astonished to hear the hated name of Butch Lassiter coming from his favorite uncle's lips, that he stumbled and almost fell.

"Uncle, how do you know anything about that lying son of a bitch? The next thing I know, you'll be telling me something about Rita Goldstein."

Morgan grinned and said softly, "Oh I know just about everything. I even know about the beautiful, lovely, Rita Goldstein, the master of the cornet, the darling of the concert stage."

Sam took a deep breath, and said, "Uncle you have amazed me with your stories all my life, but this one beats all. How in tarnation do you know about Rita Goldstein? And how do you know about that scoundrel Lassiter?"

When Sam said the name Butch Lassiter, Morgan spat into the ground and spoke rapidly.

"I don't exactly know Lassiter. I just know of him. From what I've heard, I think he is a no good, quadrilateral son of a bitch. How could any man treat a lovely woman like that? But if Rita loves him, maybe he can't be all bad. Maybe she sees something we don't. Maybe she thinks she can reform him somehow. "When lovely woman stoops to folly..."

Sam looked at the ground and whispered, "You've got it right uncle. This lovely woman has stooped to folly, but I love her so much, that I am going to help her stoop. Lassiter is not doing much to help. Poor Rita doesn't even know where he is."

"Well of course she don't. Blame it all. He don't want her to know."

"So how come you know so much about this, Uncle?"

"Sit down, and I'll tell you all about it." Then Morgan told of his meeting with Rita at Hoover's Gap and her determination to reach Butch at Tullahoma. "By the way," he said, "She sure had some nice things to say about you. She said what a nice young man you were, so full of kindness and good manners. I said, If Sam's so good, how come you're hoofing after this no good Lassiter? I was joking of course, but she started to cry. 'Please don't tease me Mr. Davis. My heart's about broken as it is.' So I put her on the train to Tullahoma, and if you're still looking for Lassiter, I suppose she made it."

Morgan clapped his nephew on the shoulder and said with a smile, "But if I were you I would do everything I could to make her forget Lassiter. Buy her flowers, sing her songs, take her to the theater."

Sam laughed nervously and said, "We're just good friends. She's my cornet teacher, and I'm like her big brother. If she wants Butch Lassiter I will find him for her." He thought, *I love her so much, that I will even give her away to the man she loves.*

Morgan led Sam to the 123rd Illinois, and in a few minutes, a private led him to a dugout shelter. Inside, Sam could hear giggling and a woman's laughter.

"I don't suppose he will be too happy to see you, but if your message is really that important, just pull back the flap and holler."

When Sam pulled back the flap, he saw a naked woman and man celebrating the rites of Venus, and he was about to step back, when the man screamed at him, "What the hell do you want?"

Something exploded inside Sam, and the dark anger enveloped him like a fury. He tore off the flap, grabbed the man by the arm and threw him on the ground in front of the shelter. A crowd was gathering to see the naked man sprawled in the dust with a young civilian standing over him with his fists clenched. Soon Lassiter was on his feet with his fists flying. Sam ducked the punches and landed a hard right to Lassiter's stomach, and as Lassiter doubled over in pain, Sam landed a hard left to Lassiter's jaw sending the naked man sprawling.

Sam was about to leap on Lassiter's back when he felt someone grabbing his arms and pulling him back. "Easy boy. Don't take it so hard. I'm sure ol' Betty Lou would sleep with you too if you had five bucks. It ain't worth fighting over women."

Sam struggled to pull free but found himself tightly in the grip of two tall Union soldiers. It was some time before he could finally convince Major James Connolly the nature of his mission and receive the Major's promise that Butch Lassiter would either marry Rita Goldstein or face a firing squad.

When Butch Lassiter appeared at the door of Mrs. Gate's cabin the next morning holding a bunch of roses, Sam was not particularly surprised, but Rita was ecstatic. "She ran to the door screaming, "I love you Sam."

"Don't you mean Butch?" asked the astonished soldier.

Butch and Rita sat together in Mrs. Gates' parlor holding hands and talking. Sam and Mrs. Gates went into the garden and did some serious weeding. When they came in about an hour later, Rita was smiling joyfully, and Butch was looking a little sheepish. She asked Mrs. Gates, "Isn't he a handsome man?" Mrs. Gates took in the six-foot tall muscular soldier with black curly hair and sparkling gray eyes and said, "Well looks ain't everything" and walked away.

Rita looked at Sam and said, "We want you to be at our wedding. In fact, Butch said that you could be his best man. What do you say?"

"I don't know," replied Sam. I may be a little busy for a while and may not have time."

"Don't be silly. The wedding isn't until September 15. You'll have lots of time to get your work done. In the meantime I'll stay here with you and Mrs. Gates, and you won't miss any lessons." She looked at Butch and smiled. "On weekends, of course, I'll be with Butch."

Butch didn't come the next Saturday or the Saturday after either. Sam watched silently as Rita dressed up in her prettiest clothes and fixed her hair and devoured the road from Wauhatchie. Butch didn't come back all of July, and when Sam looked for him again, Major Connolly told him that Butch had deserted. Sam didn't tell Rita.

He told her instead that Butch had been sent on a foraging detail somewhere around Nashville and wouldn't be back for a couple of months. And so Sam, Rita, and Mrs. Gates settled into a routine of farm work and cornet lessons.

In about a week, Sam wrote his first letter to Rita and signed it, "With all my love Butch." He took the letter to his Uncle Morgan, and the next day, a young private delivered it to Rita. Sam watched as Rita took the letter from the private's hand and tore it open. His stomach tightened as he saw Rita laughing and running back into the house.

"Sam," she screamed. I just received my first letter from Butch. I've just got to read it to you. You never believed me when I said that Butch was such a sensitive guy, but listen to this." Sam sat on the sofa and listened as Rita read him back his own words. Now I think I understand Cyrano de Bergerac and Miles Standish at last, he thought. Rita looked so sweet and beautiful that he wanted to reach out and hold her in his arms, but he just listened.

"My dearest Rita,   July 11, 1863

Every moment that we are apart is an unbearable agony to me. When I saw you in your dark blue dress in Mrs. Gates' parlor, I said to myself, "This is the woman with whom I want to spend the rest of my life. She is my East and West, my North and South. I am her Romeo, and she is my Juliet." Then just when I thought we could be together again, the war broke us apart. Believe me, my dearest, that when this cruel war is over--and the war is like the feud between the Capulets and the Montagues--we will never part again. We will buy that little farm in Iowa, and I will love you every day of the year, for you are the sweetest, dearest girl in all the world. When I see how hard you are working to convert that poor farm boy, Sam Fletcher, into a cornet player, I realize what a tender heart you have. I imagine that poor Sam can shovel manure a lot better than he can play a cornet. Most girls wouldn't give him the time of day, but you always see the good in people and would do anything to help this poor wretched creature fulfill his dreams, and I love you for it. (I should add, that I am not the least bit jealous. You have to admit that Sam is not exactly brilliant and not exactly an Adonis. Compared to me--Hyperion to a Satyr as Hamlet said--Sam is not very exciting, but he is a decent, hard-working fellow nevertheless.

I am so sorry that I had to leave without having a chance to say good-by, but my assignment near Nashville is secret and dangerous, and I am not allowed to even tell you exactly where I am. Just know that you are always in my thoughts and prayers, and the day when we will be together at last can never come too soon.

Your sincere friend, lover, and future husband,
And with all my love,
        Butch

Sam listened intently and threw his arm over Rita's shoulder. "He really loves you. I am so happy for you."

Rita said, "And how well he writes. I had no idea that he was so literate."

In about twenty minutes Rita appeared with a letter in her hand. "Sam, will you please see that this letter reaches Butch?" Then she threw her arms around Sam and kissed him. Sam could feel her firm young breasts pressing against him, and he wanted the moment to last forever, but all too soon she pushed him towards the door and said, "Go on wings of Mercury."

Sam started down the road towards Tullahoma, but as soon as he was out of sight he tore open the letter and read.

"My Dearest Butch,   July 20, 1863

    Your letter has made me so happy, that I can't ever imagine being unhappy again. I always believed in you and knew in my heart that when you left me in Iowa, you must have had a good reason. But that's all in the past. Nothing now matters except that we will be together again for ever and ever. That night in the barn when I gave myself to you was just the beginning of a lifetime of bliss. I long to feel your strong hands on my body again and to make love forever. The mere thought of you makes my heart pound in anticipation of your return. Come home to me on wings of angels but have a little of the Devil with you too

    All my love,

    Rita

PS. When I read your letter again I was a little disturbed by one thing. You seem to have a negative impression of my friend Sam. It's true that he is not as good looking as you. (Who could be? You are my Adonis,) but he is a pleasant looking young man, and I'm sure there are many girls out there who would consider him attractive. Also, he really is becoming a very good cornet player. I think that by the end of the summer, he may have a real chance to play in a military band. I hope that you and Sam will become good friends.

PSS   I love you!

Sam sat down on a log and began composing Butch's response to Rita but knew that it could not be delivered for a couple of weeks. *So I'm pleasant looking and many women would find me attractive, and I am becoming a good cornet player.*

About two weeks later a soldier arrived from Nashville with the letter.

"Dearest Rita,   August 4, 1863

You letter reached me just after a skirmish with Confederate cavalry. The rascals attacked us as we were finishing our evening meal, and one of them put a bullet through my new cap. We were so mad that we grabbed our guns and chased the devils half way to Kingdom Come. I bet they were sorry they ever messed with a squad from the 123rd Illinois. We captured nine of them, and I took a rebel flag just for you. I'll present it to you personally when we meet again which I hope will be very soon. As the poet said,

"It's not that I love thee less but that I love honor more," but that's not quite true either. In a minute I would give up this glorious fighting just to be with you.

I will try to be nicer to your friend Sam. He doesn't seem like much of a man to me, but if he's your friend he can't be all bad. I long for the time when we can be together again.

All my love,

Butch

Rita was so happy, that she threw herself into the cornet lessons with the passion of a woman in love. Every evening she worked with Sam on the major and minor scales, intervals, and long tones. "Remember to support that breath," she told him over and over again and asked him to put his hands on her stomach as she blew into the horn. Sam still loved that part the best but second best was when she put her hands on his stomach and felt him breathe. "You have great breath support," she said one day. "What a set of lungs. Now if only we had some real music to play, you'd be ready to go."

One day Morgan Davis rode up to the house with a package in his hand. He said, "Sam are you still crazy about playing that cornet, or are you ready for a real job?" Before Sam could answer, Rita said, "Why of course he's still interested. It's his passion; it's his way of dealing with this endless war."

Morgan swung down from his horse and said, "Well maybe you could find some use for this." He pushed a leather pouch in Sam's face and said, "One of the boys took this off of a rebel prisoner, but nobody could see much use in it. Someone was about to throw it into the fire when I intervened. I asked what was in the pouch, and somebody said nothing but a bunch of music. I said, "I just happen to know someone who would be most interested in a pouch of music," and so I took it for you. Enjoy it. I suspect that you will be playing for us one of these days, so don't give up. I'm counting on you." Then Morgan swung back into the saddle and rode off.

Rita and Sam tore open the pouch with the excitement of children at Christmas, but Sam was most disappointed when the first piece of music was "Dixie" for flute. "How am I going to play that?" He cried.

"Don't worry," Rita said. "It's in the key of C, but I can transpose it into Bb for your cornet." As a regular letter writer, Mrs. Gates had some sheets of paper to spare, and Rita soon had them lined for music. That evening, she had Sam playing through "Dixie." Even Mrs. Gates was delighted with the results. "That's a right lively tune," she said. "Too bad the Rebs like it so much."

"Music is music," replied Sam. "Music does not know North or South. It is a universal language of peace." It was a good thing because the pouch contained the best of the Confederate musical arsenal: "Lorena," "Goober Peas," "The Bonny Blue Flag," "When Johnny Comes Marching Home Again," and mysteriously enough, "The Battle Hymn of the Republic." Sam later learned that this last beautiful melody had been written by a Southerner but had been taken over by the Yankees with the words of Julia Ward Howe. The Rebs preferred the words to "John Brown's Body" or some of the bawdy parodies, but nothing could hide the power of the melody. Soon Rita had transcribed the entire pack, and after playing his scales, every evening, Sam enjoyed playing the pieces for an enthusiastic audience of two. Each evening ended with a gradually improving rendition of the "Haydn Trumpet Concerto."

Like a nineteenth-century Adam and Eve, Sam and Rita worked all day in the fields around Mrs. Gates' seven- acre farm. They got up at dawn and milked the goats and cows. Then they gathered the eggs, chopped the wood, drew the water from the well, hoed the corn, and mended the fences. Sam could not wait for each day to begin because Rita would be at his side, and he could be her teacher. "When you're on that farm with Butch," he said, you'll need to know how to do a few things." He guided her hands in the milking of the goats and cows and showed her the proper way to hoe. Mrs. Gates taught her how to can vegetables, and by the middle of August, Rita was a fairly competent farmer.

Every couple of weeks Sam wrote a letter for Butch, and Rita answered it, and soon the corn had been harvested and stored to dry in the cribs, and the beans, peas, and potatoes had been harvested and canned. On a bright and sunny day in late August, Mrs. Gates said, "Well most of the work's done for this year, and I reckon that Sam needs to get on with his musical career."

"Are you asking me to leave?" asked Sam.

"Heaven knows I've loved having you around, but you've got a life to live. Rita and I been talking, and we've decided that it's time."

Rita put her arms around Sam and kissed him. "Mrs. Gates and I agree that you are ready for the army band now. Find that idiot Schmertz and tell him that you can play the Haydn." Before

Sam started down the road to Tullahoma on the hot dry morning of August 21, 1863, Rita threw her arms around him and kissed him. "You're good Sam. Just believe in yourself." Then she disappeared in the house, and Sam was alone on the dusty road. As he walked, he hummed the Haydn, and choruses of birds sang their ancient airs. Before there was man, there was music thought Sam.

CHAPTER FOURTEEN
On the Road Again

> "Just before the battle, Mother,
> I am thinking of you;
> While on the field we're watching,
> With the enemy in view."

Song, "Just Before the Battle," George F. Root

When Sam reached the Federal camp at Tullahoma, he was ready to play the Haydn, but no one was there to hear him. A strange stillness hung over the deserted fort and outlying earthworks. Where 120,000 men had once made the ground shake, only an occasional squirrel rattled the dry leaves of an acre of fallen trees, trees. Sam surveyed the wasteland of trees cut down to slow the inexorable advance of the Yankees, and felt absolutely alone, the last man on the face of a dying earth. He considered going back to Mrs. Gates' and getting a hug from Rita but decided there was no going back now. As Sam stood in a reverie, an old man suddenly appeared out of the underbrush carrying an Enfield rifle. He had shaggy white hair down to his shoulders, a snow-white beard to his waist, and a battered slouch hat. He pointed his gun at Sam, and said, "What you want boy?"

Sam was so happy to hear a human voice, that he laughed and said, "I thought the whole world had died. But you're alive. Put your gun down. My only weapon's a cornet."

"Ya some kind of loony?" the old man asked.

"In a way. I play the cornet in a war. What in hell happened to the army?"

The old man, seeing no harm in this slightly crazy young man, leaned on his gun like a walking stick and began to speak. "Why the whole damned army took off a week ago for Chattanooga. Got a railroad right next door, but three divisions took off on foot towards the Cumberland Mountains. I expect by now the Rebs is tearing 'em up pretty good outside Chattanooga. If you want to be killed with the rest of them fellers, I reckon you're too late. But if you want to catch up with their remains, I suggest you head off yonder." He pointed to some distant mountains and said, "Eventually you'll reach the Tennessee River. Just follow it north, and you'll be in the city in about three or four days. I reckon it's about 80 to 100 miles, just 60 as the crow flies."

"Why not just follow the railroad tracks?" asked Sam

"Well suit yourself," the old man replied. "But the road through the mountains is a little shorter, and you're less likely to meet up with Bedford Forrest or any of those other licensed killers and robbers."

"Well I've heard of Forrest, and he doesn't scare me much. What use would he have for a cornet player and not a very good one at that?"

"He could melt down the cornet into bullets." The old man grinned at spat a wad of tobacco at the ground.

"So how come you know so much about Bedford Forrest? You work for him?"

"Hell no, the old man said. I'm a private in the old sense of the word. I don't belong to either side and can steal from both of them. Take this Tullahoma, for example. You wouldn't believe all the good stuff that got left behind. Enough to feed an army, if ya know what I mean. The Rebs stocked the place before they left, and I carried off three wagon loads before the Feds moved in. Now that the Feds is gone I got three more wagon loads."

The old man's tone softened as he looked at the seemingly simple and helpless cornet player. "Boy, I suggest that you take some victuals with you if you intend to take off into them mountains. Here. Take this knapsack. Some fool left it behind, but it's full of hardtack, corn meal, and bacon. It's also got a fry pan, knife, and a good old U.S. Army canteen."

Sam said, "I can't take it. It would be like stealing from my own country."

"Stealing. Hell. It's borrowing. You can pay it back someday."

As Sam started down the tracks of the Nashville-Tennessee Railroad, on this hot and humid August morning, he checked his father's old pocket watch, and it told him that the time was nine. The sun was just over the crest of the distant mountains like a gold watch on a field of blue velvet. *A good time to start a hundred mile stroll. A good time to start a musical career. A good time to be young. A good time to be in love.* He looked back, but the old man had vanished like the old men in the fairy tales.

The hot August sun was directly overhead when Sam sat down on a rock in the shade of a willow tree and tasted his first bite of government hardtack. As his jaws closed on that flat little cracker that had energized armies for centuries, he cried out in pain. "Damn near busted a tooth." He hurled the offending biscuit into the grass and took a swallow of Duck River water from his U.S. Army canteen. *This stuff is like rock. How can anyone eat it?* His heart ached for one of Mrs. Gates' home-cooked chicken dinners, but such not being offered, he found instead the biscuit in the grass and dusted it against his shirt. He took a tin cup from the knapsack, poured in some Duck River water from the canteen and dropped in the hardtack. When strands of cracker floated to the surface, he drank it down in three or four swallows, and when he had finished felt much better. *It sure ain't a chicken dinner, but it will serve. Not so wide as a church door, but it will serve.* As he continued along the railroad track, he tried to recite as much of Romeo and Juliet as he could remember. For the war he thought, "A plague upon both of your houses." In the distance, the Cumberland Mountains looked beautiful but formidable in the noon day sun. *They sure look big. Maybe there's an easier way to Chattanooga.*

But there was no easier way, and as Sam approached the little town of Cowan, his feet were blistered and sore, and the hot afternoon sun burned his face and made his eyes water. Then he had a decision to make. Should he follow the railroad tracks through a tunnel or go over the mountain? When he thought of dragging his weary body up over a pile of rocks and climbing into the sun, he said to himself. *I'll take the tunnel. What are the chances of a train coming along?*

The tunnel was so dark, that he couldn't see anything. It was, he thought, "darkness visible." He felt his way along the damp, slippery walls and was a little uneasy when he realized how close the wall was to the track. *Not much room to maneuver here. But I will fly through this place faster than Dante did the Inferno.* In the darkness he thought he heard the screams of the damned and looked to see those many tormented souls reaching out for him but suddenly realized that the screams of the damned were actually only a train whistle. He touched the rail with his foot and could feel the unmistakable vibrations of a train.

He started to run, but tripped over the rail and fell on his face pinned by the forty-pound pack. The trembling of the rail rumbled through his stomach, and he struggled to his feet. He could feel blood dribbling into his eyes and wiped it away with his sleeve, *I've got to keep moving.* He felt sick to the stomach but lurched forward in the darkness. The rumbling was becoming distinctly louder as he fell for a second time on the rail, and as he struggled to his feet, he saw a distant lantern casting an eerie glow in the depths of the tunnel. Sam ran as hard as he could in the center of the track this time. Each cross tie was an obstacle to trip him, but it was also a more certain footing than the slippery path along the sides of the tunnel. His side hurt, and his lungs seemed ready to burst when he saw sunlight ahead of him. He tried to run even faster now, but his legs were shaky, and he almost fell. But he stumbled on towards the light, and when he reached it, he rolled off the tracks towards the right side and lay still. In no time at all, he heard the hissing of steam and the roar of a locomotive and then felt the rush of air as this hissing monster of steel rushed by his head knocking off his hat and swirling through his hair. He lay still for what seemed to be hours and at last heard the chirping of a blue bird in a nearby poplar tree. When he rose to his knees, Sam saw the end of the train in the distance and heard the trailing sound of a screaming whistle. He was soaked in sweat, and his knees were shaking when he went over and leaned uncertainly against the poplar. "Mrs. Bluebird, I believe your music is the sweetest I've ever heard." But the bird flew away.

Sam took a deep breath and began walking along the tracks for the Old Coal Railroad, and in about two hours, he reached the Old Coal Mines. He saw the gaping hole torn into the side of the mountain and empty coal cars, but there was no one there. Once again he was alone in the world. His feet ached, and he felt the pain of the pack straps cutting into his shoulder, and with every step the cornet banged against his leg, but it was too early to stop now. The next five miles were agony for Sam, but as long as there was sunlight, he didn't want to stop.

In about three hours, darkness was beginning to descend on Tennessee, but Sam was at least nearing the foothills of the Cumberland Mountains. He was looking for a clearing to set up his shelter when he saw that the whole mountain had been cleared. He had reached Dorn's Stand. A vast Union army had stripped the woods for miles around. Everywhere he looked, he found the charred remains of campfires. There were piles of hardtack boxes strewn across the landscape and discarded clothing and magazines. "This was once a beautiful place," thought Sam, "but 120,000 men can undo nature's work in an hour."

Sam had more clearing than he needed, and so he found a stand of pines near a little brook and began to unpack the haversack the old man had given him. He found the rubber mat and spread it on the ground near the stream and covered it with a wool blanket. Then he searched the depths for food. There was a wooden box of hardtack, some corn meal, and a small slab of bacon, and Sam decided to go for the hardtack and remembered to mix it with water and swallowed it quickly. He was too tired to make a fire. And besides, there was already too much fire in the beautiful mountains.

As he munched the hardtack, he emptied the knapsack on the ground in front of him, and out came a deck of cards, a dime novel, and a daguerreotype of a naked woman reclining on a couch. She was a young woman with her hair pulled tightly behind her head and smiling coyly at the camera. She has a nice face thought Sam. And her breasts and buttocks aren't so bad either. Sam had seen daguerreotypes of families before but never anything quite like this one. Give her clothes, and she could be somebody's sister. But why would a woman let someone take her picture without clothes? Would Rita have allowed someone to take such a picture he wondered? And then, knowing in his heart that she would not, he created just such a picture in his mind.

There was the naked Rita stretched out on a Victorian couch. She had a cornet in one hand and held it coyly to conceal her private places. But a cornet can't cover everything, and her lovely firm breasts rose up on either side of the mouthpiece inviting his lips to caress their loveliness. He could almost feel the heft of her breasts and her soft breath in his hair when he suddenly realized that such thoughts were dangerous. He knew from his minister that sexual thoughts could cause madness. Nevertheless, in the last light of the sun, Sam started to read the book, *The Libertine Enchantress* to get his mind off Rita.

After a fitful night of erotic dreams, Sam rose with the sun, ate some more hardtack and continued the long winding trail into the mountains. Progress was much slower now as each step was against gravity, and the pack seemed to have doubled in weight. In places he had to climb over boulders and pull himself up with trees. The ten miles to Sweeden's Cove seemed endless, but the ten miles through a field of clover were a little easier. By late afternoon Sam had his first glimpse of the Tennessee River, blue and lovely wrapped around the green mountains like a shawl. And as the woods were descending into dusk, Sam arrived opposite Sequatchie Island. *I will camp in Eden tonight. The Euphrates could not be more lovely.*

Sam spread out the rubber mat in a stand of hemlock trees and opened the wool blanket on top. This time he decided to build a fire and cook some real food. He looked for an open space and made a circle of rocks to contain his fire, and for the next two nights, he built fires and cooked bacon and johnnie cakes. And on the evening of the third day he came upon an opening in the trees and saw his promised land. A beautiful river wound its way through mountains which seemed to reach the clouds, and Sam knew that he was either in heaven or near Chattanooga.

Sam knew that he could follow the river right into Chattanooga, but the trail ran through the mountains, and his feet were so swollen and sore, that he could barely stand. Floating on the river was a much more appealing prospect, but he didn't have a boat and didn't have an ax to make a raft. He knew that in a Cooper novel, Deerslayer would find a canoe, and so he looked in places a Cooper Indian would hide one, somewhere craftily concealed among the vines. And that is exactly what happened. Sam saw the battered nose of a birch bark canoe peering at him through the underbrush, and when he had pulled it free of the cradle of vines that held it, he saw that it would still float. The white of the bark had all been stained a reddish color by long exposure to the river, and the ribs had blackened from the air and water, but the water in the bottom was not leaking out. And most amazing and improbable of all, there was a paddle carved from a birch limb lashed beneath the crossbars with vine.

Sam pulled the canoe on the sandy shore, turned it on its side, and watched the dark water pour over the gunwale. When the boat was empty, he settled his haversack in the bow, and pushed the boat into the water. Keeping his hands on the gunwales, he crouched as low as he possibly could, put one foot in the canoe and pushed with the other foot from the shore. The canoe glided out into the cold quick current, and Sam lowered himself softly onto the bottom of the stern. He could feel water seeping into the rear of his pants, but could see no water leaking in. Then he seized the paddle in both hands and with quick firm strokes drove the canoe into the center of the river.

It was lovely in the early morning light floating down the Tennessee River surrounded by the Cumberland Mountains, and for a moment Sam forgot that a war was going on. The only sounds were the birds singing in the trees along the shore. Where there is music, thought Sam, there is peace. And birds are certainly musicians. He watched bluebirds darting from tree to tree and heard the point counterpoint of Mockingbirds birds singing. Suddenly he heard the pate, pate of a woodpecker and thought that he saw an ivory bill hammering away on an old dead maple tree. *If only Rita could have shared this moment with him, he would have been in perfect bliss.*

About an hour had passed before Sam heard the first shots. At first he thought the roaring sounds were thunder, but as he listened more intently, the music of Hoover's Gap came back into his memory. In their own kind of antiphony, cannons were again playing a more deadly kind of music. Sam paddled close to shore and tried to be as invisible as possible as he floated inexorably towards Chattanooga.

At first he thought bees were buzzing around his head, but when he heard the hissing sounds and saw still water boiling, he thought for a minute that he was back in the Duck River near Tullahoma with the Confederates shooting at him. But suddenly a loud Yankee voice screamed, "Pull that damned canoe in here before I put a bullet through you." As a man grown accustomed to being captured at gun point, Sam did as he was told. When he had stepped on the shore, he found himself surrounded by a squad of Union soldiers all pointing their Springfields at him.

A tall thin soldier with Corporals bars on his arm spat a chaw of tobacco into the ground and asked, "What are you doing poking around a Union camp?" The question must have been rhetorical because before Sam could answer, the young Corporal said, "I'll tell you why. You're one of them damned Reb spies that's been giving away our position to Bragg. Because of scum like you, the Rebs lobbed a few rounds into our camp this morning. Killed three men. Fortunately one was only a musician, cornet player at that. Damndest, loudest son of a bitch that ever lived." As the corporal rambled on, Sam's captors were leading him up a trail that finally ended on a bluff overlooking the river.

They came to a clearing in the middle of a stand of cedars, and Sam saw rows and rows of white canvas tents that sheltered a large encampment of Union troops. Near the center was a much larger tent, and Sam knew that the commanding officer was probably inside drinking or discussing military strategy with his staff. As Sam and his captors approached, the tent flap opened, and a tall, burley, officer with a think black beard, and his suspenders drooping down at his sides, stepped out to meet the delegation.

"So what's going on here Cooper?" He directed his question at the young Corporal, and Cooper stopped, stood erect and saluted.

"Sir, we found this man in a canoe poking along the river just below the camp. I figure he's a Reb spy."

The officer looked at Sam, and asked, "So is that what you are, a spy? We shoot spies around here you know."

Sam looked the officer right in the eye and said, "Hell no. I'm not even a southerner. I was born and raised in Pennsylvania. My uncle's in the 7th Pennsylvania, and I'm trying to find him."

The officer grinned and said, "Well you sure don't talk like a Reb. But for some reason I can hardly fathom, some people from the north are spying for the south. Don't want the niggers to be free. Don't care about the union. How do I know you're not one of them?"

Before Sam could answer, a voice with a thick German accent rang out, "Fletcher, mein friend. How glad I am to see you." Then from around the officer's tent came a large, extended hand followed by the portly form of Schmertz. The high-plumed shako hat was on his head, and his uniform still looked clean and neat. As Sam shook Schmertz's hand, the officer asked, "You know this man?" Schmertz laughed, and said of course. He is a cornet player."

With Schmertz's endorsement, the young Corporal released Sam, and Sam and Schmertz walked off together with Schmetz's hand over Sam's shoulder. A stranger would have thought they were the best of friends.

"So how's the music coming along?" Schmertz asked.

"Wonderful" said Sam "Let me play the Haydn for you." He started to pull the cornet off his back, but Schmertz said, "Nein, Nein. This is no time for Haydn. I need somebody to play the bugle calls. My bugler was killed this morning, and we got nobody to play "Charge," "Water the Horses," "Retreat." What do you say? Can you do that?"

Hoping that a job as a bugler would lead to a job in the band, Sam had learned all the calls, and without thinking of the consequences said, "Sure. When can I start? Any job with a cornet is better than one without it." And so Sam was officially inducted into the Federal

Army and given a uniform that almost fit. His predecessor, the slain bugler, had been a little shorter than Sam, and so Sam's arms, hung several inches out of the sleeves, and the pants didn't quite reach his socks, but he was at last playing his cornet for the Union cause. When the 7th Cavalry finally entered the streets of Chattanooga, Sam was with them.

CHAPTER FIFTEEN
A Band Without Instruments

"Yes we'll rally round the flag, boys,
We'll rally once again,
Shouting the Battle Cry of Freedom."

Song, "The Battle Cry of Freedom," George F. Root

The band members scooped up the fallen flour in their hands and dumped it back into the barrels, but much had been lost in the weeds, and for months afterward their biscuits tasted like dirt and straw. As tired as they were, no one could sleep, and so they broke camp and started down the road to Manchester in the light of a full moon. As they moved along, they discussed what they would do to Forrest's raiders if they should come upon them suddenly. By all accounts those raiders were doomed men.

The sun was just beginning to cast an eerie glow over the low wooden buildings of Manchester as the Ira Goldstein Band staggered into the Main Street of town. There was no plan of action, only the dim sense that their instruments were in Manchester and that they needed to get them back. If Forrest's raiders were there, the band would fight them barehanded.

Hancock led the procession and reflected on the madness, futility, and yes the glory of the enterprise. He had seen men die for nothing. He had seen strong, healthy human beings transformed in an instant to bleeding masses of protoplasm with no more sense of purpose than taking a flag or a corner of somebody's cornfield. But here the purpose was clear. Without instruments, there would be no music, and without music only chaos and madness. Somehow music would end all the hatred that fueled this terrible war, for hadn't God created the entire universe with music? And wasn't God love? "With music He tuned the skies." Didn't Dryden say something like that? And at the end of time he would untune them again. But, by God that time was not now. Hancock wanted to put his cornet to his lips and play for God's glory, but there was nothing to play it with, and so he started to sing. His clear, rich baritone voice broke the morning silence with, "Mine eyes have seen the glory of the coming of the Lord." And the entire band joined him with, "He is trampling out the vintage where the grapes of wrath are born," and the powerful words bounced off the wooden fronts of the buildings in the dim light of dawn. The sound was not pretty with its mix of guttural, grating, piercing wails, but it was loud and, it was music. Singing together, they all felt closer and stronger and knew that they could handle anything that Forrest's raiders could throw at them.

But the raiders were long gone. The sheriff of Manchester told them that as he rushed out into the street with a La Mott in his hand and his night shirt tucked into his trousers. He asked the band what they were doing disturbing the peace like that, but reassured by Hancock's bright smile and extended hand, he listened to the band's story. When Hancock explained the case of the missing instruments, the sheriff nodded his head knowingly.

"Yep. Forrest's boys did show here yesterday with a whole wagon load of brass plumbing. They wanted to have it melted down into bullets or some such truck, but a feller named Ben Snyder knew they was music instruments and offered to pay a whole bunch of money for them. He bought the whole lot for 100 Federal dollars. Says he'll use them to start a Rebel band."

In a few minutes Hancock and Goldstein were pounding on the heavy wooden door of Snyder's shotgun house. When Snyder emerged in his night shirt, Hancock said rather bluntly, "We're here about some music instruments." Snyder was a short heavy man and needed a few seconds to get his breath, but the word music always got him very excited. There was nobody in Manchester who really understood his passion for music. People wanted to know if he could shoot a gun or plow a field. This is what they expected of a citizen of their town. And when he arrived two years ago wanting to give music lessons to the children of Manchester, most people in the town thought that he was an idiot. But like children, they knew that idiots need to be protected, and so they let him play the little piano in the church on Sundays. For that they kept him fed with produce from their farms and gave him a little spending money every now and then. He also ran errands and wrote letters for people. When some legal document needed reading, he read it, but he never got much respect for his music education.

When Hancock and Goldstein sat down in his living room and started talking music, Snyder came alive again. The initial question of, "How much do you want for those instruments" turned to, "Have you ever heard the Gilmore Band?" They talked of instrumentation, arrangements, composers, best practice techniques, until Hancock, finally asked again, "How much do you want for those instruments?"

Snyder said, "They're not for sale. I want to start a Rebel Band."

Hancock replied, "Why a Rebel band? You got your education in New England, and the people around here sure don't seem to appreciate you all that much. In fact, where are you going to find musicians in this town?"

Snyder sighed and said softly, "My mother was from Dixie, South Carolina to be exact. She taught me a deep love for the South and its people. My Dad was a Connecticut Yankee, and he loved the South too because he loved my mother. I like the regal manners of the people, the gentle climate, the relaxed pace of life. And I really believe that this war is all about States Rights. Thomas Jefferson expected that states would separate from the Union if the Federal Government wasn't protecting life, liberty and property. And you've got to admit that freeing the slaves is not exactly protecting property." He looked up triumphantly at Hancock, but Hancock's face had suddenly turned red.

"Slaves aren't property. How can you own another human being? Under the skin the blood runs red, and these Africans are just as much people as we are. And I've heard all I ever want to hear about States Rights. Do you want this great North American Continent to be a bunch of quarreling little two-bit nations, or do you want it to be the home of the greatest nation on the face of the earth?" Hancock was standing up and shouting now, and only when Goldstein pulled on his sleeve did he finally sit down.

"Now Mr. Snyder," said Goldstein gently. "We should never talk politics and never religion. We want to get along, so we should just talk music. The devil with politics. Now Mr. Hancock, tell Mr. Snyder you're sorry for yelling at him."

Hancock had calmed down by now, and extended his hand to Snyder. "I'm sorry, my friend. This war is just getting to me."

Ira continued the negotiations. "So, Mr. Snyder, you want to have a band, but you have no musicians. I've got the musicians but no instruments. Maybe we could work together on this. If you're uncomfortable with the politics, forget it. In music there ain't no North or South, just music. My band plays concerts for everybody, North and South. If you want to help such a band, sell us our instruments back. I'll give you 60 U.S. dollars, all the money we got. Give the money to Jeff Davis for all I care. Just give us our instruments back."

Snyder was silent for what seemed to be a long time, but finally he said, "I'll give you your instruments back, but on one condition."

"And what's that," asked Ira.

"You let me play with the band."

Goldstein's sad face brightened like the sun emerging from the clouds, and he said cheerfully, "Well of course you can play in the band. What instrument you want?"

"I've always had an affection for the bass saxhorn. If you've got an extra one, I'd like to play it in the band."

"Of course you can play it. Now pack your gear. We're going to play a concert in Hillsboro next week, another in Pelham after that, and before you know it, we'll be playing before packed houses in Chattanooga. This band has got a future."

On the morning of July 7, the Ira Goldstein Band, with Ben Snyder as the assistant band master and principal bass saxhorn player, started down the dusty road towards Hillsboro, Tennessee.

Throughout the months of July and August, the Ira Goldstein Band played a series of concerts and made about fifty dollars profit, but Ira expected that the big money would be in Chattanooga. In the hot humid days of late summer, they reached the Coal Railroad and walked the twenty miles to Cowan and played a concert to a few cows and about five people. Ira said, "Enough of this. We got to play the big towns. Let's take our money and ride the train to Chattanooga." They took the railroad to Stevenson and then got on board the battered drafty carriages of the Nashville/Chattanooga. On the morning of September 10, the band disembarked expectantly in the great city of Chattanooga, Tennessee, but the great city was not in a festive mood. Rosecrans' Army of the Cumberland had taken up residence for a couple of weeks but now had left in pursuit of the retreating Bragg. Everyone said that Bragg was doomed and that the Union would soon win a great victory, but there was not much to celebrate or mourn yet. Half the people in Chattanooga were rooting for Bragg and the other half for Rosecrans, and so when the Ira Goldstein Band gave its first concert on a hot summer afternoon, it played tunes that would appeal to both sides. They played the "Battle Hymn," but followed it with "Dixie," and the non-partisan crowd cheered enthusiastically. When Ira counted the cash at the end, he found almost fifty dollars, mostly Confederate.

Ellen Richards, or Allen Richards as she was known in the band, practiced more than anyone. When the other band members were horsing around and telling crude jokes, Ellen would disappear into the woods, and soon everyone would hear the major scales floating plaintively through the leaves. It was a pretty sound, and no one in the band objected to her playing, but there was a kind of desperation that made even someone as strong as Hancock a little bit uneasy. "She's playing as if her life depended on it," he said to no one in particular," and someone else said, "You've got it there. That boy, he don't know when to stop." Everybody, except maybe Flambeau and Little, knew that Bandsman Richards was a girl, but no one said so. They respected her so much, that they let her be what ever she wanted to be.

Hancock tried to talk with her a few times, but she just drew back into herself. Finally Goldstein said to Ted Brown, "You know him best. What makes him try so hard?"

Ted shrugged his shoulders and said, "If you had had a life like hers, I suppose you'd work hard too."

"What in thunder do you mean by that? Ain't everybody had a hard life? You see old Jeff Little over there? Why he thinks his wife's been unfaithful to him. Hasn't had a letter in more than a year. He's about heart broken, but you don't see him practicing all the time. Hell no. He just drinks a little white lightening and everything's fine. Why is this Allen Richards such a special guy? And why do you spend so much time with him? You even sleep together sometimes. You ain't sweet on him are you? You ain't one of them there Sodomites are you?"

Ellen was off in the woods practicing and wouldn't be back for a couple of hours, so Ted said, "I suppose I can tell you guys a few things in confidence. Now don't go blabbing this around or Allen might be upset with me for telling you, but I ain't no homosexual and neither is Allen. Fact is, he ain't even a guy. He's a gal."

"Damn," said Flambeau. "You mean I've been without a woman for nigh unto two weeks, and we got a real live woman right here in this camp? Why I could have been plowing those grassy fields instead of looking at all them wretched daguerreotypes of naked women Little picked up in Nashville."

"She ain't for the likes of you," Ted said with more firmness than anyone expected. She's a real lady. Worth a hundred of guys like you."

Ted waved his fist in Flambeau's face and Flambeau pulled out a Bowie knife, but Goldstein intervened with his own body. "Ain't going to be no fighting in my band. Now let the boy tell his story. The members of the band curled up Indian style on the ground, and as Ted began to speak the notes of the tenor saxhorn fell among them like leaves.

"Allen, or rather Ellen, comes from a rather prominent New York family. Her father's a congressman of some kind and can buy just about anything he wants, everything except a son. He's just the worst kind of congressman too, a Northern Democrat, a damned Copperhead."

"Damn it! I knew there was something wrong with that guy. Hell I ain't going to play in a band with a Copperhead."

"Shut up Myers and listen," said Hancock. "Ted didn't say Allen was a Copperhead. Don't judge the child by the sins of the father."

Suddenly Ellen appeared. She was not wearing her campaign hat, and her long golden hair cascaded to her shoulders. Then her sweet sad voice came forth like the music from a flute. "Thanks for the buildup Ted, but I'm really not anybody special, just a farm girl from Iowa. My Pa enlisted in the 123rd Illinois early in the war, and my brother Tom, Ma and I had to do all the work on the farm. Times was tough, and we barely had enough to get by. Then we got the letter, 'We regret to inform you that Jacob Richards was killed in action fighting for his country on April 12, 1862. He died a hero single-handedly attacking an enemy cannon emplacement and destroying the cannon before he was shot. President Lincoln sends his sincere sorrow for your entire family.'

"After receiving the letter, Ma just lost interest in life and died, and Tom vowed that he was going to join the Union Army and avenge his father's death. When he disappeared down that dusty road, I was all by myself on this big farm. Tom told me to sell the farm and to move in with our Aunt Sara in Lincoln, and I said I would, but after sitting alone for a few days on the old rocker on the porch, I decided that I needed something else in my life: war. My father and brother went to war to save the union and to free the slaves. Why couldn't I? I had just finished reading <u>Uncle Tom's Cabin</u> and was willing to lay down my life to save a poor, sweet old Uncle Tom from any wicked Simon Legree. The only problem was, I am a girl, and girls were supposed to stay home and make flags and send food baskets to the boys in the front. Also I had never shot a gun in my life or knew the first thing about combat.

"I could play a saxhorn though, and it suddenly struck me that I could play the saxhorn in an Army Band and maybe see some action. When I went to try out for the regimental band, however, they told me the same old story: no girls allowed. And so I came back the next day as a boy and played so well that they put me right on tenor saxhorn. Since then, I have just about driven myself crazy trying to act like a boy. I imitated my brother's actions and tried to speak in a lower voice, but I was always afraid that something would give me away. When the boys go skinny dipping in the river, I'm terrified that someone will force me into the water. When the guys piss against a tree, I worry that someone will see me squat. But now my worries are over. You know who and what I am. Are you going to shoot me or send me to my aunt in Lincoln?"

Hancock stood up and said firmly, "Neither. As far as we're concerned your name is Allen Richards, and you are a young man who plays flute in the Ira Goldstein Band. Ira don't care what sex you are as long as you can play. Ain't that right Ira?"

Ira was grinning and said, "She'll be like a daughter to me. When we find my Rita we'll have two girls in the band, two angels."

From then on Ellen wore her hair down and everyone called her Ellen, but she still wore the army pants and shirt. "Once you get rid of those hoop skirts," she said, "you never want to go back again."

Flambeau suddenly developed an interest in the saxhorn and was very attentive to Ellen, but Ellen preferred the company of Ted.

CHAPTER SIXTEEN
A Pastoral Interregnum

"We must cultivate our garden."

Voltaire

Rita threw herself into work on the farm with an energy that would have pleased the most demanding overseer, but Mrs. Gates was alarmed. It's good to get up early and fight the weeds and gather the crops, but something was not quite right. At first Mrs. Gates joked about it. "Reckon I can get myself some rest if you're doing all the work," but as the early days of September brought with them the first hint of fall, she said to Rita, "Tell me what's wrong, child. You're working as if your life depended on it."

Rita burst into tears and said, "I'm so worried about Sam. Wouldn't you think he would have written by now? I just know he's sick or hurt somewhere. How would they ever find us to tell?"

Mrs. Gates tried to reassure her that all men were like that. They wouldn't write you a letter unless they wanted something, but Rita was inconsolable. "Sam was not like that. He was a real gentleman and would write if he were able." Finally the inevitable happened. Rita packed some clothes and a little food in her reticule bag and started the long walk to Chattanooga.

The easiest route, she thought, was to follow the railroad tracks. Why take a chance on being lost in the mountains? And so wearing her long gray dress, bonnet, and apron, and carrying her reticule bag, this determined young woman started the sixty-mile hike to Chattanooga as day broke over the distant mountains on September 9, 1863. The long dress was insufferably hot in the September sun, and she longed to tear it off and walk naked, but the nineteenth-century woman didn't even have the luxury of casual clothing. It was long dress or nothing, and Rita was too modest for nothing.

She walked until about noon and was about to find a place in the shade to eat her apple and corn bread when she heard the rumble of a train coming down the railroad tracks. She was going to run and hide, but it was too late, and the train was upon her. Would soldiers leap out and attack her? In war time, all women were often considered fair game for soldiers who had already lost the veneer of civilization. When it becomes commendable to kill the men, it is also considered acceptable to rape the women. Rape and pillage; pillage and rape. How can men go back to their homes and wives after this? Behind those pressed suits and ties, and those smiling faces, were animals ready to break from their cages.

But wild animals didn't spring from the train as it screeched to a halt. "Rita?" a friendly male voice asked. "Is that you Rita?" Then she recognized her friend, the young engineer who had brought her safely to Tullahoma. "What's a nice girl like you still doing in the middle of a ugly war like this?" Rita told him that she needed to get to Chattanooga, and the young man took her hand and led her up into the engine compartment. "No need for you to ride with the rabble in the back. Bunch of Confederates who haven't seen a civilized woman in months. No telling what they might do."

Rita sat on the narrow bench and looked at all the dials and gauges that marked the soul of this force of the modern. There was no flesh and no bone, and no blood, only steam and veins of steel. This monster could never really die, because it had never really lived and yet it dwarfed the men who drove it and rode in it. Rita watched the sweaty fireman as he opened the furnace door and hurled in three shovels full of coal. As the sweat poured over his face, he seemed to be a servant rather than a master. "Oh where is mankind headed?" asked Rita?

"I don't know about mankind," said Roger, but we're headed to Chattanooga.

It was late morning of September 9th when the big locomotive screeched to a halt in downtown Chattanooga, the railroad center of the Confederacy. Rita scanned the plateau between the mountains and didn't see any people, but as the train dumped its human cargo, she saw the streets suddenly filling with men in gray. They were mostly young men burdened with heavy haversacks and long Enfield muskets. They chattered and joked and seemed like young men everywhere, but Rita knew in her heart that they were the enemy. Soon those muskets would be pointing at the men she loved.

Officers began to bellow orders, and soon the scattered clusters of gray formed into a single animal with many feet, and as drums beat the feet began to move as one.

"Pretty sight, ain't it Mam?" said the engineer.

Rita smiled and responded, "I just wish they were on our side. I wish all those men in gray were on our side."

"Wouldn't be much of a war if they was all on the same side," drawled the engineer.

"And wouldn't that be nice?" replied Rita sweetly. "Maybe the lion could lie down with the lamb."

"I don't know nothin' about them lions and lambs, but these Rebs ain't gonna lie down with no one--excepting maybe a pretty girl or two--until they've won their rights."

"It's just all too sad," said Rita. "Let's all just make music together not war."

Rita hugged the young engineer and stepped off into the autumn sunshine. As she scanned the rows of little wooden houses piled in the front of the massive and beautiful Cumberland Mountains, she said to herself, "and so this is what men are dying for." She started walking in the direction of a large wooden building, a hotel perhaps, and heard the sounds of distant explosions. "Nothing to worry about," said an old man emerging from the shadows of a broken wall. "Just them damned Yankees trying to scare us Southern folks a bit. Can I help you find somebody?" Rita told him she needed to find a place to stay for a night or two, and the old man said, "Follow me." In a moment, the two of them were climbing the rickety wooden staircase of Sadie Smith's Boarding House.

"I live here myself," the old man said. "No better place in all of Chattanooga."

She lay on the corn husk mattress to rest up for a minute or so, but when she opened her eyes again, darkness had fallen on the little town, and she heard the distant sounds of band music rising out of the river. She listened for the unmistakable sounds of Sam

Fletcher's cornet, but hearing nothing in particular, she raced out of the boarding house towards the music.

The river looked cold and dark in the immense shadow of Lookout Mountain, and in the foreground, she saw a band playing and heard the sweet happy bars of "Dixie" rising out of the cold darkness. "What a happy tune," she thought, "What a shame it wastes its sweetness on the desert air of battlefields." From across the river came the sounds of another band playing "The battle Hymn of the Republic," and the two songs seemed to wrestle over the dark cool water of the Tennessee.

She heard somebody shout, "Hey you, Yanks, over there. Why don't you play some of our songs?" Then from out of the darkness on the far side of the beautiful Tennessee, the strains of "Dixie" drifted across the water, and the sounds of hundreds of rough male voices began to sing the words. When the last words had been sung, someone shouted, "Why don't we try to play it together?" The band across the river started playing "Dixie" again, and the band on her side of the river picked it up, and soon the bands were creating a massive sound that filled the space over the river. The notes from across the river came a little bit after the ones on her side and created a kind of echo.

Rita was still listening for the unmistakable sound of Sam's cornet when she suddenly noticed a large heavy man brandishing a baton and said, "Oh my God, that looks like my father." About the same moment, she heard the boom of cannon and shells began bursting everywhere. People began to scatter, and she found herself in the midst of a massive block of humanity moving inexorably forward. "Stop" she screamed, but no one listened, and she was dragged forward until she found herself right in front of Sadie Smith's Rooming House. Rita forced herself to the side of the crowd and was soon back in her tiny white washed room. "What's my father doing here? I should find him, but then he might take me home to Iowa."

When Rita looked out her window the next morning, all the gray coats had disappeared and had been replaced by blue ones. Chattanooga had fallen to the Yankees without a fight. That night she heard a distant bugle blowing taps and for a moment she thought she recognized the sound. "It's certainly loud enough and clear enough to be Sam. But Sam would never play bugle calls. He's a classical musician." She fell asleep dreaming of her protégé playing Haydn in the White House for President Lincoln.

CHAPTER SEVENTEEN
Chickamauga

"Hurrah! Hurrah! for Southern Rights Hurrah!
Hurrah! for the Bonnie Blue Flag
That bears a single star!"

Song, "The Bonnie Blue Flag," Harry Macarthy

Chattanooga was an exciting place for a young, pretty, northern girl to be visiting on September 10, 1863. The Union Army had taken over everything, and there was a general sense of good will and optimism. Chattanooga may have been in a Rebel state, but at least half its inhabitants were cheering for the union. And so when the Union troops poured out of the city like a huge pack of hounds in pursuit of the fleeing southern rabbits, Rita could sense the electricity in the air. Her old gentleman friend told her that the war was as good as over.

"Old Rosie's gonna round up them rebels and send them packing. You mark my words; there's gonna be a big battle, and when it's over, the Union will be restored." Rita hoped that he was right and that she would at last settle her affair with Butch Lassiter and be reunited with her good friend--"almost a brother"--Sam Fletcher. She also hoped that all this would happen before her father found her. The band director by the river was not Ira Goldstein, but he looked enough like him to make Rita uncomfortable.

She sat down at the little deal table in her room and began composing a letter to Mrs. Gates.

My Dear Friend,

I just want you to know that I have arrived in Chattanooga safely and to assure you that this wonderful city is now in the hands of the Union Army. Glory be to God. I haven't seen Sam or Butch but may have caught a glimpse of my father at a concert last night. I wanted him to know that I am all right but feared that he would take me home before my mission is accomplished, and so I slipped away in the night without speaking. I know that I am being unkind and will try to make it up to him some day. But I am so afraid for Sam. He is such an innocent, that I fear he has no idea how evil this world is. Butch can do fine without me, but poor Sam needs me. I know this sounds like a profession of love, but Sam is just like a brother to me.

I hope that you are well and that the animals don't miss me too much. Please give Jerry the horse a hug for me and feed him an extra portion of oats.

Your sincere friend,
Rita

As Rita sealed the envelope, she didn't notice the blue riders of the 7th Pennsylvania Cavalry galloping past her window with the late summer sun glinting on their polished scabbards. Most importantly, she didn't see Sam Fletcher sitting tall in the saddle, dressed in a stiff new blue uniform, and the newly--polished cornet swinging by his side.

Sam was officially in the Pennsylvania 7th Cavalry now, and as the young troopers dashed after the fleeing Confederates, Sam's cheers of victory joined theirs. Like them he believed in his heart that Bragg's troops were running like scared rabbits and that he would be among the glorious heroes who rounded them up and brought the traitors to justice. As they thundered down the dust-covered road to Georgia, waving their hats and cheering, they were only a part of the 44,000-man machine that would soon crush the Confederacy, but each man knew that his presence was essential for success.

Old Rosie knew that he had his old enemy just where he wanted him and that before the first snow fell, the terrible war would be over. However, hubris is a terrible thing, and the gods of war seem to have a deep appreciation of irony. Unknown to the Union Army, Longstreet and about 20,000 Confederates had just arrived from Richmond. Because the Union Army held eastern Tennessee, Longstreet had to go the long way around through Atlanta, but he completed his improbable journey just in time for the arrival of the unsuspecting Yankees. For one of the few times in the war, the South was meeting the north with a slight numerical advantage, and even worst news for Sam Fletcher and his boys was the fact that the Union armies were scattered, but the Confederates were concentrated and waiting along a little stream known as Chickamauga Creek.

The night of September 17th was cold and crisp as the Seventh Pennsylvania cavalry set up camp in a grove of hemlocks. As they sat around their campfires cooking their government issued salt beef and baking a few potatoes borrowed from a nearby barn, they heard the mournful sound of a train whistle somewhere off in the distance. "Almost sounds like music," said Sam. "I think I could play that tune on my horn."

"Hell," said the harsh voice of Schmertz from the darkness. "If it's noise you want, play a saxhorn. The cornet should be pretty, like a beautiful woman singing."

Then another locomotive spoke from the distance soulfully, like it was looking for a mate. When the third whistle swept out of the darkness a few moments later, a young lieutenant stood up and said, "Them Rebs is up to something. I got to talk to Minty."

"What's he talking about?" asked Sam. "Does he think the Rebs are going to attack us in locomotives?"

An old grizzled fellow spat into the fire and said, "Nope. No such luck. Every one of them trains is bringing in a load of Rebs from somewhere. You mark my words, there's gonna be hell to pay tomorrow. Them Rebs ain't runnin' away. They's laying a trap for us, and we're gonna walk right into it like a pack of fools."

"So how do you know this old man?" asked Sam.

"I been around. The Rebs may be devils, but they ain't stupid. The Devil hisself ain't stupid."

Sam pulled the army blanket up to his chin, but still he felt the frost descending on the world like a cold blanket of death. And throughout the night were the screams of train whistles.

On the crisp Friday morning of September 18th 1863, the 7th Pennsylvania rose from the rubber mats and blankets to a world transformed by frost. After a breakfast of hard tack and coffee, they fed and watered the horses and started moving slowly through a flatland covered by underbrush and trees. "If the enemy wanted to surprise us it could do so easily," thought Sam. "Can't see three feet on either side, and the road ahead disappears in a tunnel of trees." After riding for about twenty minutes, they passed through the trees and came to a little wooden bridge which stretched picturesquely across a quiet little stream. The bridge was anchored on each end by stone piers and held up on the middle by a pair of wooden trellises. The planking was of various lengths and seemed to be just piled there loosely like someone was soon going to carry it away and build something with it. Along either side was a handrail, and the space between the rails could barely accommodate two horses side by side. Sam thought how lovely it would be to paddle down this quiet little stream with Rita and have a little picnic lunch in the shadow of the bridge. However, this was Reed's Bridge and the stream was Chickamauga Creek. Sam's life would never be quite the same again.

Colonel Minty rode quickly up to the head of the column and spoke in a clear loud voice. "Boys, we've got to hold this bridge at all costs. In a few minutes, Old Bushrod Johnson and about 7,000 infantry are going to try to cross this creek. If they succeed, the whole darned Union Army is doomed. They'll turn Rosie's flank and drive the army into McLemore's Cove like a bunch of sheep for the slaughter. There are less than a thousand of us, but if we dig in and let them have it with our Spencers, we can buy the Army time enough to regroup."

"Sort of like Horatio at the Bridge," thought Sam, but before he could savor this thought, he saw a long dust cloud moving towards them and soon saw that the cloud had many feet. "Here they come," someone shouted. And just as suddenly the roar of Union cannon broke the peace of the early morning, and long rows of gray- coated men settled to the ground in a grizzly slumber. Then Colonel Minty shouted, "Bugler, play 'Forward,'" and as if the cornet had a mind of its own it sprang to Sam's lips and the stirring staccato of charge vibrated through the still, cool air of the early morning. Before the echo had died in the trees and fallen into the still water of the creek, about a hundred horsemen of the Seventh Pennsylvania and the 4th Michigan cavalry surged across the narrow bridge like a great blue wave foaming with sparkling sabers, and Sam rode the crest of this great wave blasting cold brassy notes on his cornet as it burst upon the butternut men who were frantically trying to dig trenches into the hard earth. The deep base of the roaring cannons resounded against the rapid patter of musket balls and the screaming of men and the neighing of horses. This was no place for a cornet, and so Sam dropped the cornet to his side and pulled his carbine from the scabbard and fired into the brown mass of humanity in his front and fired again and again, but the mass of brown just became larger, until he heard the command, "Blow 'In Retreat.'" Minie balls were flying around his head like mosquitoes, as Sam reached for the cornet, and then, as in a dream, the mournful notes of "In Retreat" carried above the roar of battle, and the wave of blue horsemen was almost lost in the vast cacophony of sound, as they ebbed backwards towards the too distant bridge.

Sam looked back and saw a small band of the 4th Michigan going in the opposite direction, sabers glittering in the sunlight, horses at full gallop towards the swarming gray mass stopping it for a few precious moments as the Seventh Cavalry clattered back across the bridge two abreast.

The Union troopers had thrown up breast works of fence rails, tree branches, and rocks and waited silently for the inevitable return of the Confederate infantry. The cannon of the Chicago Trade Guild were lined up in the relative protection of a log house that overlooked the creek. Inside the house were Mrs. Reed and her three small children. Minty had tried to get them to leave, but Mrs. Reed was a stubborn rebel woman and would not let up on her curses of the damned Yankees. "My boys is coming across this creek," she screamed, "and when they does, they're gonna whip you and look after me." She was screaming something about the damn Yankees when a ball from Bushrod Johnson's Confederate artillery whistled through the roof of her log house and sent her to meet her maker.

Sam leaped off his horse along with the rest of his troop and fell down on his belly behind the hastily-dug earthworks and pieces of split rail fences. The earth smelled cool and damp like a freshly-dug grave, and Sam thought how close he had come to being in one. "If those Michigan boys hadn't charged, we would have all been goners, he said to the mud."

In a few minutes the survivors of the 4th Michigan galloped across the bridge to the wild cheers of the 7th Pennsylvania, and soon the entire brigade of a little over 900 men dug in and awaited the inexorable advance of about 7000 Confederates. With the other young men, Sam ducked down low near the edge of the creek, and with the others he peered anxiously at the slowly moving brown cloud. As he lay with his belly on the frosted ground, he heard the distinctive cry of a solitary crow in the branches of a scrawny pine tree and thought of home. There was an old crow in the big pine behind the house in Iowa, and when he was a little boy his mother told him the crow was laughing at him for being so clumsy. One morning he was trying to split logs for the iron stove and missed, hitting the ground with the axe. When the crow went Ha! Ha! Ha! He got so mad, that he chased the crow with the axe, but the crow laughed all the louder. As the laughter echoed in his memory, Sam noticed that the brown cloud not only had feet; it also had faces, faces of young boys and old grizzled men carrying rifles and moving slowly and cautiously towards the bridge.

Sam saw an officer on a big white horse moving ahead of the rest and felt a sudden sickness in his stomach. The officer was tall and heavy with a thick black beard and mustache and looked a little like his Uncle Ed. Sam watched as the long line of blue soldiers on either side of him slowly raised their rifles and pointed them in the direction of the brown cloud, and as if part of a machine, he felt his own hand tightening on his Spencer. *Like shooting rabbits,* he thought, *but these rabbits were men.* He pointed the barrel at the officer and squeezed the trigger. There was a loud blast from the mouth of his weapon, and all along the line the young men began to shoot, but the gray cloud was untouched, and the officer shouted, "Fall back men. We're in an ambush." From the brown cloud came spurts of flame and the young man next to him became suddenly still as blood began to ooze from his head and trickle down his front.

The men in the brown cloud began to pull away from the creek, but Johnson soon realized that the force in front of him was not a brigade but only a bunch of dismounted cavalry and began to move his men towards Reed's Bridge on the double quick. The Seventh Pennsylvania held its breath like a single beast, and when faces began to appear in the brown cloud, the blue coats began to fire. With their Spencers, the fire was intense and steady, and the butternuts were falling like wheat before the mowers in a field. The boys in blue heard the Confederate bugler blow "In Retreat," and soon the field was empty except for the dead and dying.

Sam shouted, "We won!" But the old grizzled fellow said, "Don't count on it sonny. They'll be back" And before Sam could even get his breath, the brown mass was moving towards the bridge once again. Again and again the brown mass moved against the bridge, and each time, the men in blue drove it back with their Spencers and with canister from the Chicago Board of Trade cannon. No one ate, no one drank, and it seemed like time had stood still and that the same picture was merely repeating itself in the same frame, when Colonel Minty rode up and said, "Bugler play 'Recall' we're going to withdraw to Lee and Gordon's Mills." Sam leaped up and played the call and soon the 7th Pennsylvania and 4th Michigan were galloping through the woods to join Colonel Wilder at Lee and Gordon Mills. For ten hours this little band had held off almost the entire rebel army and in so doing had given Rosecrans time to save the Army of the Cumberland. There would be no glorious Northern victory, but at least the army had been saved from slaughter in McLemore's Cove.

That was the end of the Battle of Chickamauga for Sam and the 7th Cavalry. From Lee and Gordon Mills, they moved in the growing darkness north towards Chattanooga and set up camp near Rossville. They were supposed to guard the trains heading to Chattanooga, but after resting on the 19th, the only trains they saw were thousands of Union soldiers streaming in total panic and disarray in the general direction of the North. The word heard from retreating soldiers was, "We have been badly defeated. You better run for yours lives, because the Rebs is close on our heels."

Fortunately, the reports were somewhat exaggerated. The entire union army had not been routed. General Thomas--later to be called, "The Rock of Chickamauga"-- held his position on "Snodgrass Hill," and the demoralized but largely intact Union Army was able to crawl back into the defensive position of Chattanooga and nurse its many wounds. The cost had been enormous--about 28,000 casualties--but the army had been saved, and Sam knew that his stand at Reed's Bridge had helped prevent total destruction. *If Rita could only have seen me.*

CHAPTER EIGHTEEN
Love Rises from the Ashes of Chickamauga

"Cherry-Ripe, ripe,

Full and fair ones; come and buy

If so be you ask me where

They do grow? I answer, there

Where my Julia's lips do smile;--

There's the land, or cherry isle;

Whose plantations fully show

All the year where cherries grow."

Robert Herrick, "Cherry Ripe"

As Rita looked out her hotel window on the evening of September 20, 1863, she was astonished to see the vanguard of the Army of the Cumberland surging through the streets of Chattanooga in anything but triumph. She rushed down the stairs and out onto the porch and grabbed the sleeve of a passing blue-coated trooper. "What has happened?" she cried. "Nothin' but trouble Mam." he responded. "Them Rebs was just too many for us. We're lucky to have escaped with our lives."

"Do you know anything of the 7th Pennsylvania?" She pleaded.

"I don't rightly know, but if you're expecting to see somebody coming back, I wouldn't count on it. Powerful lot of our boys laying dead on the field."

Rita wanted to ask him more, but he pulled away from her and disappeared in a haze of blue.

For the rest of September, all of October, and about half of November, the Army of the Cumberland lay in Chattanooga slowly starving as the victorious Confederates did all they could to stop the flow of supplies from the so-called, "Cracker Trail." Horses were walking skeletons, and the men who cared for them stole their pathetic rations of corn and oats and consumed them like hungry wolves. Tedious hungry days rolled past each other without even the prospects of heroic "enterprises of great pitch and moment"

On October 23rd, however, the man who would turn the world upside down, arrived in a railroad car in the dark. He could barely stand because his horse had fallen on him, and General Howard did not even recognize him, at first, as the man who had taken Vicksburg, but when Grant spoke, Howard recognized him at once. Inauspiciously, Grant took over the Union Army from Rosecrans, and from now on, the hopes of the Confederacy would sink inexorably.

The good news for Rita, however, was not Grant, whom she did not know, but the realization that the men she wanted to find could not go anywhere outside the small river community of Chattanooga, Tennessee. They were trapped, and given time enough, she would find them.

It was also good news for the Ira Goldstein Band. As they rolled into town on the evening of September 30, 1863, they found thousands of people desperate for entertainment. The band set up camp on the edge of a low neck of land called Moccasin Bend, and from their campsite, the band members could see the lights of Confederate campfires like thousands of stars sparkling on the dark flank of Lookout Mountain.

"Looks like we're in a fine mess now," grumbled Flambeau. "We've just walked into a box, and the Rebs are sitting on the lid."

"That's your trouble," replied Goldstein cheerfully. "We've got a captive audience, so to speak. Ain't anyone going anywhere, and all you do is gripe." At noon on October 1st, Rosecrans received the grim news that the dreaded rebel cavalryman Wheeler had fallen upon a Federal supply train of 800 wagons and destroyed it. Now, with the cold weather coming on, the Federal Army found itself desperately short of food and ammunition. The civilians suffered with the army, and anyone who had an ear of corn or two to eat was a rich person. Goldstein's band was willing to play for food, but people only brought money.

Spending all day in a hotel room waiting for something to happen was not Rita's idea of living, and so she went to one of the few places where something was happening, the camp hospital, or what passed for a hospital. It was actually an old church that had been gutted of all its pews and was now filled with row after row of sick and dying young men. As Rita walked out of the clear sunshine into the darkness of the church, she was immediately overwhelmed by the stench of mortifying wounds and unwashed bodies.

Three or four women were moving from cot to cot administering to the needs of the living and trying to bring consolation to the dying. Finally a stout woman of about fifty 50 looked up and seeing Rita standing there, shouted,

"What do you want here?"

Rita smiled sweetly and said, "I want to help."

As she rolled back the filthy bandage from the stump of an amputated leg, the stout woman blurted out, "What would a fine woman like you know about all this? Come here sweetheart, and I'll show you what we do here."

Rita looked at the wounded man and almost fainted from the sight of maggots crawling over the raw stump of a leg. The smell was so overwhelming, that she almost threw up, but when the sweet voice of a young man, hardly more than a boy, whispered, "Mam, I'd be obliged if you could bring me a cup of water," Rita felt a new strength filling her body Without another word to the stout woman. Rita went outside and returned with a tin cup filled to the brim with water.

All day Rita returned with cups of water and went from cot to cot administering to the needs of the men, and the stout woman would occasionally say to her, "Could you help me roll this man over?" Or, "Could you spell for a minute while I get a bite to eat?" It was late at night when Rita returned to her hotel and fell into a deep sleep, but at the first light of day, she was back at the hospital. The next night, she didn't leave but just took catnaps on a straw tick in a corner. Finally the stout woman said, "Child you need to get away from this place every once in a while. You'll go insane. There's a band playing down by the river tonight. I want you to go."

Rita protested, "But you need me here."

"Go," said the woman.

It was a cool night in mid October, and the band had set up on a platform near Lookout Creek. Everyone was pretty hungry, and the music now served to get everyone's mind off food. Hancock was walking through the heavy brush near the river trying to dip out a bucket of water when a voice broke out from the land on the other side.

"Hey Yank," drawled a deep Southern voice. "You boys want to do some tradin'?"

Hancock was so startled, that he dropped the bucket but knew at once that he had run into some good luck.

"What you got to trade Reb?" asked Hancock.

"How about some tobacco for a can of that good Union Coffee?"

"We can't eat tobacco. What about some ears of corn?"

In a few minutes, Hancock was carrying the last of the band coffee to a rocky shallow place in the middle of Lookout Creek, and a tall thin Confederate was meeting him with a full bushel of corn.

"Name's Zeb," said the Confederate cheerfully. "I understand you boys is getting mighty hungry over there."

Hancock extended his hand and shook the Confederate's and said, "Sure am glad to do business with you."

"So what unit you with?" the Confederate asked cordially.

"No unit. I play in a civilian band. We're going to play tomorrow night out by Brown's Ferry. Bring some of your boys and take a listen."

"Tell you what Yank," play some of our songs and me and some of the boys will be there singing along with you."

Hancock saw the gray back fade into the darkness and heard the splashing of his feet as the young soldier made it to the other bank. Then the southern drawl fought its way through the darkness. "See you boys tomorrow night."

The night of the concert, the rebels were across the Tennessee in large numbers, but no shots were fired. The applause of the Rebs joined the applause of the Yanks as the sweet notes of "Annie Laurie" drifted across the water.

Rita eagerly scanned the hundreds of concert goers who fanned out in the darkness around the band platform but didn't see Sam. Rita knew that where there was music, there would be Sam, but in the thick blue-coated crowd dissolving into the twilight, all the men looked pretty much alike.

A deep southern voice from across the river shouted, "How about a few choruses of Dixie?" and before anyone could reply, the band was playing "Dixie." About the beginning of the third verse, Rita heard a roar from the crowd, and the music stopped. In the glow of a single camp fire two men were punching each other, and the crowd was cheering. She was about to leave when she heard someone shout, "Kill 'em Butch. Break his damned neck."

Then she elbowed her way through the crowd of men and felt rough hands squeezing her buttocks and fondling her breasts. The stench of alcohol and unwashed bodies filled her nostrils, but she fought her way to the front, and there was Butch punching a man on the ground. Butch was straddling the fallen man punching him in the face with all his might while the crowd cheered.

When Rita broke into the clearing and shouted, "Butch, let him go," the crowd became suddenly silent, and Butch dropped his hands to his side.

"Rita, what are you doing here?" mumbled the now-defeated Butch as he slowly stood up and faced her with his eyes on the ground.

"If you had only answered my letters I might not be here," she replied firmly. "First you write me all those beautiful letters and promise to return, and then I hear nothing. What am I supposed to do?"

The soldiers now circled the new combatants and began to shout words of encouragement.

"That a way to go lady. Tell him."

"I put my money on the lady. She's got a tongue like claws. She's like a little hell cat."

"So what do you have to say for yourself Butch?"

"I don't remember no letters. Maybe you could refresh my memory a little."

The man on the ground rose slowly to a sitting position and said softly, "I don't suppose you can even read and write, but for some reason beyond my understanding, the sweetest and most lovely woman in the world loves you, and I didn't want her to be disappointed. I wrote those letters."

"Sam," shrieked Rita. And she fell on the ground and threw his arms around his shoulders. What are you doing here?"

His face was masked with blood, and his eyes were so swollen, that they could hardly stay open, but his voice came out loud and strong, "I'm here to help these boys whip the Rebs." A cheer filled the darkness and thousands of hungry young men hurled their caps in the air.

A young officer broke through the crowd and asked, "What's going on here?"

A tall private in a blue uniform replied, "The band was playing 'Dixie' and this fellow Butch about had a fit. He picked up some rocks and began hurling them at the band. Then this other fellow comes forward and grabs Butch's arm. He says, 'Why do you always have to be such a damned idiot?' Or words to that effect. Then three of Butch's pals come forward and grabs the other fellow from behind and holds him while Butch punches him. Like they would have killed him if this little lady hadn't come along."

"Is that right boy?" asked the officer.

"That's right sir," said another voice from the crowd, and several other voices said, "He damn near killed him. If this little lady hadn't come along, he probably would have."

"We don't need any cowards in this army," the officer said. He grabbed Butch by the collar and dragged him to his feet. "I'm taking you to the stockade."

Butch began to scream, "But sir it's not my fault. He started it." But to a chorus of cheers, the officer dragged the still-protesting Butch into the darkness.

Rita took Sam by the hand and in silence led him along the dirt road above the deep, cold Tennessee River. They had so much to say to each other, that they said virtually nothing as hand in hand they climbed up the mountain to her room in the hotel. There she gently bathed his wounds and put him into her bed, and it was several days before she finally said, "So it was you who wrote those beautiful letters. I sort of thought so. I even hoped so."

"Hoped so?" asked Sam in a feeble voice.

"Of course I did."

"But why Rita?" asked Sam. "I thought you loved Butch."

Rita looked out the window, and tears filled her eyes. The only sound was the clock on the town square clanging out the hours and only after the ninth beat had died in the night air did Rita speak.

"I surely thought I loved him, but as I look back, I see that I was in love with an illusion. He was a phantom lover, a lover from my imagination."

Sam waited for a moment before he asked, "But what about me? How do I fit into the world of your imagination?"

Rita cradled Sam's head gently against her breast, and said softly, "You're not imaginary at all. You are a creature of flesh and blood. I had imagined working on that farm in Nebraska with Butch, but there was nothing imaginary about chopping weeds by your side on Mrs. Gates' farm. Sam, we suffered together; we rejoiced together. I will never forget how we struggled to deliver that little calf. The mother was having such a hard time, and I, this little girl from Brooklyn, was trying desperately to help her but couldn't. Then you came into the barn and knew exactly what to do. You took charge and soon we were sitting there on the barn floor holding this beautiful baby calf. You were so strong and so gentle."

"But why did you still keep looking for Butch, even then?" asked Sam.

"I'm a stubborn woman and don't give up easily. I think I needed to complete what I started and bring that man to his knees."

Sam looked into Rita's lovely face and asked, "Do you ever think of that night we spent together in Hoover's Gap?"

Rita laughed and said, "I sure do. It was one of the strangest nights of my life. I thought you must have been homosexual. Here you were snuggled up against me, and all you could talk about was Butch."

"But what if I had touched you? Wouldn't you have been mad?"

"Mad? I would have slapped you in the face, but I wish you had tried."

"I wish I had tried! I let one of the greatest opportunities slip into the past forever. Here my Dionysian body was stretching against the starchy limits of my Presbyterian soul, and I let the soul win."

"To tell you the truth," Rita said. "I thought of you as more of a sister than a lover. You were sweet to help me find information about Butch, and you were dear to go with me on my quest, but there was nothing sexual. You were almost like a little lost puppy that I found by the road."

Sam laughed and said, "I'm honored to be connected to the canine species. Dogs are among the best people I have ever known, but what do you think of me now? Let's suppose this hotel room is our campsite on Hoover's Gap? Can moments in time ever be repeated? I have dreamed of that night over and over again. Only in my dreams, we made passionate love."

Rita looked into his eyes and gently pushed the hair back on his forehead. "You were better looking then, but your face has more character now."

When she left the room, she was wearing the long hooped dress that Sam had first seen her in so long ago in Murfreesboro. But when she came back, she was naked. She stood at the head of the bed letting Sam take in all her loveliness, then she said softly, "Let's relive that night but have a better ending."

Rita slipped into the bed next to him, but this time the Dionysian body triumphed over the Presbyterian soul. Sam felt the soft heaviness of her breasts against his chest, but this time he didn't turn away. He ran his hands gently over every part of her sweet body. He nibbled her little toes, ran his hand along the soft loveliness of her legs and found at last, rising like a hill in Paradise, the mound of Venus, arrayed in a silky red garden of earthly delights. He rested his hand there at the secret portals for a few lingering moments, while his lips traveled over the soft hills of her breasts, and lapped upon the sweet red cherries which now swelled to meet his lips.

They rocked in the cradle of love until the bells on the church tower chimed twelve long resonant bongs, and then they fell asleep locked in each other's arms. When Sam awakened during the night, they did it again. And when the sun came over Lookout Mountain, they did it one more time. Finally Rita said "I need to go now. They need me in the hospital." She kissed Sam on the forehead and was gone.

Sam stayed in the hotel until his mangled face had almost healed and then tried to find the Seventh Cavalry, but it had gone to Knoxville to help Burnside. He thought about joining them, and his mind told him that he needed to be there, but his heart told that he never wanted to leave Rita again. This time he followed his heart.

Rita didn't stay at the hospital in the evenings now. She came back to the hotel and gave Sam cornet lessons. At first the other patrons pounded on the walls and complained about the blasting sounds of a cornet that was now invading their lives. But one sight of lovely Rita, and a few words of explanation soon won them over. Practice was every night in the lobby, and Rita started off the evening by playing some solos of her own. From her cornet came the sweet sounds of home and peace, and grown men wept. Then Sam began to play, and no one complained much. His versions of the songs were just too loud and uncontrolled compared to Rita's. And so with Rita as the model, and the hotel patrons as critics, Sam began to gradually improve. One evening an old timer came into the lobby while Sam was playing and said, "Why I be swan. I thought for sure Rita was playing." This moment lifted Sam's spirits for the rest of his life, and when he would get discouraged in the years ahead, he would think of that old gentleman and take hope again.

With the Seventh Pennsylvania in Nashville, Sam had time to practice, and he played every day, and every evening he took lessons from Rita. Out of kindness to the hotel patrons, he did most of his work in the woods with only the squirrels for an audience. For hours at a time, he worked on his long tones, scales, chromatics and best of all on his pouch of music. When the wind was right, downtown Chattanooga would sometimes hear faint echoes of "The Battle Hymn" or "Tenting to Night" or even "Dixie." Sam loved "Dixie." What a lovely melody," he would often say. "And it was written by a Yankee."

When he wasn't practicing, he went with Rita to the hospital and tried to bring comfort to the sick and wounded men. He wrote letters home for them; listened to their stories, read them books. He even brought them water and helped change bandages.

One young man gained his attention in particular. He was a very diminutive fellow from Harrisburg, Pennsylvania named Flem Cook. Flem was just 17 years old and had had his right arm amputated by a field surgeon. "We were retreating when something hit me in the arm so hard, that it knocked me down. I got up and started running again, but my head felt kind of light, and the next thing I know I'm in this tent, and men are screaming bloody murder everywhere, and this huge blood-soaked man is putting a saw against my arm. I can feel the teeth starting to dig in, and I start screaming, but he tells these other two men to hold me down. Then he starts sawing, and the pain is so terrible that I'm thinking I'd just rather die, but quicker than you might think, I hear the thud of something falling into a pail, and I suddenly realize that I've just lost my arm. I'm not thinking that about half the people who have their limbs sawed off die. I think, "How the hell can I play a cornet with one arm? I start to bawl like a baby, but pretty soon I pass out, and I don't remember much for a few days. People said that I had a high fever and that I would probably die. Some of the guys cast lots to see who would get my cornet, but I fooled them all. I'm still here." He raised his left arm in triumph still holding the cornet. Say, could you write a letter to my folks and tell them that I'm all right?"

With tears in his eyes, Sam took out a piece of paper and wrote.

Dear Folks,

I know you are probably wondering what happened to me and may have been expecting to hear the worst, but I am alive and fairly well. I say fairly, because I had a little accident on the battlefield and won't be able to play in the Gilmore Band in Boston. A Rebel bullet destroyed my right arm, and you can't really do much on a cornet with one hand, particularly if that one hand is the left one. Tell Sara that I will be home again in a few weeks or so, and then we can decide what to do with our lives. Tell her to keep studying music, and I will stand by her. Maybe I can still be of some help on the farm, but don't expect too much.

I know you and mom will be disappointed that I can't use that music talent that I was born with, but something else will come along. This fellow Sam Fletcher at the hospital has been very helpful and may have a few ideas.

Give my love to Sara and tell her that I live for the day when I can see her again.

                       Love,

                          Flem

Sam sealed the letter, looked down at the pale little fellow on the straw ticking, and said, "You know I think you might be able to play that cornet with one hand better than I can with two."

Flem's eyes brightened, and he said excitedly, "You play the cornet?"

Sam smiled and said, "I sure try, but no one ever suggested that I play with Gilmore." .

"It's easy," said Flem. "Just blow into the horn, think the notes, and count the beats."

Sam laughed and said, "That's easy for you to say. I start counting the beats, and suddenly my mind wanders, and I don't know where I am. I guess I just can't help myself."

Flem looked up and said with an edge to his voice. "Of course you can help it. Don't let your mind wander. Your mind wouldn't wander if you were standing on the edge of a cliff and were ready to fall off. One false step and you would be dead. Think of playing a cornet as like standing on the edge of that cliff. You can't let your mind wander, damn it. You owe it to yourself; you owe it to the other band members; you owe it to yourself. Now if I can't play the cornet, you will. You've got two hands and no excuses." Then Flem's head fell back on the pillow, and he whispered, "I envy you Fletcher. You've got two hands."

Every day Flem and Sam talked music and cornets and particularly cornets. Flem told Sam to practice counting beats everywhere. "When you walk, count the beats. When it rains, count the drops. When the horses gallop, listen to the thumps. Fletcher, there's music everywhere. You've just got to listen for it."

When he got back to the hotel with Rita, Sam said, "Do you suppose you could play the cornet with just your left hand?"

Rita, laughed and said, "Anything is possible. If you've got the music in your head, you can figure some way to get it out. Let me see your cornet." Rita put her right hand at her side and held the instrument in her left hand. To Sam's amazement, she was able to support the instrument with her thumb and pinkie and work the valves with her fingers. He was even more amazed when she put the instrument to her mouth and played the D major scale perfectly.

"How did you do that?" asked Sam. "I didn't think it could be done."

"Now you try it," Rita insisted. And so Sam put the instrument in his left hand and, much to his amazement, was able to play the D major scale. "Well I be swan," he said. "I've got a surprise for Flem tomorrow."

The next day Sam brought his cornet to the hospital, and over the protests of the medical staff, played the D Major scale with his left hand.

"Hey, that's pretty good," said Flem. "A little loud but all the right notes."

"Now you play it," demanded Sam.

"I really can't," said Flem. "I'd never be able to meet my own standards playing left handed. I couldn't help but notice that your playing was a little erratic playing with your left hand."

"Hell," said Sam. "The left hand has nothing to do with it. I'm just erratic. Now let me hear you play something."

Reluctantly, Flem took the instrument into his left hand the way Sam had done, and moved the valves up and down. Finally he put the horn to his lips and blew a sweet clear C. He was so excited by the note, that he played the whole C scale. Then he played all the scales. Finally he played "Annie Laurie." When he was finished, cheers and clapping could be heard throughout the entire hospital.

From that point on, Flem and Sam played every day. They played solos and duets, and through it all Flem kept the beat and tapped his foot so that Sam could see it. With the return of music, Flem's health improved dramatically, and one fine autumn day he announced to Sam that he needed to get back to Sara and then to Boston. Before he finally started off on the road home, he told Sam to "practice every day, count and listen, listen and count. If you work really hard, you could be a good player some day." In some of the discouraging days ahead, Sam thought of Flem's words and refused to give up.

The weather was getting colder as the days moved on to November, and food was still very scarce. Near the end of October, Sam heard that the Yanks had crossed the river at Brown's ferry and were starting to push back the stranglehold the Rebs had over them, but food was still scarce and would be as long as the Rebs controlled Lookout Mountain and Missionary Ridge. In late November, the massive starving beast of the Union Army began to flex its limbs in a desperate effort to throw the enemy off its back. On November 24th Hooker took Lookout Mountain, and Sherman crossed the Tennessee River to attack the Confederates on Tunnel Hill. If Sherman could crush the left flank, the Confederates could be rolled off the mountain, and the food could come in once again. As these great forces moved about him, Sam grew restless, and he became impatient and irritable. One evening at his lesson, Rita asked him what was wrong.

Sam could contain himself no longer. "Here I sit in a hotel lobby with the most beautiful woman in the world and playing my cornet while those boys in blue are out there in the mud dying for the union, dying for me, dying for us. It's not right. What will I tell our grandchildren? While the most glorious battle in history was being fought, I was in a hotel playing music."

Rita paused briefly and said, "Sam there's really not much glory out there. You've seen the glory in the hospital with all the pain and misery, with all the piles of arms and legs piled by the door, with the screams of the dying. And for what? This war will end one day no matter what happens here, and life will go on. When we till the fields of our lovely farm in Iowa, what difference does it make if Tennessee is still with us or not? You can't see Tennessee from Iowa. And what kind of farmer would you be with one leg? What kind of wife and mother would I become, if you died out there on the mountain? Be grateful that we found each other and that you have a good excuse not to fight. That no good Butch at least did something right. He took you away from the fighting."

Sam pulled out a copy of a newspaper he had been reading and showed the headline to Rita. "33rd New Jersey Hides Behind Barn While the Rest of the Union Army Takes Orchard Knob." The article below the headline explained how this division, dressed as Zouaves--one of the most flamboyant uniforms of the Civil War-- had hidden behind a barn to avoid enemy fire. Even the threats and curses of their officers could not bring them out. On either side of them marched other heroic divisions, but those New Jersey boys preferred life to honor.

I know how you feel Rita, and I know you know how I feel. Do you want our children to think that their Dad had been like those cowards from New Jersey? As the good poet once said, 'It's not that I love thee less; it's that I love honor more.'"

"So you love honor more than you love me? Is that what you are saying?"

"No, that's what the poet said. But honestly Rita, how could you love a coward?"

Rita looked out the window for a moment and said, "Look the moon is gone. It's a total eclipse. This is bad news on the eve of battle. Sam, please don't go."

Sam laughed and replied, "It's bad news for the Rebs. Way up on top of that ridge they're much closer to the moon than we are. Now I know that tomorrow will be a glorious Union victory." He wrapped Rita in his arms and kissed her. "By this time tomorrow, we will all be celebrating. The Army of the Tennessee will be gone, and we will have food."

On the morning of November 25th, 1863, Sam Fletcher shouldered his haversack, picked up his cornet, kissed Rita passionately, and walked in the direction of Orchard Knob. Sam knew that when the great blue beast flexed its muscle again it would be against the Confederates on Missionary Ridge, and Orchard Knob would be the starting point. What a glorious day it would be. The Yanks would drive the Confederates from the Ridge, open the food supplies, control the railroads, and send the Federal Armies deep into the crooked heart of the Confederacy.

With all his heart, Sam wanted to be there when it all happened: the beginning of the end of the Confederacy. In his heart, he also wanted revenge for Chickamauga. In spite of the heroic stand of the Pennsylvania 7th at Reed's Bridge, a tragic blunder by Wood's Division had lost the battle and almost the war. What was Wood feeling now? Sam wanted to be with Wood on this day of vengeance.

CHAPTER NINETEEN
The Miracle of Missionary Ridge

"Amidst the din of warfare and the shrieks of hosts a-dying,
We heard a shout of triumph, saw the flag of truce a-flying
And we knew the rebel leader a petition came to tender
But our gallant General Grant-ed unconditional surrender."

Song, "The Grant Pill, or Unconditional Surrender," J.C. Beckel

On the clear, cold November morning of November 25, 1863, Sam Fletcher could hear band music in the distance, and as he came through the trees he saw long lines of men in blue in perfect formation marching as if on parade. Near the Knob a military band was playing "The Battle Hymn Quickstep," and it was all Sam could do to not put his cornet to his lips and join them. As he approached the field, Sam came upon a young officer who was searching the distant mountain with field glasses, and Sam asked him what was happening.

"Well we ain't doing much, and probably never will. Sherman's over there on the left driving the Rebs off Tunnel Hill. When he does, the whole Confederate flank will roll up like a rug, and these boys will just walk in and help themselves to anything the Confederates have left them."

Sam was disappointed that he wouldn't be in the main part of the action but was determined to be in some part of it. He wandered up and down the long ranks of union troops trying to find some place to fit in. "You guys need a bugler?" He asked a fat sergeant. "Hell no," the sergeant replied. "Got too many of those honkers now. Enough to drive a man deaf."

From out of nowhere a tall man in blue military pants but with a non-regulation black jacket stepped up to him, and asked, "Can you really play that thing?" The man was pointing at the cornet strapped on his back, and Sam replied, "I'm improving every day."

"What kind of tunes do have in that pouch?" the man asked.

"About the same as anybody's. Government issue."

"Well we could sure use a cornet player. One of our boys got into a stupid duel yesterday and was killed. If you want to join us, come around that stand of pines and we'll see if we can work you in."

The man's name was Hancock, and he was a member of the "Ira Goldstein Band." He said that he hadn't planned to do any more fighting, but the band was in town anyway to give concerts, and General Sheridan had asked if the boys would play with his unit for a few days.

"Did you say Ira Goldstein?" asked Sam incredulously.

"You know him?" asked Hancock.

"Not really, but I'm in love with his daughter," Sam blurted out.

"His daughter? You know where his daughter is? Bring him to his daughter and he will love you forever. Or maybe not forever. Fletcher doesn't seem like a Jewish name. Are you Jewish?"

"No," replied Sam. "I'm not much into circumcision."

Hancock laughed but said menacingly, "If you ain't Jewish, you better not say anything about being in love with his daughter. Goldstein's a wonderful man. He'd give you the shirt off his back, but his daughter. Don't say anything about his daughter until this day is over."

As they entered a small clearing where the Ira Goldstein Band was in the process of putting on blue dress uniforms, a big blue tick hound rushed up to challenge Sam, but Hancock said, "That's all right Blue; this is Sam. He's with us now." Sam patted Blue on the head, and Blue sniffed Sam's pants leg like a police office checking a suspect. Sam must have passed the inspection, because the dog licked Sam's hand and followed him into the camp.

A jolly fat man with flaming red hair but graying at the temples was trying to squeeze into trousers about two sizes too small, but he was in a good humor about it. "Estelle's probably up in heaven now laughing at me. 'Ira, you fool. Don't you have any sense? A man your age in the army?' But Estelle, it's only for a day, and we won't be doing any fighting. We're just here to cheer up the troops."

Hancock and Sam approached Ira, and Hancock said, "I think I have found us a cornet player to replace Fisher."

"Well blessed Moses," replied Goldstein. He's even got one of them blue uniforms. Give him Fisher's music pouch and put him to work."

The sixteen members of the Ira Goldstein Band, all in ill-fitting blue uniforms, formed a semi-circle in the trees and began to play. At first Sam was so tentative he could hardly be heard, and Goldstein shouted kindly, "Let me hear some more of that first cornet," and when he did play loud enough to be heard, Goldstein said, "Tune that thing boy before you kill us all." Sam listened harder and finally heard the pitch and could tell that he was now blending in. The band practiced for about an hour and then moved in formation to Orchard Knob. There an exasperated General Sheridan rushed out and said, "Well there you are at last. We need you now. Fall in behind that regiment over there." He pointed to a large group of soldiers that appeared to be maneuvering for no particular purpose.

The men in the ranks were joking. "I sure hope Sherman hurries up. I want to have lunch today on the top of Mission Ridge." But the sun passed the meridian, and there was still no word from Sherman. General Grant looked grim as he scanned the mile or so of open ground between Orchard Knob and the Ridge. Finally someone heard him say, "We've got to make Bragg pull some of his troops off the flank and put them in the middle. That's about the only way Sherman is going to get through."

Soon the orders were coming to get ready to attack the Confederate rife pits in front of the Ridge. The general mood of anticipation was slowly being replaced by a feeling of unspoken dread, and there were few jokes. Sam heard someone say, "Grant's not serious. We've got to cross a mile of open ground with the Rebs shootin' at us. They've got cannon all along that ridge and men with rifles aimed at us right now. Damn, we'd be like fish in a rain barrel." But Grant wasn't joking, and Sam heard the word passed along Wood's division, "There'll be six shots fired in succession from the Knob. When you hear that, start moving across the fields to the ridge."

"Which rifle pits?" someone asked. "The one's on the top, or the ones on the bottom?"

"How the hell should I Know?" replied another voice. "Maybe we'll discuss that when we get there."

"You mean if we get there."

Another message came down the line, "Take the pits on the top of the hill."

"My God," said a voice, "That hill must be 200 foot high if it's an inch. How do those goldarned generals expect us poor creatures of flesh and blood to climb it? Hell it would be tough with nobody shooting at us."

An officer on a horse rode up to Goldstein and said, "You boys follow the troops out for 100 yards or so and stop. Just keep playing. Got to keep their spirits up."

Sam looked at the distant rise of Missionary Ridge and said, "I'm not going to stop until I reach the top. Boys today will be the most glorious day in the history of our country."

As soon as he stopped speaking, six cannon shots in succession roared out from Orchard Knob, and the mass of blue lurched forward as if of one mind. Sam noticed that in front of this juggernaut, a rabbit had run across the open field, and Blue had started after it in swift pursuit. "Must be a rebel hare," said Sam. Ellen Richards laughed nervously as the band stepped forward and started to play "Yankee Doodle."

Somehow the band had ended up in front of Wood's division, the same Wood who had made the costly error at Chickamauga. Some of the boys were uneasy about this, but Sam, said, "He's got something to prove. Let's help him avenge the disaster at Chickamauga. Remember Chickamauga," Sam shouted, and soon all along the ranks men were shouting, "Remember Chickamauga!"

In their formation, Sam was in the front row with Hancock, Ellen Richards, and Jeff Little, all cornets except for the girl who played tenor saxhorn. Behind him he could hear the deep sounds of Nathaniel on the bass saxhorn and the shrill cries of Jack Wilde on the piccolo and under everything the steady boom of Leeping Deer's bass drum, and the rattle of Ted Brown's snare drum. In front was big Ira Goldstein waving his hands like a large blue bird with a flaming red crest, and shouting, "Remember, listen to each other. Stay in tune."

Behind the band came an endless mass of men in blue with bayonets sparkling like stars in the late afternoon sunlight. The regimental banners fluttered like rainbows in the slight breeze that came across the open plain, and the men stepped to the beat of the music; they seemed to be a part of a glorious pageant rather than on a mission of death.

Soon, however, another kind of music began to add a terrible dissonance. The Rebels were firing their cannons from the ridge, and the deadly lead balls were whistling overhead. "Them boys can't shoot worth a darn," said a cheerful voice. A few laughs ripped through the ranks, but then another shell seemed to almost stop over their heads and exploded in a roar. There were a few screams of agony, as a small gap opened in the ranks. But an officer rode up and said, "Close those ranks," and the blue mass surged forward as if nothing had happened. Some of those who came from behind had to step around the fallen bodies, but no one said anything. There was still a mile to go across an open field before they even reached the bottom of the ridge.

Ira said, "Boys, we can stop now. Let the soldiers go by. We done our part." Suddenly General Sheridan rode up and said, "Don't stop playing now. Give us the 'Battle Hymn Quickstep.' Let's keep up their spirits." Ira said, "If anybody wants to leave, now is the time to do it," but Hancock shouted, "Things are just getting interesting. Let's go a little further. Let's have another round of 'Battle Hymn Quickstep.'" And so the band lurched forward with the quickstep, as Rebel cannon balls whistled over their heads.

Although the top of Missionary Ridge was lined with Confederate cannon pouring out a steady stream of exploding shells onto the mass of blue coats below, something almost miraculous seemed to be happening: the shells were mostly falling behind the advancing army. Ironically, one of the first casualties was the man who had volunteered to stay behind to guard the haversacks. A piece of exploding shell punched a hole in his thigh. Miraculous or not, the Union army needed to cross a mile-wide open field and--if successful-- find itself at the base of a two-hundred foot cliff facing the guns of Confederates in rifle pits at the bottom and looking up at Confederates shooting from the top. Sam, however, didn't think of impossibilities. He was young and in love. Nothing was impossible.

The cannon balls were still flying overhead, but the band was now in range of the rifle pits below. The crack of rifled muskets added its harsh staccato to the sounds of the oft' repeated "Quickstep." Many soldiers became so excited, that they kept loading their guns without firing them. In their excitement, the band played the same piece over and over again.

Sam heard a load thunk behind him and looking back saw Nathaniel and his base saxhorn fall to the ground, but the band still surged forward without missing a beat. In a minute, Sam heard the bass saxhorn again, only this time it was totally out of tune. He looked back and saw a huge gaping hole in Nathaniel's bell, but Nathaniel was still grinning and blowing.

All around him Sam suddenly heard the rattle of Union muskets as the troops of Wood's Brigade at last opened fire. Sheets of flame poured out all round him, and clouds of smoke were so thick, that he could no longer see the rifle pits. "Double Quick" a voice roared, and the blue mass rolled forward like a giant ocean wave. Sam kept playing the march as the troops rushed ahead in a blue blur. Hours seemed to pass before he heard shouts, "Hooray. We've got 'em now. We've got the rifle pits."

As Sam came closer, he could now see patches of butternut scrambling up the side of the hill with men in blue running after them. "Stop boys," a loud, harsh voice shouted. "We've got to stop here at the pits, but Sam could see blue coats still in hot pursuit of the men in butternut. "Bugler, blow 'Assembly,'" a voice said, and from somewhere in the smoke came the harsh cry of a bugle. But the men on the ridge didn't stop. They kept climbing. Meanwhile in the rifle pits just vacated by the Confederates, other men in blue were falling in heaps like newly harvested wheat, and rifles from the ridge sent down a deadly hail of Minie balls.

Goldstein said, "What kind of dunderhead would make us stop here? Let's go up the mountain where it's safe. Anybody know 'Forward?'" Sam put the cornet to his lips, and the piercing, shrill notes of "Forward" leaped out of his cornet like bullets into the cold November air. All around him men were cheering, and the blue tide began to surge up the mountain. Then an amazing thing happened. No more bullets were plowing into the blue coats. At this angle, the men on the ridge couldn't hit them. "Well blessed Moses," said Ira panting heavily and leaning against a rock. "I think I'll stay here until it's all over."

From his place on the side of the mountain, Sam watched squirrels scampering through the brush and a solitary crow perched on the bullet shredded limb of a pine tree. To the right and left, he could hear the roar of cannon, the patter of rifles and the unforgettable screams of men, but here on the mountain there seemed to be a moment of peace.

With the Confederate defenders on the Ridge, Bugle looked down on the surging blue tide. He sniffed the air but could smell only blood and smoke, and there was so much noise that he couldn't tell one sound from another. His master went to the side of the hill with the stick that boomed and began pointing with it at the men in blue who struggled up the side of the cliff. Everywhere were the shrieks and cries of men; everywhere was the smell of blood. There was so much of everything, that he didn't know what to do. Then he heard the cries of the loud shiny thing that always made him howl when he was with Sam, and he threw back his head and sang. Then he scampered down the side of the hill towards the noise, and suddenly his nose found the man smell that he had been missing for these many darknesses, and in a moment he was sniffing Sam's pants and howling excitedly.

"Bugle," Sam shouted. "Where have you been old partner?" The familiar voice made Bugle run in circles up and down the hill," but soon a man on a horse galloped up and said, "Fall back to the rifle pits. Our orders were to stop at the rifle pits."

"What kind of half-assed order is that?" grumbled a fat sergeant on the left. "Here we're already half up the mountains and the rebels are on the run, but they want us to go back. Bugler blow 'In Retreat.'"

Sam blew "In Retreat," Bugle howled joyfully, and the mass of men on the mountain began to slide down again towards the pits at the bottom, and as they emerged near the pits, the rebel sharpshooters on the top could see them again and opened up fire. Some of them shouted derisively, "Chickamauga! Chickamauga!" as they fired into the backs of the retreating Yankees. All around him men were falling, and Sam thought of Rita and wondered if he would ever make love with her again. In his mind's eye he was back in the hotel room with her, and life was good.

Just when it looked like everyone would be killed, another man on a horse came by and said, "Take the ridge if you can." Sam played "Forward," with all his might and Wood's division once again made its painstaking way up the mountain. And just as before, they eventually found themselves out of range of the rebel guns. Hancock dropped on the ground next to Sam and said, "Those idiot generals just lost this division about 700 men. Why the hell did they bring us back into the line of fire when we were already half way up the ridge? I say just forget about the generals and let the boys fight."

Hancock put the cornet to his lips and blew "Forward," and the long line of blue coats began to make its way slowly up the ridge. The band went with them, but the instruments were silent now. Those who had carried horns across the field now carried the rifles of fallen soldiers, all except Sam who kept his cornet dangling at his waist and carried the regimental flag in both hands. The original bearer of this flag had been cut down by a bullet in the rifle pits, and Sam had jerked it from his stiffening hands.

The band was now mixed with soldiers of various regiments who were all now clawing their way up the sandy slope of the ridge. The rebel cannon were still firing, but the shells were so far over their heads, that the band hardly noticed them. They saw only the ground in front of their faces as they dug in with their hands and feet inching ever upwards to some unknown point and some unknown purpose. "What do we do when we get to the top?" someone said. "I don't know," someone answered. "We'll think of something when we get there."

All of a sudden, there was no more dirt in front of them, just open sky, and just as he was about to yell, "Chickamauga!" Sam found himself looking into the eyes of a young man in butternut pointing a rifle at him. They stared at each other for what seemed to be a long time, but an astonished look overcame the Confederate as he clutched at his heart and fell in a heap. In a second Sam leaped to the top and planted the regimental flag in the lose dirt of the now-deserted rifle pit. Everywhere men in blue were swarming over the top, and men in butternut were running backwards down the other side of the ridge. Sam shouted, "Victory to the Union. Thanks be to God." But in the euphoria of victory he had a vision of defeat.

Out of nowhere appeared an apparition like "The Dying Gladiator" on the crest of the ridge. A large fat man was lying on his side, and a young Confederate was about to run him through with a bayonet, but this was not an ordinary fat man. He wore a huge white shako with a tall blue plume and Sam knew at once that he could be no one other than his old nemesis, Carlos Schmertz. Without thinking, Sam reached for the only weapon he had, his precious cornet, and hurled it with all his might at the young Confederate, and time stood still. The cornet seemed to hang forever, a silver spear against a field of white clouds, before it suddenly darted into the young Confederate's forehead and sent him hurtling forward. At about the same time, Schmertz rolled on top of his adversary pinning him to the ground and shouting, "I now take you prisoner." When Sam picked up his cornet and saw that the bell had been knocked flat, he was about to cry, but Schmertz shouted to him, "So it's you. That's the best I've ever seen you play that damned cornet. You saved my life."

Afterwards, Sam wondered what Schmertz was doing on the Ridge that day. The 7th Pennsylvania was not there, nor was there any reason for any part of the band to be there either. The only plausible answer was the obvious: Schmertz was ubiquitous, yes ubiquitous. At crucial moments in Sam's life, no matter where he was, Schmertz seemed to appear out of nowhere dressed in that absurdly oversized shako. Some people have even seen Brady photos of the war which contain numerous pictures of the man with the shako. The pictures could be from North, South, East or West, but there would be Schmertz smiling behind his thick wire glasses, his large erect plume reaching towards the sky.

No one really knew where he came from. He claimed to be of German heritage, and stories of his childhood in Berlin, and his marriage, and the birth of little Hilda all seemed plausible enough, but there were rumors of a Spanish heritage. Why was he called Carlos? One story had him born on a Spanish freighter bound for New York, but no parents were ever found; nothing was ever proved.

It was now late afternoon, and the sun was fading behind the mountains. Everywhere union men were rounding up fleeing rebels, and one group brought in 700 prisoners. Sam couldn't find the band because it had been widely scattered along the ridge, but suddenly out of the looming darkness Goldstein and Hancock appeared like ghosts. Goldstein was most unhappy. "So I finally have a good band, and the music is back in my life, and now they are all dead."

"Wait," said Hancock, "there's our new cornet player. Hey Sam, where is everybody?"

Sam, Hancock, and Goldstein walked back in the direction of Orchard Knob, and everywhere they stepped there seemed to be a dead body. The wounded had been carried off, but the huge price of victory lingered everywhere they stepped. The three weary men waited at the Knob for a couple of hours, and miraculously, one by one, the entire band eventually returned. "God be praised," said Goldstein. "We not only win the fight, but we also still got the band."

"And that's not all," said Hancock suddenly. "Our new cornet player has something to tell you."

"So what do you have to tell me young man?" Ira asked gently.

Sam looked at the man he hoped would soon be his father-in-law and said, "I know where you can find Rita."

Goldstein looked like he had just been struck by a bullet as he lurched towards Sam sobbing.

"Rita. You've found Rita. To you goes the reward money. Bring me to her and the money is yours." Goldstein hugged Sam in his big bear-like arms and still sobbing stepped back and said. "So let's go. What are we waiting for? Take me to her."

Sam took a deep breath, and said, "There is one more thing that I want to say," but Goldstein brushed the words away with his hands, and said, "Not now, later. Take me to Rita."

CHAPTER TWENTY
The Almost Marriage

"Then be not coy, but use your time,
And, while ye may, go marry,
For, having lost but once your prime,
You may forever tarry."

Robert Herrick, "To the Virgins to Make Much of Time"

On the morning of November 26, 1863, Goldstein found at Sadie Smith's Boarding House what he considered to be his most precious possession, his daughter Rita. Even though he was perspiring heavily and winded from the walk, he sprang up the wooden steps as if he were still trying to make the top of Missionary Ridge, and he almost knocked Rita over the rail as he clasped her in his big bear-like arms.

"Oh, my baby girl, my sweet Rita," he sobbed. "Like Rachel, I been looking all over for you. Now we are together again at last. Now we can go home to Iowa, and you can comfort your father in his old age. No more talk of marriage to that no good goyim, Lassiter. May his soul rest in hell. Now you belong to Daddy again. All is forgiven."

Rita managed to pull herself free and said, "Well I'm certainly glad to see you too Dad, but let's not discuss Iowa yet. Did Sam talk with you?"

Goldstein turned to Sam, and said "So what are we supposed to be talking about? A job with the Ira Goldstein Band?"

Sam looked at the ground and then blurted out, "I want to marry your daughter Mr. Goldstein."

Goldstein staggered backwards as if he had been hit with a blast of grape shot and then leaned forward to regain his balance. "But Rita, we hardly know this boy. Is he a practicing Jew?"

Rita laughed and said, "Does it make any difference? We love each other."

"Love each other, love each other? What kind of reason is that? Love don't last, but Judaism lasts forever. Who's going to take the children to Hebrew school and make sure they celebrate the Seder?"

Sam smiled and said, "I will." Rita and her father gasped, and then Rita said, "Sam you don't need to do this."

Sam said, "Maybe circumcision isn't so bad after all. I would really do anything to have Rita as my wife."

Goldstein looked at his daughter and saw that her face was radiant with happiness; it was a look that a loving father would treasure for the rest of his life, and Ira Goldstein was one of the most loving fathers who ever lived. He grabbed Sam's outstretched hand and squeezed it in his big paw, "Any man who would do that for my Rita must be one hell of a good man. If you promise to be good to her, she's yours."

Sam and Rita fell into a deep embrace, but before they could kiss, a tall rider on a big bay horse thundered up to the front of the hotel. When the dust had cleared, Sam saw that it was his uncle, Morgan Davis.

"Morgan, where have you been?" asked Sam?"

"I might ask the same thing of you. Minty's been lookin' all over for you. Calls you a deserter and wants to have you shot. Says he'll use you as an example to all those other no good shirkers who refuse to serve their country. Let's go inside and get out of sight."

The whole party, Goldstein, Rita, Sam, Hancock, and the bridegroom-to be, or the hanged man-to be, Sam went quickly up to Rita's room.

Then Morgan addressed the group. "A couple of days ago, the 7th Pennsylvania got orders to round up some Confederate wagon trains around Stevenson, and as we were pulling out, Minty asked about you. He asked, 'Where the hell is that nephew of yours, that damned bugler Fletcher?' I told him that you'd been hurt in a fight and were recovering somewhere in town, and he said, 'If he's not here in an hour I'll have him shot when we get back.' Well we rounded up the wagon train and captured a bunch of prisoners, and now we're back, and Minty considers you a deserter."

"Deserter, my foot," exclaimed Hancock. "When you boys were rounding up a bunch of scared, unarmed Confederates, your nephew was leading the charge at Missionary Ridge. If he hadn't blown that bugle when he did, we'd still be sitting there in those rifle pits being blown to bits by the Rebs like fish in a rain barrel. Your nephew is a real hero."

"Well Sam," said Morgan, "I regret not being with you on Missionary Ridge. The rest of the 7th wasn't doing anything nearly as exciting. If you had been where you were supposed to be, you would have been in Stevenson with us. Of course we didn't get much glory and didn't have a chance to kill anyone, but you are supposed to be where your unit is. What would happen to Army discipline if everyone picked his own fights? By Army standards, you are just a low-down deserter."

"So what was going on in Stevenson?" Sam asked.

"We went down to escort a wagon train full of supplies back to Chattanooga. In case you didn't notice, food's been a little scarce back here. Anyway, when we got to Stevenson, a unit from Ohio asked us if we had any grub to spare. They hadn't had anything in three or four days and were starving to death. I asked the Captain if we could bust open one of the railroad cars, and he said we could for a good cause. The Ohio boys said they had a bunch of prisoners and were bringing them back to Chattanooga and wanted to feed them too. So we threw them some cases of hardtack, a few barrels of bacon and some tins of coffee. By and by, I walked over to where they were cooking the bacon and coffee, and there was this tall feller in a Confederate uniform standing by the fire drinking a cup of coffee and gassing with the boys from Ohio. I asked, 'Which of you boys are the prisoners and which ones are the guards?' I heard a lot of people laughing, and then the tall guy in the Confederate uniform smiled and said, "We are all children of God. In a way we are all prisoners of this war, and only God's love can set us free."'Hear, Hear!' shouted a voice in the darkness. 'We are all brothers, and God loves us all.'

"A young Lieutenant with a Federal uniform came up to me and said, 'Well I see you have met the preacher. He may be in a Rebel uniform, but there ain't no harm in him anyway.'

"I talked with the preacher for a good while, and we both agreed that this whole war business had been a mistake. It was unsafe for human beings and caused endless and unnecessary suffering. He said, 'Just tell old Jeff Davis to set the slaves free and let bygones be bygones. Go thy way and sin no more.'

"The Ohio boys and their prisoners pulled out early the next morning, and we stayed behind to see that no one else broke into the supplies. I wonder what will ever happen to that preacher fellow. He was a mighty good man, even though he was a Reb.

"We loaded the supplies into the wagons and started back over the trail, but that rascal Wheeler came up behind us and started shooting. Some of the wagon drivers ran off into the woods, and if we hadn't regrouped and charged, we might have lost everything. When Wheeler heard our bugles blow "Charge"--and where were you, Sam, our loudest bugler?--and saw us coming after him with our sabers flashing in the sun, he took off like lightening. I did manage to capture one of his boys and this handsome Colt revolver. Here you go, Sam. Take this gun as a souvenir from your old Uncle Morgan. Keep it in the family as a reminder of when you were a deserter."

He handed the gun to Sam, and Sam slipped it into his belt. "Thanks Morgan," said Sam. "This gun will always remind me that I should have been in Stevenson guarding a wagon full of hardtack instead of up on Missionary Ridge bathing in the sun."

Suddenly there was a pounding on the door, and when no one opened it, there was a loud crash and the sound of splintering wood as four young soldiers in blue pushed their way into the room with their Enfields pointed at Sam's chest, and one of them said, "You're under arrest Fletcher. Come with us."

Rita shouted, "No! He's not a deserter. He's a hero. Let him stay." She pushed herself between Sam and the Enfields, but Goldstein put his arm around her and pulled her back. "Gentlemen, we want no more violence. When you understand the facts of the case, I am sure that you will send this young man back to us with your blessings. But for now, he must go. Good bye Sam. Shalom. We will find you and explain everything." And Sam disappeared in the haze of four blue-coated soldiers.

Finding Sam was harder that they thought it would be, and it was noon when somebody on Minty's staff told them that Sam had been led away to be shot for desertion. Rita, Hancock, and Goldstein rushed to a field outside the town limits, and heard the sound of drums playing a funeral dirge. They tried to get closer, but a ring of men in blue pushed them back saying that no civilians were allowed any closer.

All seemed hopeless until Rita heard a familiar voice. "I might shoot him for the way he plays the cornet, but he ain't no deserter. He saved my damned life up on the Ridge." It was Schmertz, and he was arguing with an officer on a horse.

The officer said, "You mean to tell me that this young fellow was on the Ridge yesterday?"

"You're damned right. He threw his cornet at a man who was going to kill me, and believe me he loves that cornet as much as his life."

The officer turned to the four soldiers leading Sam away and said, "Bring me the prisoner." The men dragged Sam in chains to the young officer, and about the same time Colonel Minty rode up in a cloud of dust and demanded, "Why hasn't this man been executed yet?"

Meanwhile Schmertz joined the group as did Rita, Hancock, and Goldstein. For a few moments the battle for Sam's life hung in the balance, but in the end Minty relented. "All right. I suppose we have a hero here instead of a deserter. But it ain't going to be easy to explain to the boys why he wasn't with us at Stevenson. Orders is orders." Then he galloped off leaving Sam with his deliverers.

The young officer said, "Now you folks have good reason to celebrate Thanksgiving today."

"Thanksgiving? What's that?" asked Hancock.

"Why haven't you heard? President Lincoln himself declared that today will be the first national Thanksgiving, and every year all Americans will celebrate it."

"Well I'll be damned," said Hancock. "We do have a lot to be thankful for. Not only are we all still alive, and not only do we still have our band, but the Rebs are out of Chattanooga, and we can eat again. Let's go to Sadie Smith's and have us a wedding feast. We can have all the hardtack we want."

They heard a movement in the bushes, and there was Bugle with a rabbit in his mouth. Sam said,"Now we can all celebrate." And so

Rita, Sam, Goldstein, Hancock, the young officer, and Schmertz, headed to the Smith House for their first Thanksgiving.

While they ate, they discussed the future. Would Sam be able to marry Rita and play with the band, or would he need to go to Nashville with the 7th Pennsylvania Cavalry? The young officer was of the opinion that if you were enlisted in the Army, you needed to stay until your enlistment was up. Rita argued that if you had done meritorious service such as Sam had done on Missionary Ridge they would let you out for good behavior.

The discussion ended when an aide from Minty rode up to the Inn and said, "Minty wants Fletcher to report for duty by one p.m. this afternoon. The 7th will move on to Nashville."

Sam said, "I'm not leaving until Rita and I are officially man and wife. Does anybody know a preacher in town?"

Hancock said, "Sure there's that fellow that preached the Trumpets sermon in Shelbyville. I saw him hanging around the hotel the other day. I'm sure that he'll do anything for a buck."

Goldstein interjected, "But is he a Rabbi?"

"Dad," answered Rita, "In a time of emergency, he is a Rabbi. And as Hancock said, 'He'd do anything for a buck,' even be Jewish."

Goldstein laughed and said, "If you're happy, I'm happy."

They found Brother Belcher in the Red Dog saloon, and he promised to be at the hotel by noon, but by 12:30, he had still not arrived, and Sam knew that he had to go soon. Hancock played the Haydn on his cornet for the music, and Goldstein gave a few words about the lovely bride, but when the clock struck 1:00 p.m., a horse thundered up to the front of the hotel, and a Yankee voice yelled, "Fletcher, we've got to go now. Uncle Sam waits for no man." Rita said sadly, "Well at least the bridegroom is here this time." Goldstein said, "Well at least I can give you this wedding gift," and he presented Sam with a new cornet. "This is the best cornet I have in the wagon. All German silver. rotary valves. You'll need it when you come back to play in the band."

Sam kissed the twice-abandoned bride and looking at his watch said sadly, "I've got to go." Rita followed him outside the door, and they had one last deep passionate embrace before Sam broke from her arms and walked slowly to his horse. "I will not forget you. I promise I will come back to marry you."

"Take care of yourself, Sam," she said. "Don't try to be a hero. Stay in the back of the regiment whenever you can." Then as Sam disappeared into the darkness she said, "And don't forget to practice. When this war is over I want to play music with you. We will play together in the Ira Goldstein Band. When you practice, think of me."

"I love you," he shouted through his tears. And then he was gone, and Rita was alone on the porch.

The next morning, Goldstein called the band together, and they had a practice session outside the hotel before deciding what to do next. As they were warming up, a young man in butternut came up and asked if he could play with them.

"Ain't you one of them traitors?" asked Goldstein.

"Ain't no more." The young man replied. "I been pardoned." Then he showed them the piece of paper certifying that he was a kind of born-again American with the paper to prove it.

"So what do you play?" asked Goldstein.

"I can do a pretty good job with a keyed bugle," he replied, "but I really play just about anything. Just give me an instrument, and I can figure it out."

He played a few lovely airs on one of Goldstein's keyed bugles and a few marches on a bass saxhorn, and Goldstein said, "Congratulations. You are now in the Ira Goldstein Concert Band."

After practice, Goldstein called a meeting to discuss future plans, and Rita suggested following the 7th Pennsylvania to Nashville. Just about everyone shouted, "No." Goldstein said, "I don't want to go where there is any more shooting. Let's go back to Shelbyville. They loved us there, and the pay was good."

On the bright sunny morning of November 27, 1863, the band started on the road for Shelbyville. Seated next to a sobbing Rita, Ira led the way in his covered wagon. The rest of the band followed on foot behind, and as they passed the last clapboard houses of Chattanooga, they played a few choruses of "Tenting Tonight." As the road narrowed and faded into the shadows of Raccoon Mountain, the music stopped, but the chattering of Mocking birds and the cawing of crows took over.

When the 7th Pennsylvania bivouacked in a Tennessee woods that night, Sam took out the cornet that Ira had given him as a wedding present and began to play. As the notes of the Haydn concerto broke through the chill night air, sounds of cursing came from the ranks of sleeping men, but Sam played on, and with each note he felt the presence of his lover and best friend, Rita.

CHAPTER TWENTY-ONE
On to Atlanta

> "Bring the good old bugle, boys
> We'll sing another song--
> Sing it with a spirit that will
> Start the world along
> Sing it as we used to sing it
> Fifty thousand strong,
> While we were marching through Georgia."

Song, "Marching Through Georgia," Henry Clay Work

With Rita heading West to Shelbyville, and he heading North West to Nashville, Sam didn't think that he had much to be thankful for. (So much for the first National Thanksgiving.) Not only was his best friend and lover--not to mention his only cornet teacher--leaving him, but she was entering a world of music and he the world of war. She would be going where brass instruments played pretty tunes for happy civilians; he was going where the sound of brass signaled destruction and death. He was officially one of the four buglers assigned to the Seventh and had no prospects of playing in the brigade band. At Chickamauga he had achieved a celebrity of sorts. He was universally known as "the loudest damned bugle in the whole Union Army." Men shook his hand and congratulated him for saving the day at Reed's Bridge.

An old Sergeant rode up to him and said, "If you hadn't blowed that thing like the world was comin' to an end, we never would have made it back across the bridge in time. You're a regular Gabriel. You saved our lives."

Sam smiled and said, "Thanks," but he was deeply troubled. Real musicians don't want to be known as the loudest. They want to have the sweetest sound and the best musical techniques, but mere loudness is enough to keep you on the outside looking in. As his big black horse clopped along the Nashville Pike, Sam thought of the words of his friend Flem: there is music everywhere. And in the beat of his horse's hooves, he heard a beautiful melody in his head. The horse was sort of like a drummer playing a counterpoint to the beats of the other horses around him, and suddenly there was music, dear sweet music. As the beat went on, Sam fell into a reverie and suddenly he was playing the Haydn for Mr. Lincoln in the White House. The president's sad homely face broke into a smile, and when Sam had completed the last note, Mr. Lincoln applauded vigorously and put one of his huge hands on Sam's shoulder. Then he spoke, "Son, that's the loudest cornet I ever heard. How do you do it?"

An icy hand seemed to have seized all of Tennessee, and as the Seventh Cavalry at last trotted into the fortification at Nashville, on January 8, 1864, every man tumbled into the warmest dwelling he could find. Some ended up in the infamous houses of ill repute that lined every thoroughfare; others found inns and taverns; Sam found a concert hall. The walls were covered with crimson and gold, and the roof was held by gilded pillars of wood. A vast chandelier cast a golden glow over the crowd of blue-coated soldiers who huddled in the plush seats. Finally a military band moved out on to the stage, and the audience, like a single blue being, rose in unison and applauded. A tall man in a military uniform stood in front, bowed to the crowd, turned to the band, raised his baton, brought it down and the sounds of brass music filled the golden hall For what seemed to be only minutes Sam had traveled to realms of gold. But all too soon it was over, and he was swept by the crowd into the cold streets of Nashville.

The sweet sounds of brass music gave way to the din of a raucous mob, and Sam was in the midst of a sea of drunken soldiers cursing and screaming and brandishing clubs. They had destroyed the hotel and were now on the way to destroy the music hall, and Sam wished that he could disassociate himself from this barbaric horde, but he too was wearing the uniform of the Seventh Pennsylvania and like his unwelcome comrades found himself locked in the stockade. The Sergeant said, "These boys just need some Rebs to fight. They've got a lot of spirit. Just send 'em South and they'll be alright." And so on January 12, 1863, the Seventh Pennsylvania headed South and chased General Hood and the Confederates all the way to Gravelly Springs, Alabama. And Sam, the loudest cornet in the Union Army was with them.

In the long tedium of daily camp activities, Sam's only music consisted of the bugle calls. He blasted everyone off the bedrolls with reveille and soothed them back to sleep at night with the new Daniel Butterfield "Taps." In between these events he signaled the watering of the horses, mess call, sick call, church call, and the thousand and one tedious activities that filled the hours of a soldier in camp. But there was no real music, and not even the calls of battle that stirred the blood and sent men running like maniacs across fields of blood relieved the tedium.

On March 22, the 7th crossed the swollen Black Warrior River and lost one man and forty horses; then they crossed the Locust and the Catawba and were deep in the heart of the enemy. Still there was no real music and no real fighting. Sam wished he were with Rita and the Ira Goldstein Band.

July descended on these men from the North like the fires of hell, and most would give anything to be back in the cool mountains of Pennsylvania. In the 100 degree heat, the fires they built to heat railroad tracks didn't add to their comfort either. The main job of these fighting men for the past several weeks had been to destroy the southern railroad system, and the technique involved fire. One group would pry the tracks off the ties with crow bars, and another group would drag them onto fires. After the tracks had been softened by the heat, the men twisted them into pretzels by bending them around trees.

As the sweat poured down the blue wool jackets which—contrary to military regulation, hung open—one young man expressed the opinions of the group, " Breakin' up this damned railroad is more work than buildin' one, but if old Jeff Davis has got to walk now, I suppose it's worth it."

On July 18, 1863, Sam had a little good news. The Colonel wanted the band to play some music to brighten the lives of those men toiling in the sun, but the regular cornet player had just disappeared. He walked off into the woods one day and never came back. And so old Schmertz came up to Sam and said, "Can you play some tunes on that cornet or just bugle calls?" Sam felt his chest tighten and the air rush from his lungs, but he still managed to throw his cap into the air and yell, "Hallelujah! My hour has come at last. Of course I will play."

As Schmertz extricated himself from Sam's embrace, he muttered, "I didn't say you was any good. I just need someone to play the part." But Sam only heard Rita's voice in his head saying, "You can do it. Watch the conductor; listen to the other musicians and try to match their pitch. Don't get nervous. Keep good breath support and play clear pretty notes. And don't blow too loud."

When the fifteen musicians assembled near the bed of the Southern Railroad, Sam was with them. And when Schmertz gave the downbeat, Sam's C sharp was the first note to rise above the din of men destroying a railroad, and in a fraction of a second, he was joined by the rest of the band. Schmertz glared at him, but Sam was happy nevertheless. He was playing "Yankee Doodle" with a real band, and in the next piece, "Hail Columbia" he would have the first solo of his career.

As the last notes of "Yankee Doodle" died in the heavy air, Schmertz, looked at Sam and Said, "Vel Fletcher. This is der big chance. Let us see vat you do with it."

The first cornet was supposed to play the first verse alone, and then the rest of the band would come in for the rest of the verses, but as Schmertz raised his baton, Sam felt sick to his stomach, and he thought he was suffocating. But Rita's voice came into his head and said, "Breathe in and breathe out. Take deep breaths; hold the last one, and when the baton comes down, let the air rush into the horn." Sam was about to let the air go rushing into the cornet, when the boom of cannon and the spattering of rifle fire stopped the baton in mid-air, and the whole band, with Schmertz in the lead scattered into the woods.

In a few seconds a Union cavalryman rode up and shouted, "The Rebs are attacking us from the rear." Since the union line stretched along the railroad tracks for about two miles, news of the attack had spread slowly, but the sound of guns was getting much closer now. Sam rushed out into the open and said, "Where is I Company?" And the horseman whirled and said, "Follow me." Sam untethered his big bay horse from a tree, swung into the saddle, and soon caught up with the speeding cavalryman.

When he reached his company, Sam found General Kilpatrick quickly organizing his men and preparing a whirlwind counter attack.

The 7th Pennsylvania was known as "The Saber Regiment," because rather than firing their carbines, the troopers preferred to rush against the enemy swinging their sabers. Kilpatrick shouted, "Bugler, blow 'Charge,'" and without thinking, Sam put the cornet to his lips and shook the world with one of the loudest renditions of "Charge" ever heard. With his first note, the horses bearing men with sabers glittering in the sun, rolled like thunder, and the men on their backs gave a death-defying yell and charged against the ranks of their attackers.

The sight of the glittering sabers, and the roar of thundering horses and screaming men, must have been indeed terrifying, because the attacking Confederates began to retreat as rapidly as they could. Troopers of the 7th overran the fleeing enemy cutting them down with sabers and capturing all those who surrendered. And Sam Fletcher was right out in front. To his knowledge, he had never actually killed anyone yet. His first shot at Chickamauga had sailed harmlessly over the Confederate General's head, and the only injury he had inflicted at Missionary Ridge had been with his cornet, but as he was racing towards the woods, a young Confederate, perhaps too tired to run any further, had stopped and aimed a pistol right at Sam's face. Sam never thought that he could kill anyone, for he deeply believed that all men are brothers, and that music would eventually convince all nations to beat their swords into plow shares, but without thinking, he brought his saber down in the middle of the young Confederates head and split it like a pumpkin. It wasn't until afterwards that he thought about it, and wondered how such a peaceful man as himself could have ever committed such a ghastly deed. Didn't Jesus say, "Turn the other cheek," but if he had followed that injunction, Sam knew that he would be the one lying by the side of the road.

The fight wasn't over yet. As a heavy rain soaked the fields and trees, the Confederates fell behind a breastwork of fallen trees, and Kilpatrick stopped his troopers to plan some strategy. He considered flanking the position, but before he could put the order into effect, he heard cannon fire in his rear. His troops were now pinned between two Confederate forces and could have been squeezed in a vice until they surrendered. Fortunately for the 7th Pennsylvania, Kilpartrick made the right decision instantly: turn around and counter-attack the troops who were charging from the rear. Sam blew the proper calls, and everyone heard them above the roar of the cannon. Following the rapid fire of Sam's bugle, the 7th Pennsylvania charged back over the same ground, once again scattering, destroying, and capturing the Confederate attackers. Sam could feel the weight of his boots that were now filled with water, and realized that he had faced death twice in just a few hours and had never even noticed that it was raining. Everyone told Sam how loud he sounded and slapped him on the back, but no one even mentioned the concert. No one ever told Sam that he had played well or had played beautifully. He desperately wanted to hear these words from someone, but not even Rita had ever said them.

Thanks to the valiant efforts of the 4th Michigan and the 7th Pennsylvania, the work of destroying the railroad continued peacefully as the noose around Atlanta continued to tighten. Sam continued to play in the regimental band but never did perform a solo. Shortly after the Battle of Lovejoy, a new cornetist came into the camp and astonished everyone with his virtuosity. No one knew where he came from or where he was going next, but no one ever forgot his name, Hoss Jensen.

Hoss was a big Swede, six feet tall and all of 250 pounds. He had a full black beard and vague brown eyes that peered dimly through glasses as think as the ice on the pond in winter. He played an old beaten up cornet with a style and confidence and precision that made Sam envy him. He made Sam Fletcher sound like a sick moose by comparison, and there were times when Sam wished Hoss would just disappear, but he didn't really want that to happen. When Hoss wasn't there, the whole band sounded sick.

Hoss was the only one in the band who carried a sword at concerts, and before any performance, he would pull it out of its scabbard, swing it over his head a few times and shout, "If anyone screws up, they're going to get a taste of this fine steel blade." Then he looked at Sam and said, "Fletcher, you're the main one I'm talking about. If you speed up one more time, this blade is coming at you." Then he would poke the long blade in Sam's face, and Sam could see the fine engravings on it and on the gold hilt, the initials CSA. Sam was tempted to say, "I'm not going to die by a damned rebel sword," but when he looked into the eyeless glasses glinting in the sun and the shimmering blade, he decided to play perfectly.

Of course he didn't play perfectly. How could he? The whole time he was trying to play the right notes, he was thinking about that silver blade and watching Hoss out of the corner of his eye for any sign of movement. But as Sam raced through passages a half a beat ahead of the band, Hoss just sat there playing perfectly as usual and never made a move for the sword.

It actually wasn't the sword Sam was worried about. He just wanted to please Hoss. He figured if he could ever get a compliment out of him, it would be the same as winning a medal of honor. Hoss could do by instinct, or maybe it was sprezzatura, what he had tried so hard to learn, and he desperately wanted to be like him. He wanted to be able to step forward and play the solos the way Hoss did, and so he practiced a little harder each day.

However, some of the other boys in the band weren't quite as impressed by Hoss. Some of them resented Hoss's ability and some had the audacity to think that they should have been chosen to play the solos. One day in late June of 1864, the band had a concert in Jonesboro, not too far from Atlanta. In an effort to show the people of the South that Yankees weren't totally uncivilized, the Mayor of this sleepy little village had actually arranged to have the concert. If Atlanta was to be lost anyway, the mayor was of the opinion, that "If you can't beat them; join them." More and more southerners were becoming of the same opinion. They were so weary of the war that had taken so many lives and destroyed so much property, that they didn't care who won. They just wanted peace.

Peace, however, was not necessarily what the band wanted. As the Confederate enemies diminished in strength, the animosities of the band members towards each other increased. And just as Rita had said, about two years before, "The better you play, the more they hate you," and so did some of the cornet players turn against Hoss. When Hoss laid his cornet on the ground and left it untended for a few minutes before the concert, the second cornet player, picked it up and poured a cup of lard into the bell. Sam didn't know about this and certainly would have warned Hoss if he had known, but he was there when Hoss stood up to play "Lorena," and nothing came out of the horn. His proud confident face took on a look of total panic, and for the first time Sam had ever seen, Hoss seemed uncertain of what to do next.

Sam was already to play the third cornet part, but in one of those rare musical inspirations, he grabbed the ruined cornet from Hoss's shaking hands and inserted in its place his fine German silver model. Hoss hesitated for a second, but when the director stopped the piece and started it again, Hoss began to play, and the notes soared from his horn like they had never soared before. Even though Sam was just standing there with no horn to play, he never wanted the music to stop. "Lorena" had never sounded more beautiful to him.

When he finished the piece, Hoss handed Sam his cornet and said, "Thanks pardner. You saved my ass." Sam told him to keep it for the rest of the concert, but Hoss said, "No. It's about time that you show some guts. Here's my pouch." Then he handed Sam the pouch of music for the solo cornet part and said, "Play that thing right. Just remember I've still got my sword right here, and I aim to use it."

And so Sam played solo cornet for the rest of the concert with Hoss right next to him directing his every move and poking him in the ribs with the hilt of the sword whenever he made a mistake.

When it was over, Hoss clapped Sam on the back but didn't say anything. He walked over to the second cornet player and decked him with one punch. The director said that kind of behavior was intolerable in the Federal Army. The Federal Army was a peaceful organization and no violence of any sort was acceptable. Hoss came to see Sam before he left. He said, "Don't be so damned afraid of everything Fletcher. Play that horn as if you mean it. If you make a mistake, who cares? And practice every day. If anyone needs practice, it is you." He clapped Sam on the back and disappeared in the night. Sam never saw him again.

From that time on, Sam's playing improved. The second cornet took Hoss's pouch from him, but from then on he played second. Of course, he wanted to play first. He had had a taste of glory and didn't want to fade back into the group, but he wasn't willing to sabotage the current soloist who, was like a satyr to Hoss's Hyperion. In a fair tryout Sam knew that he could beat this guy some day.

CHAPTER TWENTY-TWO
The Serpent Enters Paradise

"Now the serpent was more subtle than
any beast of the field which the Lord had made.
And he said unto the woman, Yea, hath God
said, Ye shall not eat of every tree of the garden?

Genesis 3:1

News of the Battle of Lovejoy eventually reached the Ira Goldstein Band in Nashville, and of particular interest was news of the death of the cornet player. The man who had disappeared was named Sam Filcher, but when the news crossed all those many miles, it strangely evolved into a more ominous story. The man didn't disappear; he had been killed in the Battle of Lovejoy, and his name was not Filcher; it was Fletcher.

A young cornet player in the Ira Goldstein Band was a little too eager to give Rita this sad news. Most of the young men in the band couldn't keep their eyes off Sam Fletcher's beautiful fiancée, and most cursed the fact that she was already "taken." But this news added a new element to the chemistry of the group: hope. Now they all hoped that Rita might honor their advances instead of repulsing them as she had done so vigorously before. But how should they plan their attack?

That old snake Henry Flambeau figured that he had the best approach: sympathy. And as soon as he heard the news, he wanted to be sure that he was the one to tell Rita, and that he would be the first to offer her comfort.

Now Rita had always had a strong dislike for Flambeau. She hated his exalted sense of his own ability and even more hated the way he was always disparaging Sam. "You know, he would often tell her, "Sam has no sense of rhythm at all. I think he should give it up." And Rita would always give him the same response. "He works ten times as hard as you do and someday will make you sound sick." Then she would do a disdainful pivot and walk away.

But today was different. Flambeau spoke to her gently, "Rita, I have something I need to talk with you about, something that concerns Sam." He used his sweetest kindest voice, and Rita was uncertain how to respond.

"So what do you need to tell me about Sam that I don't already know?"

Flambeau put his hand gently on her shoulder and said, "Come with me to a place where we can talk." Rita was suddenly numb with fear and meekly followed him like a small bird mesmerized by a snake. They sat down on a bench in a little park, and Flambeau put his arm over her shoulder and like a lover whispering beautiful words into his beloved's ears, Flambeau gave the dreadful words.

"Rita, I really hate to tell you this, but I would rather you hear it from me than from a stranger. I have bad news. Sam was killed in Lovejoy."

Rita shrieked and jumped up from the bench. "No! NO! It can't be. He's a musician. He's too gentle, too good. God would not allow this to happen."

Flambeau wrapped Rita in his big perfumed arms and whispered, "There, there. I'll always be with you. I won't allow anything to happen to you." And Rita collapsed in his arms.

Suddenly she drew back and said, "But how do I know this is true? You would love to have Sam dead wouldn't you?" And then Flambeau pulled out the little newspaper clipping which said, "In the Union victory at Lovejoy on July 18, Union casualties were light, but they included a musician, Sam Fletcher."

Rita grabbed the clipping from Flambeau's hand and tore it to pieces. "It can't be," she sobbed. "We have so much to live for."

After the battle, Sam wrote a letter to Rita:

Dearest Rita,

I finally got a chance to play in the band. I remembered everything you said and tried to play pretty. Unfortunately the concert was cut short by a Confederate attack. Damn inconsiderate Rebs didn't know how to behave at a concert, but we beat them badly and moved that much closer to ending this terrible war. I live for the day when we will be in each other's arms once again. I feel your body next to mine and can almost hear the beat of your heart (3/4 I believe, the beat of romance).

We and Sherman are pushing them to the sea and burning everything in sight. It would make you sick to see what we are doing to this country. Pretty farms, like the one you and I are going to have soon, looking like the wasteland of hell, the barns and fields in flames, the animals gunned down, the people hiding. Sherman says it has to be like this. We need to break the will of the people to fight. Still I would rather build than destroy. Soon you and I will build beautiful things and have beautiful children who all look like you. I live for the day when we will be together again.

All my love,

Sam

P.S. The battle wasn't too bad. I survived it without a scratch.

The letter reached Nashville on August first, but Flambeau picked up the mail for the band and decided not to give Rita the letter. "It would just break her heart," he reasoned. To make sure that Sam stayed dead, Flambeau printed a letter and forged Rita's name. The letter informed Sam that Rita no longer loved him but loved Flambeau instead.

In the weeks to follow, Flambeau was most attentive to Rita and consoled her in any way he could. He encouraged her playing and even arranged to play some duets with her. He plied her with drink and tried to tempt her into his bed, but Rita always insisted, "I know Sam is coming back." Although Flambeau was actually the spoiled only child of rich parents who doted on him and praised even his very farts, he told Rita that he was an orphan.

"You know, Rita," he said one day. "Lots of people think that I am an arrogant snob, but if they knew my story they might be more understanding." Rita, who was always receptive to hearing about other people's troubles, listened intently to Flambeau's story.

"They found me in a handbag hanging from a doorknob in a pub. No one could figure out where I had come from, and so the pub owner took me to St. Bede's Orphanage in New York City. Life was not easy in that orphanage. Up at dawn, scrubbing the floors when I was just four years old, beaten for stealing a scrap of bread so that I would not starve. When I was nine years old, I began to slip away at night to hear concerts at Wilson Hall. Of course, I couldn't pay to get in. I waited until the ticket-taker left and crawled into a seat in the back. Everything was like magic there, so different from the drab emptiness of the orphanage. Soon I began to notice the cornet players and knew at once that I wanted to be one of them. I began moving closer and closer to the front, and one night after a concert I dared go back stage to meet one of the musicians.

"He was a little, fat man with a thin moustache, and when I tried to speak with him, he said, 'What the hell do you want?' I was crushed, but not so crushed as to not speak.

"'Mr. Lutz, your music was just about the prettiest thing that I ever heard.' That brought a smile to his face, and he reached out and shook my hand.

"'Boy,' he said, 'you have good taste in music. You could go far. Come and hear me play tomorrow night.' From then I went to just about all the concerts, and the cornet player eventually took me back to his apartment. It was a small place in the Upper East Side, but it was filled with cornets of all types. He said, 'Henry, pick one out and I'll show you how to play it.'

"I picked up a beautiful German silver model, put it to my lips and blew, and out came a clear sweet sound. 'Henry, you're a natural. With a little work, you'll go right to the top.' He presented me with one of his least expensive horns and gave me lessons in the afternoons. I had to sneak away from the orphanage, but I was progressing rapidly through the major and minor scales and could play a few simple tunes. Unfortunately, the master of the orphanage noticed that I was sneaking out and began to lock me in my room. After three days in my room, late one night, I grabbed my cornet, made a rope of my sheets, and slipped out the window. It was dark and cold on the sidewalk, but I figured I could go and stay with my friend the cornetist, Mr. Lutz, but when I knocked on his door, no one answered. The janitor saw me, and said, 'Ain't no use knocking. Mr. Lutz died last night.'

"Died! My benefactor had died, and I had nowhere to turn. I would never go back to the orphanage, and so I walked out on the street clutching my cornet. I sat on a bench and began to play just to get my spirits up, and before I knew it, people were stopping to listen. Some of them began handing me money, and when I finally could play no more I counted the money in my pocket and found five dollars. With that I had enough for some food and a place to stay for the night. At the age of ten, I was living in a rooming house by myself and playing the cornet on the streets every day. I was a very lonely child, but the cornet kept me going for the next ten years, and when the war started, I figured I could serve my country with my cornet."

Flambeau was weeping as he finished his story, and Rita looked on in wonder. Either Flambeau was the greatest liar she ever heard, or else he was a wonderful sad man who needed love. She decided to give him the benefit of doubt and began spending her days with him

CHAPTER TWENTY-THREE
The Temptation of Music at Mrs. Murphy's Bordello

> "If music be the food of love, play on
> Give me excess of it, that surfeiting,
> The appetite may sicken, and so die.
> That strain again! It had a dying fall;
> O' it came o'er my ear like the sweet sound
> That breathes upon a bank of violets,
> Stealing and giving odor."
>
> Shakespeare, <u>Twelfth Night</u>

For much of the summer, Sherman's Army had probed at the crouching town of Atlanta like it was a powerful dragon, and each day time raced with the terror of sudden death. But now that the Confederates had graciously moved out, and the Yanks had moved in, time hung like heavy weights around the neck of the Union Army. Outside of the routines of camp life there wasn't much to do. The band played fairly frequent concerts, but playing the same songs over and over again, particularly the second cornet part, was ultimately unsatisfying. Playing that solo for Mr. Lincoln seemed as far away as the moon. In fact playing any kind of solo for anyone was beginning to seem like an impossibility. Sam felt sorry for himself as he thought of his dream ending right there in Atlanta, ending not in a burst of glory but just dissolving in the Atlanta mud. Where was his future?

A bunch of the boys began talking about a great piano player in Mrs. Murphy's Haven, a bordello in the middle of Atlanta. He was an ex-slave named Caesar, and he could play just about any tune you could imagine. Sometimes he would let somebody play an instrument along with him. The music part sounded great to Sam, but he wasn't too sure about going to a bordello. His true love was in Nashville, and even if she weren't, he had seen enough of his fellow soldiers grossly destroyed by venereal disease to not be tempted. Faces rotted away; bodies, covered with sores, just wasted away to nothing. And the one prescribed cure of the day, mercury, didn't really help all that much. Still there was the music, and music prevailed.

One night in early September, Sam picked up his cornet and went with some of the boys to Mrs. Murphy's Haven. As they approached the wooden steps, they could hear the sounds of a piano playing "Kingdom Coming," and Sam bounded up the stairs ahead of the rest to find the source of the music. He knocked on the door, and a large woman in petticoats opened the door a crack, and asked him what he wanted. Sam laughed nervously and said, "I just came to hear the music." Thinking that Sam had just made a joke, the woman laughed like a braying mule and flung open the door. "Why do come in then. We have just what you want right inside."

Sam entered a large living room lined with fancy stuffed chairs and sofas, and on every one of them sat sirens in various states of dress and repose, Mrs. Murphy's soiled doves. But Sam hardly noticed the sirens. He went right to a black upright piano where a large black man was hunched over and massaging the keys with his immense fingers. Light from the oil lamps glistened on the large diamond ring on his finger, and the music seemed to glisten too.

Sam just stood by the piano as Caesar finished the last chorus of "Home Sweet Home," and then said, "Mr. Caesar, someone said that you sometimes let people play along with you. Is that so?"

Caesar just grinned revealing a mouth full of big white teeth. "Dat all depend son. Is you any good?"

Sam blushed and said, "Some people say I'm not too bad."

"Not too bad huh? What's dat supposta mean? I'm gonna play, "Aura Lea." If you wants to play 'long, den play. We'll know soon enough whether you is good or bad."

Sam began rummaging through the pouch to find "Aura Lea," and Caesar laughed. "What's you need music for? Just play da horn."

Sam had never played without music before and was about to rummage some more when Caesar said again, "Just play da horn."

Sam was aware of about fifteen young women looking at him as he worked the valves and blew some air through the cornet. The chatter of the young soldiers had stopped suddenly, and the room was so silent, that he could hear the air going through his instrument. When he turned around, Sam saw that the room seemed filled with blue coats and long dresses. His hands started to shake, and he felt like he was going to suffocate, but when Caesar played through the first line of the song, Sam took several deep breaths, and when Caesar came back to the top again, Sam let the air rush into the horn, and much to his astonishment, his fingers began to press down the right keys and the unmistakable sounds of "Aura Lea" began to pour from his cornet. Sam had played the piece so many times with the music, that the horn seemed to be playing itself. When Sam speeded up Caesar followed him, and the two men galloped together through the first three verses like a horse and rider. Sam was thinking to himself, "This is not bad, but how am I doing this without music? What is the actual starting point for this piece?" When he started the second verse, he was thinking the song started on a D natural, but as soon as he played the note, he realized that he was wrong and that every note after it fell randomly into space. He was fishing for notes now, and Caesar just stopped. When Sam dropped the cornet to his side, the blood was rushing to his face, and he felt sick to his stomach, but from somewhere behind him he heard a solitary pair of hands clapping.

When he turned around to look, he saw that the entire room had cleared of people except for a petite black-haired woman who remained alone on a small divan. "Where did everyone go?" He asked sadly. The woman stood up and said, "Your music was so lovely, that you turned them all to thoughts of love. They've all gone upstairs to celebrate the rites of Venus."

Caesar got up from the piano bench and said, "Yer jus' like Peter in the Bible. You was walking on water until you didn't believe no more. Then kerplunk, ya falls right in." Then he patted Sam on the shoulder and said, "Throw away dat music. Jus play fro da heart." Then he walked out of the room. Sam was about to move towards the door, when the pretty dark--haired girl on the divan got up and stood by his side. "You sure can play pretty," she said. "Do you suppose you could play me some more of those tunes?"

Sam couldn't remember anyone ever having told him that he played pretty, and so he was mesmerized at once by the young woman who looked at him so disarmingly. "So what would you like to hear?" Sam asked eagerly.

"Why don't you just pull some of that music out of your pouch and play something romantic like maybe 'Lorena.' It's such a pretty song. Don't you think so? It makes me feel in love."

Sam fumbled from his music pouch and held up the music for "Lorena." Here it is." He cried like a child finding a long-lost toy and placed it on the piano. "Sit up here on the bench, and I will play it for you." The dark-haired girl did as she was asked, and Sam put the cornet to his lips and played one of his best renditions of the song. For once the notes were sweet and soft and not shrill. When he was finished, the dark-haired girl clapped excitedly and said, "That was good, real good."

"So you know music?" asked Sam excitedly.

"Oh, yes," she replied excitedly. "I am a student of music."

"Let's sit on the divan and talk." The girl smiled and said, "Sure. Let's talk about music." When Sam sat down, she sat right next to him so that her thigh touched his leg, and she looked right into his eyes. Then Sam talked about music while she listened. He told her about all the great songs that he knew. He told her about the proper techniques for playing a cornet. He told her about famous bands and musicians. And for everything he said, she smiled sweetly and said, "Oh yes. I think so too."

It wasn't until she suggested to Sam that they go upstairs for a little rest, that he suddenly realized where he was. "Oh, no, mam. I could never do that. You see I am engaged to a fine, lovely woman in Nashville, and I could never do that to her." The dark-haired girl laughed and said, "You're kidding aren't you? With her way up in Nashville and all, and you way down here. Don't you see? You've both got needs. Why right now she's probably got some man between her thighs telling him she loves him, and he's doing the same. In her position I know that's what I would be doing."

Sam felt his fists tightening at his side, and he came close to striking the lady in the face, but she sure was pretty, and she had said some nice things about his playing. He relaxed his fists and said, "I'm sorry you feel that way. When you really love some one, you wouldn't do such a thing. I know that Rita's up there in Nashville, alone waiting for me to come back. We're going to get married as soon as this war is over."

The dark-haired girl smiled and said, "Don't talk to me about marriage. When I was fifteen, this no good skunk promised to marry me, and we had a few lovely romps in the hayfield, but when he found out I was pregnant, he ran off and joined the army. I don't even know which one. This girl of yours may be pretty special, but maybe she ain't. Anyways, she's way up there in Nashville, and I'm right here. Just follow me up those stairs, and I'll give you the time of your life. I may be young, but I know every trick of the trade."

Sam stood up abruptly and said, "You sure are pretty, and I would really love to have the rites of Venus with you, but it wouldn't be right. I've got to go now before I do something I might regret."

Then he stood up, bowed politely, and as he went out the door said, "Good night to you mam. I sure hope that you will find love in your life someday." The crickets were playing their own kind of night music as Sam made his way back towards the Union Camp.

A young red-faced Sergeant came down the stairs shortly after Sam left and saw the dark-haired girl still sitting on the divan. He grinned and said, "Well I be swan, Abby. You sure are fast tonight. In an out of bed and ready for another customer before old Louisa here can do one. I've got to hand it to you."

"Shut up Swede. He left without doing nothing. Where the hell did you ever find him, some monastery?"

Swede laughed and said, "So you're losing some of your charm is it?"

"Charm, Hell. I think he's probably one of them homosexuals."

Like a pneumatic nymph, the large round figure of Mrs. Murphy floated from the plush red interior and said, "I never seen anything like it in my whole darned life. This musician comes to a whore house for the music, not the girls. I send him my prettiest girl, and she doesn't even get a rise out of him. I tell you, that man don't have an ounce of red-blooded man-hood in his bones."

"And I'm saying he does," said Swede. "I'll tell you what. I get him in bed with Abby, you give me a free one on the house, and Abby gets an extra ten bucks. I don't get Abby in bed with him, I pay you 20 dollars. What do you say?"

"Mrs. Murphy laughed and said, "I don't see how I can lose that one. You're on." Then she shook hands with Swede to seal the bargain. Abby punched Swede in the arm and said, "You fool; she's got us."

"No she don't. I've known you a long time Abby, and I just know you can pull this one off. You got a lot of sand, and you know how to have a good time. Just do as I say."

"So what are you gonna do? Kidnap him and tie him to a tree so I can rape him?"

"I've got a better idea. Meet me by the mess tent at the camp in 20 minutes."

Swede ran to the Union encampment and went right for Fletcher's tent. "Say Fletch, we've got us a little problem and thought that maybe you could help us." Anyone who had a problem knew that Sam Fletcher was the one who would do just about anything to solve it, and so Sam slipped on his clothes and followed Swede across the campground. "Seems old Bill Bates got a letter from his girl. She busted up with him, and Bill is talkin' about shootin' hisself. I thought maybe you could talk some sense in his head."

"I'll sure try," said Sam. "I'd hate to see old Bill do something that foolish."

Bill Bates was sitting on a log in front of his tent looking into the fire and smoking his pipe when Sam arrived. Sam put his hand on Bill's shoulder and said, "Sorry to hear about your girl."

Bill looked up and replied, "What the hell you talking about Fletcher?"

"The problem with your girl." Swede said , "You got one of those bad news letters from your girl."

"Well that's no body's business but my own. And just to set the record straight, I ain't even got a girl. And if I did, I certainly wouldn't tell Swede about it. He would likely steal her for himself."

As Sam returned to his own tent, he was deeply puzzled and was about to confront Swede when one of the soldiers who had been at Mrs. Murphy's whispered, "Sam. I've got great news for you. Rita just got here from Nashville. She's in your tent waiting for you."

Sam shouted, "Rita! Thank the Lord. I was hoping she would come." He was about to plunge through the opening of the tent when the soldier grabbed his arm and whispered, "Don't talk. The General's been pretty angry about girls in the tents. Says the next man he finds with a girl goes right to the stockade. Sentry's been walking around with his ears to the ground. I wouldn't say nothin." Sam patted the soldier's arm and dived into the tent like an eagle catching a fish, and landed on top of a naked female body.

Ben Franklin once said that in the dark, you couldn't tell one cat from another, and in that truest of all books, <u>The Works of Thomas Malory</u>, Lancelot spent an entire night in the arms of Elaine of the White Hands, thinking all the while that he was with his darling Guinevere. Now here was the virtuous Sam Fletcher--on a pitch black night, a moonless night so dark, that he couldn't see his hands in front of his face--in the arms of a lovely woman most likely not the woman he loved. What happened next was not in any book.

A crowd of soldiers had gathered around the tent waiting to see the outcome. Most of them had placed bets on one side or the other, and Swede stood in the front of the tent holding the wagers. In just seconds, however, Sam came flying out of the tent as if he had been shot by a cannon and knocked Swede to the ground. A mixture of cheers and boos fought with each other over the fallen Swede, and then the arguments began.

"I won because he slept with her," said a loud gruff voice.

"Hell no," said a high-pitched tenor. "Sleeping with her means having sexual relations with her. There ain't no way he could have done it that fast."

"Well let's ask her," said another voice in the darkness.

And so they dragged Abby from the tent draped in an army blanket and asked her.

"Damned son of a bitch," she shrieked like a banshee. "I've never been so insulted in my life." Then, dragging the blanket behind her, she disappeared into the darkness.

"We won," said the tenor voice. "I take that to be a no."

"I say we ask Sam first. No man alive would be in a tent with a beautiful woman like that and not make love to her. What do you say Sam? Are you one of those homosexuals, or did you have her?"

Sam was on his feet now and ready to punch the first man who came into range, and he couldn't get words to come from his mouth. But finally he managed to say, "Damn you all. You almost made me untrue to my beloved Rita. Damn you all."

The men continued to argue about who had won the bet. Swede insisted that Sam had been in bed with Abby, although admittedly for a short time, and being in bed together was what counted. The men who had lost argued hotly that it was clearly understood, if not stated directly, that being in bed meant having sexual relations, and so they went as a group to let Mrs. Murphy settle it.

Mrs. Murphy was by all accounts a fair woman, and she declared the evidence inconclusive. The men were pretty unhappy with this arrangement, but she said, " Let's have a new bet. I will wager that before a year is out, Sam and Abby will be husband and wife." Swede laughed and said, "That's one I can't lose. Let's draw up an agreement." If Sam doesn't marry Abby, I will give you $100 and a free pass to all activities in the house for one year. If he does marry her, you owe me $200 Federal dollars."

Sam's anger never lasted long, and he had already forgiven those who had played the trick on him. He was just happy that he had discovered the deception in time. A young soldier finally had the nerve to ask Sam how, in the dark, you could tell one cat from another. Sam smiled and said, "It was easy. Rita's right breast is slightly larger than her left one. On this girl, the opposite was true. Anybody could have told the difference."

The next day Flambeau's letter arrived signed by Rita, and Sam considered killing himself.

Dear Sam,

Please excuse me for printing this letter. I burned my right hand in the fire and needed to print with my left hand. I could have waited until my hand healed but wanted to get this news to you as soon as I could because I didn't want to hurt you any more than I need to.

Sam, you are a wonderful man, and I will always treasure those moments we spent together, but you will never play the cornet as well as Flambeau does. Let's face it, you work hard but don't have the talent. Henry and I have been spending a lot of time with each other. We practice together, eat together, and--I almost hesitate to say--sleep together. We also make beautiful music together as you and I never could do.

I know this hurts, but it is the truth. The good news is that I am releasing you to find some wonderful girl who doesn't care how well you play the cornet.

Affectionately always, Rita

"Why would she drop me for that arrogant bastard, Flambeau?" he cried to the trees. A more skeptical man might have laughed at the transparent deception of the letter and said. "Sure she hurt her hand and had to print left-handed. Do you think I was born yesterday? This whole thing smells of that rascal Flambeau, and if I find out he did it, I'll kill him." But as Rita often said, "Sam had no guile." He was as trusting of the world as a new-born baby, and if someone gave his word, Sam believed it. Being honest himself, he thought all the world was honest, and he had no knowledge of evil. Rita used to argue with him about this.

Rita had told him once, "As innocent as he was, Jesus Christ himself could spot evil a mile away. Whenever those Pharisees came up with a plot to trick him, he always saw through it. Remember the woman caught in adultery? The Pharisees wanted to trap him. One of them said, 'We caught this woman committing adultery. The law says she should be put to death. What do you say?' They figured that Jesus would fall into their trap. If he said 'Stone her,' he would be going against everything he stood for: love and forgiveness. If he said, 'let her go,' he would be going against the laws of Moses and could be put to death himself. Yes, they knew they had their nemesis at last.

"But Jesus looked at the ground and wrote with a stick in the earth as if sounding the depths of their vicious hearts and said, 'Yes stone her. But he that is without sin, let him cast the first stone.' And so Jesus triumphed over evil by understanding it. Sam, you need to understand evil before those Pharisees get you at last." Sam didn't think of those Pharisees now. He could not imagine that anyone could be so evil as to destroy someone else's happiness. Above all he could not believe that the love he and Rita had for each other would be the envy of those who lacked the capacity for love. And because he still loved Rita with all his heart, he wrote back.

Dearest Rita,

    I would never do anything to make you unhappy. If you and Flambeau really love each other, I wish you the best in everything. If there is anything I can do, please let me know. Just know that I still love you, and if you change your mind, I will still marry you.

Love,
Sam

When Sam's letter arrived in Nashville, Flambeau intercepted it, read it, laughed, and tore it to shreds. He did not bother to answer it. "I've won," he said. And he danced a little jig on the way back to the band.

Sam checked the mail every day, but when Rita hadn't answered in two weeks, he stopped looking. Life seemed particularly dreary with the love of his life gone and the only music the playing of bugle calls. When Swede came up to him one day and said, "You know, Old Caesar says he misses you. He says you need to bring your cornet up to Mrs. Murphy's place and play some tunes with him," Sam said "What do I have to lose?" He knew that Rita would say, "The Pharisees are planning another trap," but not much mattered to him now. All he had was music, and the only show in town was at Mrs. Murphy's.

And so on a bitter cold, starlit night in early November, Sam picked up his cornet and for a second time walked into Mrs. Murphy's drawing room. Caesar was at the piano playing "Darling Nelly Gray," and he nodded when he saw Sam. When he was finished playing, he smiled and told Sam to pick a song and start to play it. Sam worked his valves, blew some air through the horn, and tried to remember what Rita would have said to him, but at the thought of Rita, his eyes teared up and he couldn't see anything. Fortunately, he had played the "Battle Hymn" so many times, that he could play it by heart, and the notes began to flow from his cornet as if by magic. He felt that he was outside his body watching someone else play, but it was lovely. In his sadness, Sam's music seemed to have become richer and deeper, and when Caesar joined him on the second verse, Sam had never heard anything more beautiful. When he finished, he heard a smattering of applause by the few girls and men who still remained in the parlor, and he bowed politely before starting the next piece. He played "Just Before the Battle, Mother," and before he could think about it too much, followed with "Kingdom Coming," and "Listen for the Mocking Bird." He started each piece by himself without music, and Caesar joined him and played to the end. If Sam played faster, Caesar caught up with him; if Sam slowed down, Caesar slowed down with him. For a few minutes, Sam felt happy. The music was lifting him out of his sadness, and all seemed right with the world. But all too soon, Caesar said, "That's 'nuff fer now." and walked off into the back of the house. Sam thought that he was all alone until he heard the clapping of two hands and saw, much to his amazement, Abby sitting on the divan.

"That was just lovely she said. I do declare Sam that you are just about the best cornet player I ever heard." Sam was about to say, "You're not going to fool me again" when a little boy walked into the room. He was about eight years old and was wearing homespun pants and a baggy shirt all about three sizes too big for him, and he was barefoot. "Sam, I'd like you to meet my son Willie. Willie, say hello to the nice man who played all that pretty music."

The boy walked up to Sam and extended his hand for a shake, and as Sam was shaking the tiny hand in his own huge paw, the boy said. "I sure wish I could see that cornet." Sam handed him the cornet, and the boy said, "How do you play it?" Sam made a buzzing sound with his lips and told the boy to do the same thing with his lips pressed against the mouthpiece, and when the boy blew, a blast of sound came out of the end of the cornet.

"Isn't that wonderful?" shrieked Abby. "My boy is playing the cornet."

The next thing Sam knew, he was sitting on the divan with Abby and Willie, and giving Willie his first lesson on the cornet. After a while, Abby said, "Willie, you've practiced long enough today. Why don't you run off and play now. Mr. Fletcher and I have some important things to discuss."

"Yes, Mam," the boy said and ran excitedly through the door.

"Mr. Fletcher, I just wanted to tell you how sorry I am about the other night. I had no idea the boys had been up to some mischief. I really thought you wanted to see me." She started to cry as she said this and seemed to be having a hard time getting out the words. "I just want you to know that I really admire you and wouldn't do anything to make you feel uncomfortable."

Sam put his hand on her shoulder and said, "I hate to see people cry. Don't fret so. I'm not mad at you, just a little surprised and disappointed."

"Disappointed?" she sobbed.

"Yes, disappointed. We should at least have gotten to know each other first before we got in bed together."

Abby suppressed a laugh and said sadly, "But Mr. Fletcher, I'm a soiled dove, a lady of the night. What man would want to get to know me better?"

"Abby, you shouldn't be so hard on yourself. I bet there are thousands of men who would like to know you better. With such a wonderful little boy, you must be a good person at heart. I'm sure you wouldn't have accepted employment with Mrs. Murphy if you had had any other options."

Abby dabbed at her eyes with a handkerchief, and said softly, "You're right Sam. If my husband had not been killed at Chickamauga, I wouldn't be here now. I was a good wife, and we had a nice little farm in the Wauhatchie Valley, but when the word came to me that Abner had been killed, I knew that I couldn't keep up with the farm by myself. I had a child to feed and clothe, and there was no money. I met Mrs. Murphy in a tavern, and she told me that I could have a job with her. She said she was in the entertainment business and thought that I would fit right in. She told me I could sing along with her piano player in her "Haven." I assumed, of course that the "Haven" was kind of like a theatre of some sort. You can imagine how shocked I was when I arrived at the establishment and found out what it really was.

"When I saw those handsome young men in the pretty blue uniforms, I assumed that they were there to hear me sing, and when a tall fellow came up to me with a sweet smile on his face and offered me his arm, I assumed that he was going to escort me to the piano. You can imagine how shocked I was when he led me upstairs into a little room with a bed in it. "What are we doing here?" I asked. He laughed as if I had made a joke, and said, "After we have both removed our clothes I'm sure we will think of something." I yelled for Mrs. Murphy, but she never came, and before I knew it the handsome young gentleman had his way with me. If you don't know what I mean, I will tell you."

Sam said, "I think I know what you are going to tell me, but tell me anyway."

Abby sobbed and said, "He tore off my clothes; tore off his own clothes, and when we were standing there like Adam and Eve, he pushed me down of the bed and had his way with me again and again. Believe me I told him what I thought. I told him, 'Get off me you brute.' But he refused to desist. After he was finished, he led me down the stairs, and much to my surprise, there was another officer standing there offering me his arm. I said, 'What are you doing?' And he answered sweetly, 'Let's go upstairs, and we'll think of something.' I called for Mrs. Murphy, but she didn't answer, and the next thing I knew I was in the same little room with another naked Yankee. This went on all night, and when the sun came up over the mountains, I at last settled into a deep slumber."

Sam had a pained look on his face as he asked innocently, "When you awakened, did you tell Mrs. Murphy that you no longer wished to work for her, that you had been misled by her description of the job?"

Abby wept and placed her hand on Sam's shoulder. "Yes I tried to leave, but she showed me a piece of paper that I had signed. She said that I was under contract and couldn't leave for five full years."

Sam looked at the woman dabbing at her eyes with a handkerchief, and his brain told him that he had just heard the most amazingly improbable story of all time, but in his heart he wanted to believe her. After all, anything in "this best of all possible worlds" was possible. Maybe she was a good woman who had been misled and who just needed a good man to save her from the clutches of a wicked witch. Sam put his arms around her and said, "I will get you out of this place and make an honest woman of you." Now Sam was not thinking marriage. He was thinking that somehow he would take Abby away from Mrs. Willis where she could start her life again as a respectable woman. He wasn't quite sure how he was going to do this. There weren't really that many career opportunities for reformed whores, but he would try. "Tomorrow, night at 6," he said, "I will pick you up, and I will cook you dinner. Then we'll think of something to do."

"Yes," she said, "Yes. I will be ready."

From behind the curtain where she had been listening, Mrs. Murphy had also said yes. "Yes my dear soldiers. I think I may just win this bet." When Sam came by the next morning to talk with her about Abby's contract, Mrs. Murphy said, "I was hoping a good man would come along. Abby is a sweet girl and should not be in this business at all. I just wrote up the contract for her own protection."

When, on November 16, 1864, the Union Army left Atlanta to begin its glorious march to Savannah and the sea, Sam Fletcher, had a family with him. He wasn't married, and so he insisted on separate tents, but where Sam went, Abby and her son went also. In the background was the eternal presence of Swede who was ready to report to Mrs. Murphy any progress that had been made. But like so many before him, Swede was totally baffled by the inexorable virtue of Sam. "Every night he goes to bed with this beautiful willing woman in the next tent, and he never goes to see her. It ain't natural. Maybe he is one of them homosexuals."

Abby did her best to be a virtuous companion for Sam. She let it be known that her father had been a Presbyterian minister and that she had been studying to be a medical missionary. "I originally wanted to go to Africa," she said sweetly, "but when the war came along, I went to where the fighting was going on and volunteered my services. I was seventeen years old when the bullets began to fly at Bull Run, and I walked right up to the first hospital tent I saw. The men were bleeding and screaming for help, but the big, fat hussy in charge took one look at me and said, 'Go home to your mother. You're too young.'

"Well, I didn't want to go home. I wanted to help those boys, and so I found General Custer himself. He was in his field tent sitting on a cot in his underwear when I opened the flap and said, ' General Custer, could I have a word with you?' He gave me a great big smile and said, 'Anything you want sweetheart. I don't know whether to put these pants on or take them off. I'll let you decide.'

"I told him to take them off if he was sick and needed nursing care but to put them on if he wanted to help a lady serve her country in an honorable way. Custer paused for a moment as if not knowing which way to turn, but eventually he slipped on his trousers and led me from the tent. He led me back to the big hussy who had ordered me to go home and asked her to find a place for me. The woman was furious for Custer's intervention, but soon she had put up a tent of my own right next to General Custer's tent. From then on, wherever Custer's regiment went, I went also.

"I soon became a favorite of the officers who seemed to be much entertained by my conversation. Then one day I met Hank. Hank was a tall, dark-haired Captain in Custer's regiment, and I fell in love with him at first sight; the feeling seemed to be mutual because in no time I was spending time in his tent. Like Custer, he promised me a position in the nursing corps, but he told me it would take time, and the next thing I knew I was with child."

Sam didn't know how much to believe, but he interrupted her story and said, "But Willie's eight years old; how could he have been born in 1861? And what happened to the story about the farm in Wauhatchie and the farmer husband?"

"Sam, will you let me finish? I'll get to that soon. I gave birth to a little boy in early 1862. He was a beautiful child named Ted, and Hank said that we would get married as soon as the war was over, but within a week, Hank had disappeared, and I tried to find him. I packed up Ted and headed west but found myself lost in the midst of vast bodies of troops. Finally I made my way to Chattanooga and decided to give up on Hank and start a life of my own for Ted. I met Abner at church one Sunday in Wauhatchie, and we felt an immediate attraction for each other. He had a boy, Willie, who you see with me now. His wife had died of consumption in 1860, and he wanted a mother for his son as well as a wife for himself. We got married in the church, and Ted and I moved in with him. He was a deacon in the church as well as a farmer, and so I found my old spiritual life coming alive once again. The Lord certainly works in mysterious ways. Life was good for a while, but little Ted died of small pox, and my dear Abner was killed at Chickamauga. Rest his soul." Here she dabbed at her eyes with a handkerchief and sighed.

Sam was deeply touched by her story and hoped that he might be able to lead her back to a respectable life, but he still loved Rita. She might love another man--that bastard Flambeau--but he would love her always. He believed that he would never marry. But he soon became a father to Willie. Whenever he could, he showed Willie how to play the cornet, and within a couple of weeks, Willie could even play a couple of simple tunes. Willie told Abby, "I sure do wish that Sam could be my Dad."

Sam and Willie became inseparable, and whenever Sam played, Willie was there to listen. Every now and then the band would play a concert, but Sam was still playing the second cornet part. Willie kept telling everybody that Sam should be playing first, but most people just laughed. Sam said, "No matter how hard you practice, or how much you improve, it's almost impossible to change people's opinions of you. A prophet is not without honor, except in his own country."

Abby soon grew bored with her role as virtuous companion, and when Sam and Willie went to the concerts, she started to scout the camp for business opportunities. By early August she had found about a half dozen willing clients, and when the sutler came to camp, she bought a few luxuries for her family table. "Real butter!" said Sam enthusiastically.

"Yes," Abby said. "The General likes your playing so much, that he sent it with his compliments."

Sam wanted desperately to believe her, but one day he came back to his tent, and there was obviously something going on next door. He heard a woman giggling and a man snorting, and when the tent had stopped shaking, a young lieutenant emerged into the sunlight. Sam waited until the young officer had left, and then he went to confront Abby.

"I thought you were a reformed woman now," he said sadly.

Abby smiled and said sweetly, " I am reformed. I only sleep with officers now. And I charge ten dollars. Except of course when I do it for free."

"Dang it Abby, will you ever become a virtuous woman?"

"Only when I am in love, and I think I am in love now."

"But what about me?"

"Sam, you are a really nice follow, but you never make love with me. After a while, I start thinking there is something wrong with me. I wonder, does Sam just consider me a two-dollar whore? But then I realize that you are still in love with that Rita and know that I don't stand a chance. You need to find her and love her. Don't let another man have her without a fight. Find her or you will never be happy again."

"But she said she doesn't want me."

"Damn it. She needs to say it to your face. Don't believe in a letter."

"But if I show up again in her life, I will just embarrass her, and I don't want to do anything to hurt her."

"Damn it again Sam, women aren't that fragile. Be a man. Take her."

Sam pondered what Abby had said, but in the end decided that the best thing he could do for the woman he loved was to leave her. The young lieutenant was now a regular visitor to Abby's tent, and Sam eventually realized that he was a non-paying customer. And when Abby invited Sam to her wedding, Sam wasn't totally surprised.

The chaplain performed the ceremony on the parade ground on a beautiful May morning with Willie as the ring bearer and Sam the best man. The bride wore white, and when Sam questioned the message it sent, Abby told him that virginity was actually just a state of mind. When Abby and Willie moved in with young Lieutenant Philip Hayes, Sam felt happy for helping Abby reform her life but sad for creating the emptiness in his own. He often wondered if he could have loved Abby, and if she could have replaced Rita as his bride, but it was all too late now. He filled his time practicing his cornet.

He found an old army musician, Zeke Brown, who had played the piccolo in his youth but who now agreed to give Sam cornet lessons for fifty cents each. They worked on long tones and the major scales, but everything Zeke told him to do, he knew Rita could do better. The worst part was when old Zeke put his hand on Sam's stomach and asked him to breathe in and breathe out. It was not the same.

CHAPTER TWENTY-FOUR
Wherein Flambeau Turns Up the Heat

"Many a green-gown has been given;
Many a kiss both odd and even;
Many a glance, too has been sent
From out the eye, love's firmament."

Robert Herrick, "Corinna's Going A-Maying"

Summer turned into another bitter cold Nashville winter, and Flambeau and Rita spent so much time together, that their relationship was the gossip of the whole band. People would report the latest sightings of Rita and Flambeau. Someone even reported seeing them coming out of a Nashville Hotel together early one morning, but Ira Goldstein didn't believe it. "Not my Rita. She's a good girl."

By the spring of 1865, Ira began to have concerns for his grieving daughter's reputation. "You know," he said, "if you're going to sleep with him you might as well get married."

"Sleep with him! No, no, no," she cried. " I am still grieving for Sam."

Goldstein held his daughter in his arms and said, "You can't grieve for ever. You're young. You've got to get on with your life. You and this Flambeau fellow have something in common. You both love music. You both play the cornet. He seems to adore you. Maybe you should consider making it permanent."

Rita burst into tears and blurted out, "But I still love Sam. Flambeau can never be Sam."

In any event, Flambeau and Goldstein talked and suggested that when spring came to Nashville Rita should seriously consider marrying Flambeau. "After all," Ira said, "nothing can bring him back. You might as well get on with your life." Sobbing, Rita agreed that if Sam didn't come back by May 25th, she would marry Flambeau.

The Goldstein Band was doing so well in Nashville, that they decided to stay there as long as business was good. They did regular concerts at the music hall and supplemented their incomes with weddings, bar mitzvahs, church services, and private parties. From a musical point of view, the world had never looked better for the Ira Goldstein Band. But still Rita grieved and dreaded the coming of May 25th.

Hancock had noticed what was going on, and he didn't like it. One day he took Rita aside, and said "I need to talk with you." Rita knew how much Sam respected Hancock, and so she sat down to listen.

"I know you are grieving for Sam, but you don't need to get involved with that snake Flambeau. I'm speaking to you as if you were my own sister. That man is no good. He is so rotten, that I wouldn't be surprised if he fabricated that whole story about Sam's death just so he could seduce you. He has fooled more women than King Solomon himself, and I don't want you to be one of them."

Rita stood up with her teeth clenched and her eyes ablaze. "Don't try to tell me how to live my life. I am a grown woman and certainly know how to judge character. Flambeau has had a difficult life and has reasons for being the way he is. If you had grown up an orphan, you might be a little more sympathetic."

"An orphan?" asked Hancock incredulously. "He said he was an orphan?"

"Yes he is," said Rita defensively. "And I don't appreciate your inference that he would be mean enough to fabricate Sam's death. He showed me the clipping."

"Yes, that son of a bitch would be crafty enough to fabricate the evidence."

"Fabricate the evidence? Your problem, Charles, is that you are too cynical. No one would be mean enough or low enough to fabricate someone's death. Especially someone as kind as Henry Flambeau. Henry has been like a brother to me through all my grief. I wish you could understand."

Hancock gave Rita a big hug and said, "I sure hope you are right," but he was more convinced than ever that Flambeau had somehow contrived the whole thing. He didn't say anything more to Rita. He just began asking questions and checking the casualty lists in newspapers. One afternoon, he told Ira Goldstein that he needed some time off for personal reasons. Ira told him the band was no good without him, but Hancock insisted. The next morning Charles Hancock slipped out of Nashville without saying a word to anyone. He knew that the 7th Pennsylvania was somewhere in Georgia in search of Jefferson Davis, and he wanted to be sure about the fate of his friend Sam. "Was it Fletcher or Filcher?" he asked himself.

CHAPTER TWENTY-FIVE
Charles Hancock Tries to Make the Crooked Straight

"Every valley shall be exalted, and every mountain and hill shall be made low; and the crooked shall be made straight, and the rough places plain...."

Isaiah 40:4

By April 30th, 1865 the great war was essentially over. The armies of Lee and Johnston had surrendered, and only the army of E. Kirby Smith remained as a glimmering hope for the always sanguine Jefferson Davis. Davis still believed that if he could cross the Mississippi and go west perhaps the war might still be won. However as Charles Hancock started down the 249-mile road to Atlanta, Jefferson Davis was inexorably falling into the Union net.

It was a bright sunny May morning as Charles Hancock stepped out onto the road to Chattanooga. It wasn't much of a road at all, just the cleared area next to The Western and Atlantic Railway, but at least there was no danger of being lost. In about 100 miles, he would be in Chattanooga and in another 150 miles beyond that in Atlanta. Sherman was somewhere down there, and if he could find Sherman, perhaps he could find some news of Sam. The casualty list in the Nashville paper had clearly said "Filcher," not "Fletcher."

At first he enjoyed the brisk walk on such a beautiful morning, but before the sun reached the zenith, he began thinking of how nice it would be to lie down in the shade and take a nap, but there was no shade. He thought that maybe a train would come down the track from Nashville, but there were no trains. Just when he thought he could not take another step, he felt the unmistakable beat of horses' hooves on the hard ground, and in a few minutes, he saw a dust cloud coming towards him. From the cloud emerged a man dressed in overalls, a home-spun shirt and a tattered slouch hat perched on the top of his greasy, shoulder-length hair. He was riding on a brown mare and leading a roan stallion.

"Howdy friend," the man said cordially. It looks you're about tuckered out. Been walking long?"

"Long enough," said Hancock.

"Well this is your lucky day, that is if you have ten bucks on you. I have the finest piece of horse flesh in Tennessee, and you can have him for the low price of ten dollars."

"So where did you steal him?" asked Hancock.

"Steal him? Do you think I look like a horse thief? Why I'm a preacher in my spare time. I've got Jesus in my heart."

"Well, you've probably got the devil in you somewhere else, but I'm really tired, and I do have the ten dollars."

"You are talking Federal dollars? Don't want none of that Confederate trash. Ain't worth the paper it's printed on."

Hancock reached into his pocket and pulled out ten silver dollars and handed him to the preacher. "You can bite them if you like, but they're all silver."

The preacher put one in his mouth and bit down on it and then said, "Stranger, you just bought yourself a horse. Take care of him. He's a mighty good piece of horse flesh." Then he handed Hancock the reins and galloped off in a cloud of dust. Hancock pulled himself up on the animal's back, grasped the reins and turned the horse's head towards Atlanta.

The path along the railroad track was level and smooth, and when the sun was settling behind the Cumberland Mountains, Hancock was entering the dust-covered streets of Franklin, Tennessee. About six months before, the Confederates under General Hood had hurled themselves against the entrenched Yankees of General Schofield, but in just five hours, 1,750 of them, including the capable Patrick Cleburne, would lie dead on the battlefield. It was if the Confederacy was a prize fighter who had been beaten almost to submission but had one last punch before he went down for the count. With that flailing, ineffective punch of Hood's army, the Confederacy was almost down for good. As Hancock rode into town he could see whole stands of pines that had been shattered by the hail of cannon and artillery fire on that awful Indian Summer day of November 30th, 1864.

As Hancock rode slowly into town, he scanned both sides of the street looking for a room for the night. He had never noticed the CSA brand on his horse's left flank, but a black whiskered man sitting on a porch noticed it at once. Within seconds he was in the house and out again with an Enfield rifle in his hand. His name was Sam Cook, and he had ridden with Joseph Wheeler in the days when the greatest authority in Tennessee was the Confederate cavalry.

With Wheeler now gone, a few of his crew remained in the shadows looking for opportunities to revive the southern cause. Sam Cook was one such man, and Hancock was his opportunity. Cook stepped into the street, took aim and fired. The bullet tore through the folds of Hancock's coat and almost dragged him from the saddle, but as the horse reared in panic, Hancock recovered his seat in the saddle, kicked the horse's flank, and shot through the main street of Franklin like an errant cannon ball.

Cook reloaded, saddled a horse, and was soon in rapid pursuit. Hancock reached the Harpeth River, the back of the old Union line in the Battle of Franklin, and began to search for the ford in the growing darkness. Twice the river rose up his horse's stomach, and twice Hancock returned to the river bank. But just when all seemed lost, his horse's feet found the shallow of the ford, and made his way slowly across. In the distance, Hancock could hear the thunder of a horse's hooves beating against the hard, dry earth.

Hancock slept in the woods just south of Franklin, and the next morning, not seeing Cook anywhere around, he continued down the pike inexorably towards Atlanta. Just South of Murfreesboro, he saw a cloud of dust behind him and felt the thunder of hooves and slipped off quickly into the woods. From behind his leafy screen, Hancock saw Cook and five seedy looking characters in tattered Confederate uniforms riding by. With these remnants of Wheeler's cavalry prowling along the pike, Hancock knew that his chances of reaching Atlanta by the road were a bit dubious, and so he turned his horse's head through the woods in the general direction of the railroad. He came to a clearing and was about to ride along the deserted road bed when he heard the unmistakable sound of a locomotive in the distance. At the same time he saw Cook and his gang riding out of the trees just below him. Hancock turned his horse into the woods, dismounted and hid himself in a little glen of hemlock trees.

From his hiding place he heard the sound of men's voices. "He can't be too far from here. Hell, there's the damned horse."

Hancock looked out and saw a tall skinny man with overalls and red suspenders leading his horse. Then Cook yelled, "Ya damned Yankee! You might as well come out and surrender yerself. We ain't goin' nowhere until you come out."

Hancock could have reached out and touched Cook's trouser leg, but he tried not to move a muscle. He tried to even suspend his breathing, but then a fly landed on his nose, and he felt ready to sneeze. By and by Cook said, "Hell he ain't goin' nowhere, and I'm getting powerful thirsty. You men poke around through the bushes for awhile. I'm goin' down to the creek and fill my canteen." Then he galloped off leaving Hancock the smallest of openings to the railroad track.

The train was much closer now, and the roar of the engine and the shriek of the whistle shook the trees, and the five riders dashed out of the woods to get a look. They got off their horses and stood idly by the track. The train was upon them now, and as the horrible sound eclipsed the chatter of the squirrels and the call of blue jays, Hancock dashed out in the open and grabbed the handle on a box car door. He thought he saw the men running down the track and shouting at him, but he was soon swallowed by the train and found himself lying on the hard wooden floor of a boxcar. He was breathing heavily as he heard bullets smashing through the door, but in a few seconds, all he heard was the clatter of the wheels beating against the tracks. He closed his eyes and before he knew it he had fallen into a deep slumber. The next thing he knew the wheels were grinding to a screeching stop, and he leaped to his feet ready to confront Wheeler's men. But as he peered through the cracks in the side of the box car, all he saw was darkness.

When he leaped into the night from the boxcar, Hancock found himself in the streets of Atlanta. Most of the Union Army had gone on the march to the sea, but there was a small occupying force, and when a nervous young private had fixed Hancock in the sights of his Enfield, it looked like Hancock's mission was over, but the young soldier didn't shoot. He just asked Hancock to identify himself, and when Hancock's brisk Yankee voice had said, "Bandsman Hancock, formerly of the 123rd Illinois Mounted Infantry," the young soldier lowered his gun.

Hancock soon learned of the direction of Sherman's Army and of the probable location of his friend Sam, and when he had purchased his second horse--this time a big black stallion with U S burned into his flank--he headed towards the sea. This time the journey was uneventful until he came to a field outside Macon, Georgia. In the distance, he heard the unmistakable howl of a dog singing along with a cornet, and he spurred his horse in the direction of the sound.

CHAPTER TWENTY-SIX
The End of the Road for Jefferson Davis; The Beginning of the Road for Sam Fletcher

"Jefferson Davis was a hero bold,
You've heard of him I know, He tried to make himself a king
Where Southern breezes blow
But Uncle Sam, he laid the youth
Across his mighty knee
And spanked him well,
And that's the end of brave old Jeffy D."

Song, "Jeff in Petticoats," George Cooper

Sam went further and further into that great heart of darkness, the Confederacy, and when Atlanta fell on September 3, Sam was there. On April 2nd of the next year, he played the cornet before the gates of Selma and was there as the Southern Masons gave a Masonic burial to a fallen Yankee Mason cavalryman, Lieutenant Sigmund. Resistance was becoming weaker and weaker, and this charge against a strong Confederate defensive position—unlike those disasters at Fredericksburg and Cold Harbor—led to victory. There was hardly anyone left to stop them. Sam played mainly bugle calls now, but he still dreamed of playing the Haydn for Mr. Lincoln. When the news arrived that Lee had surrendered on April 9th, and that only Johnson and Davis stood in the way of total victory, the men were jubilant. "The joyous mood ended, however, when the disheartening telegraph dispatch reached the Union Army near Selma: "The President Has Been Killed by an Assassin's Bullet."

At first everyone was too dispirited to move, but Sam's despair turned to anger. He blew "Assembly" and shouted, "Revenge for Mr. Lincoln." The men cheered, and the great blue Army moved on into Macon, Georgia in search of the elusive and still dangerous Jefferson Davis.

On May 9th the 7th Pennsylvania and the 4th Michigan closed in on a clearing where a lone camp fire burned. There was a large woman wearing a shawl hovering by the fire, and a younger woman and four small children stood nearby. The sound of musket fire suddenly erupted, but soon everyone realized that the Pennsylvania boys and the Michigan boys were just shooting at each other. There were no more Confederates to kill. And most astonishing of all was the sudden realization that the tall woman by the campfire was none other than the first and last of the Confederates himself, Jefferson Davis.

In the early morning light of May 10th, 1865 the Union Soldiers moved in with their guns pointing at the last Confederate, but no shots were fired. As the sweet smell of magnolias drifted across the Ocmulgee River about a mile from Irwinsville, Sam saw the weeping children huddling around their surrounded father and felt a surge of pity. Of all those hundreds of thousands of troops who had once followed his every command, only thirteen remained for this last supper of the Confederacy. With these thirteen soldiers were the remains of the Davis cabinet: John Reagan, the Postmaster General: Burton N. Harrison Davis' private secretary and about four officers. But Sam saw only the fallen President ridiculously attired in his wife's shawl and the weeping children.

As Davis and his army marched from the camp surrounded by Union guards, someone said to Sam, "Play 'The Rogues March.' If anyone deserves it, he does."

Sam put his cornet to his lips and was about to play the infamous "Rogue's March," when he suddenly stopped and put the cornet at his side. The guards with Davis in the middle stopped too, and everyone looked at Sam expectantly. The same voice shouted, "Well let's hear 'The Rogues March' damn it." But instead of playing, Sam stepped up on a tree stump and said, "Gentlemen, this is no time for 'The Rogue's March.' I have waited all my life for this moment, and it has nothing to do with rogues. I have wanted to play a solo that has profound meaning for the future of our country and thought that I would play it for Mr. Lincoln. I will now play it for Mr. Davis instead."

"Just play the March," someone shouted. But Sam said in a loud booming voice, "Just hear me out. This has been a long bitter war, and many people have died on both sides. In a lot of ways I think this was all unnecessary. We could have resolved our differences peacefully. We are all Americans, and we all love the same music. I am going to play something and dedicate it to both Mr. Lincoln and Mr. Davis."

Sam took three deep breaths, worked his rotary valves, blew some air through the mouthpiece, and finally put the cornet to his lips. Instead of playing "The Rogue's March," he played the "Haydn Trumpet Concerto." The sound was sweet and clear as Sam's silver notes rose above the river and blended with the fresh spring flowers and the chirping of the birds. As Sam played, the little dog at his side threw back his head, and sang his song, and the notes blended in a kind of harmony, not the harmony of a Mozart or a Beethoven, but the harmony of man and dog. When Sam had finished the third movement, and the last note had quivered among the trees, Davis turned to him and said, "Thank you Son. That's the kindest thing anyone has ever done for me. You could have sent me out with 'The Rogue's March,' but you gave me Haydn instead. Bless you, and may you have a brilliant career as a cornet player" As Davis was being led away by the guards, he turned around and added, "The dog is pretty good too. Bring him with you when you play." Davis turned his head, and the procession moved forward and out of sight. Sam never saw him again but never forgot his words. He was savoring his triumph, when he heard the sound of a horse's hooves.

Just then Hancock galloped into the clearing, leaped off his horse, and grabbed Sam's hand. "Sam, you jackass. You are still alive. I knew it."

"Charles. What are you doing here? Did you hear me play the Haydn?"

"What kind of question is that? Of course I heard it. You and that dog are a real team now. He's even learned to match your pitch. But, damn it all, that's not why I came all this way to see you. You are about to lose Rita to that son of a bitch Flambeau."

Hancock gave Sam a full account of the wedding plans, and Sam was about to throw up. "Why, I sent her letters. What happened to the letters?"

"Flambeau was the one who picked up the mail. Why didn't I see that coming?" lamented Hancock. "Rita thinks you are dead. We've got to get you back to Nashville before it is too late. We could send a telegraph, but that bastard would make sure it never arrived. Let's get you a horse and start riding. Nashville is more than three hundred miles away, but with a little luck, we could make it on time."

"I wish it were that easy," replied Sam. "The war may be over, but I am still officially in the army."

The war was officially over now, and small bands of paroled Confederates sometimes stayed in the Union camps a night or two for food and shelter and then made their way to what remained of their homes and families. The Seventh Pennsylvania stayed in Georgia until August 23rd before making its way to Harrisburg. But Sam made his case to Colonel Minty. "Sir I have an emergency at home. My girl is about to marry another man, and I need to stop her."

Minty roared, "So you're down here fighting for your country while some son of a bitch coward is up there sweet-talking your gal! Go now! Take a pistol! Kiss the bride, your bride, for me. Now go. Take the best horse you can find. Here take my horse. Now go!" And so on the very day Davis fell into Union hands, Hancock and

Sam started the long journey back to Nashville. They tried to find a telegraph office on the way but without success, and they followed the railroad tracks in hopes of a train, but none came. The best they could do was to travel as man had traveled for thousands of years, on horseback.

If they could make thirty miles a day on a three-hundred and forty mile trip, they figured that they could be in Nashville by about May 20th, and the wedding wasn't until June 9th, but progress was slow, and the horses got tired. After four days on the road, the horses were so exhausted, that Sam and Hancock realized that no horses who ever lived could maintain that pace for that many days. And so just north of Atlanta, somewhere between Rossville and Rome, they traded their wonderful but exhausted U S horses for a couple of farm animals. The old farmer who made the deal showed off his new horses to his friends, and for years afterwards, he was known as the best horse trader in all of Georgia.

Sam and Hancock didn't fare quite as well. Sam had a roan mare that limped, and Hancock an undersized bay stallion that often stopped to ponder the nature of his existence. Now they rested often and traveled about twenty miles a day. However, they moved inexorably north, and in five days, they were riding into the main street of Manchester, Tennessee. "In about four days we'll be there," Sam shouted to no one in particular. "Rita, I will be there like Lancelot was there for Guinevere."

As they reached the other side of Manchester, Sam and Hancock set up their camp in a small clearing. It was a most pleasant spot with a little stream running near where they pitched their tent. They had been in such a hurry, that they didn't often take the time for the amenities of a tent, but now they were in a celebratory mood. The end was in sight. They were going to be there to save Rita. Sam even pulled a little flask from his pocket, and he and Hancock had a small libation to toast Sam's bride. The warmth of the alcohol blended with the warmth of the blazing campfire, and they began to sing together, "Tenting Tonight on the Old Campground."

They had just finished the third verse when they heard a rustling in the woods and before they could reach for their guns, the threadbare remnants of Wheeler's cavalry entered the clearing. Cook was in front, and he held his Enfield cradled in his arms. He had a crooked smile on his face and spat a wad of tobacco through the black stumps that once had been teeth.

"So, looky what we have here. That dammed Yankee horse thief and his pal. Boys, we are goin' to have ourselves a party." Six other men stepped forward with the muzzles of their rifles pointing at Hancock and Sam. "Tie them up good and tight. When Wheeler sees what we have, he may want to keep this war goin' a little longer." A tall skinny man with a tattered Confederate jacket and homespun pants stepped forward and tied Hancock's hands behind his back and then did the same to Sam. Then he tied a rope around both Sam and Hancock, and taking the other end, got on his horse. "Now let's go for a little walk," said Cook." The man in the tattered jacket had spurred his horse, and the horse shot forward, dragging Sam and Hancock behind him. Sam could feel roots and rocks banging against his body, but he held his head as high as he could. "I can not die now," he muttered to himself. "I am too close to Rita to die now."

But Cook didn't want Sam and Hancock to die either. After hauling them about a hundred yards, he shouted, "Stop. Throw them on their horses and tie them on." And so Sam and Hancock were thrown across their horses like bags of grain and led off into the night. Sam's hip throbbed in pain, and his left arm felt broken, but he would not let himself drift into unconsciousness. He yelled to Hancock, "Charles, are you all right?" But Hancock did not answer.

They traveled for what seemed like hours, and then the horses stopped, and Sam felt himself being dragged from the horse's back. His hip throbbed, and his arm hurt so much, that he almost lost consciousness, but he landed on his feet and found himself staring at a small log house. In a second Hancock was standing next to him. "Sam, are you all right?" Before Sam could answer, someone grabbed him by his aching arm and threw him into the cabin. He fell heavily on the dirt floor, and before Sam could get his breath, Hancock came hurtling in and fell on top of him; the heavy door latched shut.

Outside they could hear someone, shouting, "Get out of here, ya damned mutt." Then they heard a heavy thump, the cries of a whimpering hound, and the crackle of small feet stirring dead leaves. "If you've hurt Bugle, I'll kill you," shouted Sam, but he heard only gruff laughter and the words, "You ain't goin' to kill no one. As horse thieves, I suspect that you're the ones who will be killed." Then several men laughed in unison. "We're goin' hang you at sunup." Then they laughed again.

Sam and Hancock were exhausted, and Sam's arm was aching badly. Hancock looked at it carefully and after poking it and pulling it concluded that it wasn't broken, just badly bruised. "But if we're going to be hanged in the morning, I guess it doesn't really matter, does it?"

In the long hours before dawn, Sam and Hancock checked every inch of the cabin hoping to find some means of escape, but there was nothing. Even the windows had been boarded shut. And so the two friends lay exhausted on the dirt floor and fell asleep. Sam dreamed of Rita listening to the solo he played for Jefferson Davis and telling him that it had been wonderful. "Gilmore himself couldn't have played it better," she said smiling. Then she wrapped Sam in her arms and was about to kiss him, when Sam awakened to the sound of the iron latch on the front door clanking, and the door creaking open. His hour was come around at last. Rita would marry Flambeau, and he would be hanged.

But there was no lynch party at the door. It was a young boy with some hardtack and water. "Suspect you boys must be powerful hungry and thirsty. The boss said to give you this." He handed in the food and shut the door after him. With the door shut and the windows boarded up, the room was pitch dark, but Sam and Hancock eagerly devoured the hard tack and sipped at the warm foul-smelling water. Then they waited in the dark for death to come, but many hours later, the same boy came with some more hard tack and water.

Days passed in the dark, but there was still no lynch party. Hancock calculated that about ten days had gone by because the boy had come in twenty times. To someone outside, this time would have been deadly monotonous, but to those awaiting hanging even the days of empty darkness were precious. Sam and Hancock speculated about what was taking their captors so long to do something, and one day they heard a conversation outside the window. It seemed that nothing would be done until Wheeler could be reached, and no one knew where Wheeler was.

Sam talked to Hancock incessantly about Rita and kept trying to reaffirm the date. "I figure it's about the end of May, don't you think?"

Hancock would always answer with the exact date "It's the 29th of May. We've got eleven days to get out of here and on into Nashville."

"What about you?" asked Sam one morning. "Don't you have some girl waiting for you somewhere?"

Hancock took a long time to respond, and when he finally did, the words seemed drawn out of him by a pair of tweezers.

"If I'd been thrown into this hell hole five years ago, nothing could have kept me here. I would have torn the logs apart with my bare hands and flown away on angel's wings. Or I would have died trying.

"Yes there was a girl, Laura. Before I went off for my last year at Harvard, I gave her an engagement ring, and we planned to marry in May when I got back home. We had big plans. I would open my law office and make lots of money. Then we would build a big house and have eight children, four boys and four girls. I would eventually be elected to Congress and maybe even become President of the United States."

"That last year at Harvard was more of a dream than a reality as the words of pedants were eclipsed by that beautiful face. How could I concentrate on Louis Agassiz' lectures in paleontology when instead of fossils I saw only those sparkling blue eyes? I remember there was a fellow there named Henry Adams, the grandson and great grandson of two presidents of the United States. Old Henry loved that course, and he made me study with him. Without his help, I never would have made it. He hated Harvard, but he loved those fossils."

"So what about Laura?" blurted out Sam. "This is a long preamble to a tale."

Hancock paused so long, that Sam thought that he had fallen asleep, but the words started to flow again, soft words flowing like a river in a dream. "Yes, the girl. She was a part of that dream of Harvard that haunts me still. She came all the way to Massachusetts for Christmas, and she stayed with the Adams family. Of course we were much too virtuous to share the same quarters before marriage, and so she stayed with the illustrious Adams family.

"She was impressed by these descendents of presidents and began to talk more and more about me becoming President of the United States, but the more she pressed the idea, the more I resisted. 'But Laura,' I remonstrated, 'the President of the United States is no longer his own person. He becomes the pawn of big business. To get the job I would need to lose myself.'

"'Not really,' she said and kissed me. 'Mrs. Adams said that the best years of her life were when her father was president. The only people she knew then were important people.'

"I looked into those baby blue eyes and asked, 'But who are the important people? Isn't everyone important? Even the most humble person was created by God to serve a purpose. In God's eyes, isn't everyone important?'

"'Theoretically, I suppose, but you know what I'm talking about. You don't get to be President of the United States by hanging around with working men.' Before she took the train going west, she hugged me, kissed me, and as the train was pulling out of the station, she waved and shouted, 'Good-by Mr. President.' She was so pretty, that I almost thought that I could become President to please her, but before the spring semester had ended, the guns began to fire on Fort Sumter. I never did see her again. When I got back to Illinois, I found that she had gone to Washington to become a nurse. Her mother told me that I had convinced her that God loved the common people best and that she wanted to help save the lives of the common people. That is when I decided to sign up for a military band. My folks were outraged that their son who had graduated from Harvard and who could easily afford a substitute should put his life on the line for no purpose. 'Why there's plenty of cannon fodder out there in the working classes. You don't need to go.' But I figured if she went I should go too, and maybe my music would help bring some joy into the hearts of the common soldiers."

"So why don't you find her and get married?" asked Sam. "It seems you have a lot in common."

"She's dead," Hancock cried. "She died working with Clara Barton on the battlefields of South Carolina. She and Clara walked out on the battlefield to rescue a wounded soldier, and a bullet went right through her heart. With that bullet, all my ambition died. No man would want to be President if he didn't have a woman pushing him from behind. So you can see why I'm not that eager to get home and start a law practice."

The door to the cabin creaked open again, but instead of the boy with the hardtack, it was Morgan Davis. He appeared in the doorway like an angel of deliverance, but apparently he needed deliverance himself because he stumbled through the doorway and fell against the wall.

"Morgan!" Sam cried. "What are you doing here?"

Morgan got up and dusted himself off and said, "Just making sure you are all right."

"Really?"

"No, of course not really. I got my honorable discharge from the United States Army in Columbia, Tennessee and was heading back to Pennsylvania and enjoying my life as a civilian when these jackasses came out of the woods and arrested me. I told them the war was over, but they said, 'It ain't over until every last Yankee is either dead or north of the Mason Dixon line.' Then I said, 'You lunkheads. Lee surrendered. Johnson surrendered. Davis has been captured. The war is over. You lost. There is no more Confederacy. There is only a United States of America.' This seemed to make them mad because they tied me up and dragged me here. They said, 'It ain't over until Wheeler says it is.'"

Sam laughed and said, "That's why we are sitting here. We're just waiting for Wheeler to give the word to hang us."

Sam told his uncle about Flambeau's deception and the forthcoming wedding which was now just four days away, and Morgan had one comment, "Well we've just got to get the hell out of here and on the road. We can't just sit here and let that sweet girl marry that son of a bitch."

"It's no use," said Hancock. "We've checked every corner of this cabin, and there is no way out. Even if there was, these idiots post guards around the clock. As soon as we came out, they'd shoot us."

Morgan rubbed his hands together and said, "I escaped from the Rebs twice at Stones River, and these people aren't, strictly speaking, Rebs. They're outlaws. They are breaking the law, and the law is on our side."

"That's technically speaking true," interjected Hancock, "but what law enforcement can we find to make our case?"

"Why the Union Army, of course. Tennessee is under military law, and we have about 50, 000 troops within eighty miles of us."

"But they don't even know about us," lamented Sam.

"They will," said Morgan. "As soon as I get out of this place, I'll send an army to set you free and bring justice."

"But we only have four days to be in Nashville," cried Sam. "We don't have time to wait for the Union Army."

"All right," said Morgan. "We'll leave together then."

"But how?" asked Sam.

The floor of the cabin had looked solid enough, but Morgan insisted that there must be an old root cellar in there somewhere and started crawling up and down the length of the floor pounding his fists on the ground. After about an hour of this, he said, "By gum. I think I've found it." In their haste to capture Morgan, Cook and his men had failed to take his bayonet, and so Morgan pulled it from his belt and began scraping the ground with it. Finally there was a hollow drum-like sound from the bayonet hitting wood, and when an old wooden door was at last exposed, Morgan slipped the end of his bayonet under one corner and pushed down using the bayonet as a lever. "Well old Archimedes said he could move the world with a lever if he could find a fulcrum. I reckon we can move our own world with a small one."

After he had pried the door open, Morgan stepped down into the dark hole and, after a few minutes of silence, his voice came from out of the depths, "Great news. This cellar even has an outside entrance. Boys we are free." But just as Morgan spoke, the latch on the outside door began to clank open, and Sam and Hancock had no choice but to close the lid on Morgan. There in the doorway was the boy with the hard tack and water and just behind him was Cook. Cook stepped into the room and said, "Great news boys. We found Wheeler. He said, 'We know what to do with horse thieves.' I reckon this will be your last meal. I hope you enjoy it because tomorrow morning you will hang."

As soon as the door had latched shut, Sam and Hancock opened the door to the cellar, jumped into the hole, and pulled the lid over them. Morgan whispered, "We have to dig our way out. There is a stairway to the outside, but it's covered in dirt. I've already started digging." Morgan continued to scrape away, and Hancock and Sam picked up handfuls of the loose dirt and threw it behind them. When Davis became tired of digging, he passed the bayonet to Sam who began hurling dirt like he was engaged in one of the labors of Hercules. The soil was densely packed and occasionally the bayonet would scrape a rock and make a spark. The noise seems as loud as a cannon to the men in the hole, but no one in the camp seemed to notice.

When the last layer of dirt had been cast behind them, they emerged from a world of darkness into a lighted world. The sun was just coming over the mountains, and the camp was illuminated like a magic lantern. When Morgan poked his head outside the hole, he couldn't see his captors because the cellar was on the opposite side of the house from the sleeping men. Morgan pulled himself from the hole as quietly as he could, and Sam and Hancock followed close behind. Darkness would have been helpful now, but as they rounded the corner of the cabin, the entire camp was brightly illuminated by the rising morning sun. It would be a beautiful June day in the mountains of Tennessee, but a guard was slumped over by the door with a stolen Spencer repeater between his knees. It could also be a good day to die.

The horses were tethered in a line of trees just beyond the clearing where twelve angry men were still stretched out on their blankets ready to greet another day of inactivity. Their cause was gone now, and only the irrepressible anger remained to give meaning to their lives. And all the passions of the war, all the hatred, all the glory, all the belief in the wondrous abstraction of states rights was focused on three Yankee prisoners, three men who had done them no harm and who even now wanted only to slip peaceably back into the north. One noise could unleash all that anger, and so these three northern men stepped quietly through this maze of southerners, seeking only to do that which they were accused of doing, stealing horses.

All three men were mounted on saddle-less horses when the first shot rang out, and a bullet tore Morgan's campaign hat from his head. Bullets were flying past them like enraged bees when the Yanks hit their heels into the horses' flanks and rode madly into the trees. They hadn't had time to scatter all the horses, and so as they rode, they knew they would soon be followed by this last vestige of southern revenge. "On to Nashville," shouted Sam. "Here we come, Rita. Wait for me." When they reached the pike to Franklin, they could hear their pursuers crashing through the woods, and as they approached the outskirts of Murfreesboro, they could see Cook and his band of brigands closing in on them from the rear. In front of Cook and rapidly gaining on them was a small, red, and white hound.

It all looked hopeless until they ran smack into the middle of a Union cavalry patrol from Nashville. Morgan told the young lieutenant what was happening, and before anyone could say another word, the bugler blew charge, and twenty men in blue with the guerdons flowing in the wind and their sabers glistening in the sun, rushed into the oncoming remnants of Wheeler's once formidable cavalry and scattered them like a bull charging through a market place. When they came back they had with them Cook and three of his henchmen. The rest had melted back into the brooding world of the old south. They were now about fifty miles from Nashville, and the date was June 7th, 1865. "In two days Rita is supposed to marry Flambeau," said Sam suddenly. "We need to keep moving."

"We also need saddles, food, and water," said Morgan. Two hours later, the three Union men, now ready for the last leg of their journey, left Murfreesboro along the very road that had brought Rita there about three years ago. They had saddles, good horses, water, and food, but they knew that time was running out. The sun was setting as they crossed through Franklin, and in spite of Sam's protests, they camped for the night about ten miles outside Nashville. "Suppose we are too late?" he cried. "Then we'll just have to shoot him," said Morgan laconically.

Nobody slept much that night, and at the first sign of dawn, they saddled their horses and made their way towards Nashville. Bugle was with them now as he had been on and off again throughout their journey. As he raced ahead of the men, he seemed to know that something momentous was about to happen, and he wanted to be there. When they reached the outskirts of Nashville at about eleven o'clock on this beautiful June morning, Union sentries stopped them, but this time Sam was not arrested. When Morgan spoke, the blue soldiers opened a path, and the three young men came upon the city like conquering heroes.

CHAPTER TWENTY-SEVEN
Wherein Virtue is Rewarded

"Thy firmness makes my circle just
And makes me end where I begun."

John Donne, "A Valediction: Forbidding Mourning"

Flambeau had intensified his wooing of Rita, but the more flowers he brought her, the more solos he played outside her window, the more Rita seemed to withdraw within herself. And so Flambeau intensified his attentions to Ira. "So, Ira, "he said one day in early May," what do I need to do to become Jewish?" All of a sudden Ira's opinion of Flambeau rose like the sun on a clear summer day over Lookout Mountain. Every evening Flambeau studied the Torah with Ira. And after a couple of weeks, Ira said to Rita,

"You know that boy is coming a long way with his Hebrew lessons. He may be a good Jew someday. We haven't discussed the circumcision yet, but he loves you so much that should be no problem."

But Flambeau began showing some reluctance when Ira suggested a meeting with a Rabbi.

"It'll only take a couple of minutes. Then you can be the Jew that my dear departed wife always wanted for her daughter."

"I don't know," replied Flambeau. "Does the knife ever slip? I'd hate to be a eunuch for your lovely daughter."

"No! The knife never slips, and it won't hurt a bit. They been doing it to babies for thousands of years, and they don't hurt. Why should it hurt a grown man?"

And so one day in early July of 1865, Flambeau made his own private sacrifice for the Union cause. A Rabbi sliced off his foreskin, and Flambeau walked around for a week like he had been shot in both legs. The sight of Rita or Ira sent flashes of pain into his groin, and he began to regret his loss. Only the hope of marriage to the boss's lovely daughter and a life of prosperity helped him bear the pain. He knew that within less than two weeks he would be under the canopy with Rita and smashing the ceremonial glasses. He would yet lie down in green pastures.

Every day, Rita looked down the muddy road into Nashville hoping against hope that Sam would yet ride into town on a dashing steed and carry her away. However, she also wanted to please her father and had begun to find qualities about Flambeau that she didn't really dislike. "He is kind of cute," she told friends. "And he has a good career ahead of him as a musician. He will be a good provider." But her heart still belonged to the man who was not a very good musician and whose future was anything but certain. And by July 17th, he had still not come to save her from a very ordinary future.

The morning of June 9th was hot and sunny in Nashville, Tennessee, and everyone was telling Rita, "Happy the bride the sun shines on!" But Rita took one last look down the Nashville road before she began to put on her bride's attire. Ira noticed the sad look on his daughter's face and said, "Smile, darling. Life is good. You will be very happy now."

Rita forced a happy face, and said, "I would be happy if Sam came back."

"Forget Sam," Ira said almost kindly. "He ain't coming back. Life needs to go on."

As Flambeau and Rita stood under the canopy for the rites of marriage, Rita was thinking of Lancelot rescuing Guinevere when suddenly a small beagle raced into the room. Somebody said, "Get that dog out of here. People in wedding attire began chasing the small creature around the room and yelling at him, but he was too fast, and soon he jumped on his hind legs, put his paws on Rita's dress, and with his sad beagle eyes looking into Rita's face, he sang that ancient beagle song, the melodious howl that has brought joy into the hearts of hunters for thousands of years.

"Bugle!" Rita shouted. "How did you get here?" She dropped her bouquet and embraced the dog, but the dog squirmed from her arms, yelped one more time and ran out the door. Before the service could resume, Bugle was back and by his side was Sam Fletcher.

Sam was tall and muscular, and in his Union blue uniform, he seemed like a young Hercules on a quest. Being on the road to Atlanta seemed to have been good for him. In those eight months, he had done a lot of growing, and as Rita looked at her young groom, she realized that the callow youth she knew in November had grown into a man. He was so strong, that for a moment Rita doubted who he was, but when Sam's voice boomed out at the assembled crowd, she had no doubt.

In response to the Rabbi's question, he roared, "I object. I have plenty of reasons why these two should not be joined in bonds of holy matrimony, and that ass Flambeau is all of them. That man--if you want to call him a man-- does not have the right to kiss Rita's feet. He is, in every sense of the word, a lying, cowardly, quadrilateral son of a bitch."

When Rita rushed from under the canopy and flew into Sam's arms, people in the congregation began to cheer and whistle, and no one cheered more loudly than a large fat man with a huge white shako hat and a blue plume. He rushed forward and wrapped the young couple in his bear-like arms. Flambeau slipped quietly out of the room, but no one noticed or cared. In a minute Rita and Sam were under the canopy with the Rabbi and after what seemed to have been centuries of grief, they became at last husband and wife.

They still had the reception and the dancing, and even a cornet duet played by Rita and Sam, and when the bride and groom finally slipped into the night followed by a little dog, everyone knew that a deep and genuine peace had at last settled on the United States. For now there would be music.

EPILOGUE

On a hot August night in Nashville, Tennessee, Rita gave birth to a pretty baby girl, Aura Lea, whose first sounds, according to Ira Goldstein, were the opening bars of the " Mozart Mass in C Minor." "That baby came into the world singing," he told everyone who would listen. Rita and Sam played in the Ira Goldstein Band for three years before they finally bought their farm near Hoover's Gap. The city girl from Brooklyn--inspired by her days with Mrs. Gates--developed into a first-rate farm wife, and Sam, the Iowa Farm boy--with his live-in instructor-- developed into a decent cornet player. Eventually the family consisted of three boys and three girls, and they became known locally as the Fletcher Family Band, a group much in demand for very small occasions in Eastern Tennessee. Sam ended each concert with the second movement of the Haydn Trumpet Concerto, but still "there were wars and rumors of wars."

ABOUT THE AUTHOR

With a B.A. from Middlebury College and a Ph.d. from Rutgers University, Victor Thompson has spent his entire career fighting for high levels of literacy in college English classrooms. The battle began many years ago at the University of Cincinnati and continues today at Thomas Nelson Community College in Hampton, Virginia. Dr. Thompson published a book, **Eudora Welty: A Reference Guide** and several scholarly articles and book reviews, but his greatest delight is in telling stories. He won an award for his humor column in high school and has been an enthusiastic teller of stories for generations of children, including his own. His stories derive from a life-time of reading the classics of world literature.

Printed in the United States
26048LVS00003B/46-162